Brotherhood of Bones

JM Meigs

ISBN: 978-0-9963544-2-4

This is a work of fiction. Names, characters, places and incidents either are the product of the authors' imagination or are used fictitiously, and any resemblance to actual persons, living or dead, businesses, companies, events or locales is entirely coincidental.

Acknowledgement

So many people have played a part in the development of the Rhyjl Martin Mysteries, I could write a novella just listing them.

Foremost, I want to thank my husband, Earl, who has encouraged me for the last thirty four years to turn my stories into books. My daughters and my friends, who have read so many drafts of each story and have been caring enough to be honest and critical while still encouraging me.

I want to give a special thanks to Karrie Ross who spent hours turning my ideas into an awesome book cover. Also fellow authors who have always been there to remind me that all my blood, sweat and tears are worth it.

Last of all, I want to thank all those during my academic years who taught me how to read the stories the bones tell.

Table of Contents

Prologue

Five Years Prior

The young woman was heavy with child, the rough weave of her calf-length tunic pulled tight. That she was in pain was obvious by the way she wrapped her arms around her swollen belly. It was too early! Too soon! The sling, half-filled with firewood, spoke against the thought of immediacy. She stumbled, her arm flinging wide to catch and brace herself against a huge tree, its rough bark scraping her wrist and hand. Her low groan grew into a throat-tearing scream.

Two other women, hearing the scream, ran to help her. The older, a blond with streaks of moon-kissed gray, pulled the sling from the girl's back and let it drop to the ground. Her other hand lay upon the mother-to-be's swelling. Looking grave, she nodded and spoke to the second woman, whose tunic was brightly woven and matched her colorfully braided copper hair.

Again the expectant mother screamed, her arm fighting free from the colorful woman to claw at her belly, her knees buckling. More individuals gathered, and out of the crowd a man, rough, scarred and tanned from the sun, came forward to scoop the woman up as if she were mere chaff. He carried her back along the path, the populace parting like a wave to flow in behind and follow in his wake.

~~

Rhyjl held the remnants of the femur in trembling hands. The preservation of the bones was minimal, due to the acidity of the Maine coastal soil. To find as much as the team had found was incredible! Thank the heavens and the ancients for garbage piles of shells. If not for the shell midden that had piled over the burial, neutralizing it over the next few millennia, they wouldn't have much more than a red hole like so many of the other sites.

Red ocher stained the bone, like the soil and the few artifacts surrounding it. The same red ocher which caused a hiker to phone the local police. The police, in turn, alerted the archaeologists to the site, as it seeped like a bloody pool out of the eroding ground near the estuary's bank. The team was thrilled to find a half-dozen graves had survived beneath the bleached shells.

It was not uncommon to find the burial sites of the Red-Paint People. Maine had a number of them. To find bone still intact and not disintegrated after four and a half thousand years was rare. To find six, with the artifacts and a significant amount of preserved bones, was almost unheard of. At least in this part of the country. There were other sites where individuals were intact that were significant. Most of them were located along the eastern Canadian coastline.

She placed the bone reverently in the bag beside her and wrote the coded number on the tag. Then she began again to use the soft brush and the dental tool to remove more of the ocher and soil away from the rest of the remains.

This was her first dig outside of her home state of Montana. She'd jumped at the opportunity for several reasons. The Red-Paint People were somewhat of an enigma, surrounded by a century of controversy. As a sophomore majoring in archaeology, she was excited to take what she had been learning to this dig, in hopes of bringing to light a new part of their story. She was sure that she could solve the ongoing question of where these people had mysteriously come from and disappeared to.

Then there had been her own personal agenda. She wanted to go back to New Hampshire, where she'd been born. She needed to see if she could find Mrs. Kelly, who had been so influential in keeping her out of the grasp of Child Protective Services after her mother died. The few letters she had exchanged over the years with the grandmotherly woman had never truly expressed her gratitude. Then this spring, Mrs. Kelly's letters had simply ceased.

She saw again in her mind's eye the man who carried the woman. His rust-colored beard hiding much of the concern written beneath that healthy thick growth. Dangling from his wrist on a leather cord, a small figurine caught the light. An animal? No, a bird.

Rising from the grave as though her thoughts had summoned it, she saw the carving—possibly a totem—fashioned from shell. It was a beautiful thing in its intricacy. A water bird, likely a loon with its long arched body, unusual head, and long pointed beak. A gift to the unborn child and mother? Her heart feeling heavy, she allowed a single tear to trail down her cheek.

Chapter 1

A Gathering of Bones

Alice Merks, ME, pulled on the overly large, overly ugly black rubber boots. She'd borrowed them from her office secretary as soon as the call from Detective Mike Tanner came through, telling her the situation she'd be walking into at the old farm off Highway 3.

An old farmhouse stood stoic in a large field and was flanked by a two-story barn. The roof on the barn was sagging from too many Maine winter snow loads and not enough care. Both buildings were in need of paint to replace the white strips clinging to weathered gray boards. To the left of the barn, she'd joined the three Maine state vehicles already gathered near a stone wall and a row of short sturdy white pines.

According to Mike, two sets of remains, possibly more, had been found at the edge of a sodden field bordered by pines. "Gotta love mud season," she said, squishing toward the gathering of CSI folks in their sterile white gloves moving cautiously behind the yellow crime scene tape.

The air was damp and full of the pungent scent of leaf mold, pine and new earth. It was mid -April and there were still patches of snow in the shadows. Tanner stood looking down into a raw hole just a little over three feet deep. His suit was crisp and professional. His sandy hair was close-cropped. His jaw line clean and square. It was as if he'd been cast for the leading role in some BBC mystery. Business first. Pleasure later. She slipped past the tape. "What have we got?"

"Two victims and a good start on a third, unless this one fellow had three feet." Tanner, homicide detective for the Maine State Police, answered. "My guess is there might be more, as I told you over the phone."

"Guess? Are you serious?" Alice Merks said, giving him a playful nudge to the shoulder. "You've been hanging out too long with bad company. The Detective Tanner I know would never guess. 'Facts, only facts, ma'am.'" Her voice deepened to mimic his.

He liked the way she teased him. It felt familiar, comfortable. Something he didn't feel around most people. He'd learned a long time ago to build up walls. Guess he'd been too good at it 'cause they were hard coming down. She was too good for him: Blond, leggy, a model's figure that showed off her designer clothes. Add to that, a sensuality that aroused him from head to toe just to be near her.

"If you are referring to those friends of yours, Rhyjl and Erik, you are probably right."

She stiffened, if only momentarily, but enough so he knew he'd stepped on some sacred ground.

"So what makes you think there are more than three?" She grimaced, looking down at the sprawled mix of bones. For a doctor and medical examiner, she wasn't fond of skeletal remains, especially when they were scattered about like confetti. She could foresee hours of painstaking articulation ahead of her.

"See there?" He pointed just to the right of where two of the investigators were carefully making progress on the exhumations. "There's a depression, almost making a shallow bowl."

"Gotcha. Bodies decay, the soil once mounded over them sinks in. Could we have an old graveyard here? You know these old New England folk often had their own family burial plots?" She knew it was her own wishful thinking before Tanner even opened his mouth.

"Not unless they were all buried in the last few years," he replied. "Then there is the fact of what is missing. No casket. Not even a simple shroud. Add to that, the clothing they'd been wearing—and I'm assuming they were wearing something when they died—is missing. I may not be an expert on bones like Rhyjl, but these haven't been here that long and someone didn't want to leave anything behind that would give us any clues to work on. What do you think?"

"I think you may be right." She leaned slightly over the burial site. "Does that mean I can call Rhyjl in for a consultation?"

Tanner looked down at her with a scowl. "Not up to the job, or just lazy, Alice?"

Eyes narrowing, she shot back icy daggers. "Below the belt, Mike. I thought you liked Rhyjl? Where's this animosity coming from?"

"I do like her. She's a great archaeologist. She knows her stuff, but she's an amateur when it comes to crime scenes, and *this* is a crime scene."

"You are behind the times," Alice countered. "I read just the other day that over in the UK they are using forensic archaeologists a good deal to solve crimes. Especially ones like this one." Her hand waved over the excavation. "They've been trained in the exhumation of skeletons and to look for evidence that others might overlook. Rhyjl helped a lot on that last case. Why …"

"And almost got herself killed! Look," he said, lowering his voice from the prying ears of those around them. "I know she knows bones. I'll be the first to admit she's good, but for God's sake, Alice, she's not much more than a kid. A nice kid. She shouldn't be getting messed up in stuff like this."

"Well, by that logic, neither should I. I'm only a few years older, and I thought you considered me nice."

Tanner's right hand scrubbed his face. There was just no winning with her. She had a way of twisting things around and making him regret he'd even opened his mouth. "Could we continue this later and focus on what's before us? Please!"

The next couple of hours, she forgot the mud and chilling damp as she snapped copious digital photos with her Canon 5D Mark III and filled her notebook with details. What they had were the remains of four distinct individuals. Not complete remains, as the local rodents had done a fairly good job during the winter months of dispersing the smaller bones like the phalanges, carpals, and metatarsals. They were male, possibly in their mid-thirties—she'd know more when she got them back to the lab—and one had Negroid features. She cringed as she made that last notation. But the facts were that ethnicity went far deeper than skin color. Still, with all the media hype over the last few years and the racial card being played at every turn, inferring negative and judgmental connotations, as a state employee she felt awkward making that call. She wondered what Rhyjl would think of it and decided, that for Rhyjl, it probably wasn't a problem. She had a different way of looking at things, and her future paycheck wasn't tied to being politically correct.

~~

"What do you mean you won't review my paper, Marcus?" Rhyjl Martin stood before her professor and advisor with the first draft of her doctoral dissertation.

She'd always liked this room that looked over the

ocean and was filled with a treasure trove of books and copies of artifacts collected over a lifetime. That the contents were incongruous with the rugged Maine coastal view framed by the large window at Marcus's back, suited the man. It was a testimony to the breadth and span of her mentor's experience and expertise. Mayan and Aztec, with a smattering of Navajo, possibly. She didn't know much about those peoples other than what she'd learned in her first class under Marcus. The first two were amazingly complex peoples. Peoples who had attained great heights and then appeared to fade away. To fall into obscurity.

"This isn't up for discussion, Rhyjl. We've gone over it in the past and you've been told many times that it isn't an acceptable subject." Marcus McClellan leaned back in his chair, folding his hands across his lap. He wasn't a big man, probably 160 pounds and an inch or two short of six feet, but his mannerisms made him seem so. "I warned you to steer clear of this line of research from the very first time you brought it up in your first class with me. Go back to your first choice, concerning the roles of Nordic women."

"You mean the choice you and Kendricks chose for me?"

"We directed you toward it because of your interest in Nordic life pathways and because you had already done extensive research in that area."

"*You* told me to choose it because my other choice was not acceptable."

Dr. McClellan nodded, smiled and lifted his hands palm upward before folding them again. "As I said, you were warned."

"But if you would only look!" She held the manila file folder containing her research out to him in supplication. "The research is solid. I've got proof to back my theories, with more recent work done using DNA."

"Rhyjl, listen. It doesn't matter what proof you have. If you persist in this course of action, you will destroy every chance you have of getting your doctorate and being considered a reputable archaeologist. You've worked too hard and you're too good to throw your future away for something like this."

"These people deserve to have the truth about their lives told, not muddled up in political mumbo jumbo." She leaned closer to him across the desk between them. Her muscles as taut as a fully extended bowstring. The strain of holding back was costing her. She'd come knowing this wouldn't be an easily won victory, but she'd been well armed. She could turn this battle they'd waged for the last four years. She had hard evidence. That he wouldn't even look! Wouldn't concede even that much!

"These people have been dead for over four thousand years, Rhyjl. They don't care, and to be honest, neither should we."

"How can you say that?" Rhyjl threw her thesis on his desk. "Isn't that what we, as archaeologists, do? Isn't it our job to find out how people in the past lived and died and share it with the world?"

"Sit!" Marcus McClellan, head of Archaeology and Anthropology, rose to his full height from his chair. "I'm going to overlook this outburst because of what you have recently gone through *and* ..." He held up his hand to forestall the protest he saw forming on her lips. "I'm going to try one more time to make this perfectly clear. To submit this paper is suicide. It threatens all our treaties with First Americans, possibly making them null and void."

"As if the United States government has ever done a very good job of honoring or ..."

"Enough!" His hand came down on the desk hard, sending the contents of the desk, including Rhyjl's paper, jumping. "This is politics, Rhyjl, plain and simple. You may not like it. I may not like it. To be honest, I don't much care for it, but this is the world we live in. You just can't propose that any group from Europe ever set foot on these shores prior to the accepted theory. The controversy surrounding Kennewick Man should have taught you that."

"But surely DNA should count for something even if bones are disputed?"

"Politics, Rhyjl. You'd better learn now that when it comes to politics, nothing is as it seems. Not even DNA."

~~

Jack was waiting at the door when Rhyjl came home. One hundred twenty pounds of exuberant puppy was hard to pass by. All she really wanted was to go take a hot bath. "Okay, boy. I know you've missed me all day." She ruffled the fur on the top of his massive Saint Bernard head. "Where's Erik? He must be home if you are out and about."

Jack did a happy dance, circled twice and headed toward the kitchen. Either Erik was in cheffing something, or Jack was thinking with his stomach. Most likely the latter, since she couldn't smell anything coming from that quarter. She was wrong. Erik was indeed involved with some culinary delight—a large banana split by the looks of it.

"Hey, how was your day?" Erik asked, as she and the dog entered the bright room. She adored the lovely old Cape she'd come to call home since moving in with Erik. The open floor plan. The plethora of large windows that let the morning sun come streaming in. The warm color of the varnished wood floors. The wide and unique moldings that spoke of true old-fashioned craftsmanship. But the last owners had lost that sense of history when they modernized the kitchen. Erik had told her that the woman had been somewhat of an accomplished gourmet chef. The result was a kitchen that bordered on commercial, from the eight-burner, double convection gas range with built-in griddle to the huge double-door stainless steel refrigerator and matching freezer. It wasn't Rhyjl's style, all gleaming and metallic. It suited Erik, however, and he was the one who spent the most time here when he wasn't molding the next generation of electrical engineering students or working on his new concept for a supercomputer. She was a passable cook, but Erik, when inspired past apple fritters from Perfection Confections, shone as bright as the kitchen.

This afternoon he was looking a bit ruffled. He had a habit of combing his dark curly hair back from his forehead when he was frustrated or overly focused on a tough problem. It was possible his day had been as rough as hers. Possibly.

"That ice cream had better be for me," she replied, reaching out and snatching at the elongated bowl he was holding.

"Wow! Okay! You can have it," he said, letting it slip from his grasp. "You rarely indulge like this. So I take it things didn't go too well?"

He didn't wait for her answer, but pulled another bowl from the cupboard and began the creative process over. It was just as well. She didn't want to talk about it just yet. Maybe after the dessert and a long soak in the deep Jacuzzi tub. That was one modernization she wholly supported.

Jack's metal water dish clanged. It was his way of quite literally putting his foot down and letting it be known it was empty.

Erik paused in the midst of slicing a banana and eyed the dog. "Now? Can it wait?"

"Wrooof!" Jack responded, with such emphasis that his front legs came off the ground.

"Guess not," Erik answered, setting his creation aside to fill a pitcher and empty it into the dog dish.

To the sound of lap, lap, lap, Erik replied, "You're welcome."

When he'd finished topping the second split with a bright red cherry, he joined Rhyjl at the small table in the kitchen alcove. It had become one of his favorite spots. One where he and Rhyjl shared copious discussions over their meals. Rhyjl always said he was the future and she was the past. He felt they came together here. Their minds worked along similar paths. Both analytical, they reminded him of Jack on the trail of a squirrel. There was no shortage of fodder for their discussions in a world awash with seemingly too much information. At the moment, Rhyjl appeared totally focused on her split. He knew in reality she was a long way from the spoon she dipped and swirled between the remnants of strawberry and chocolate toppings. He gazed out the window to the ocean, wondering how to pull her mind away from that far place. He took a bite, the flavor of pineapple bursting in his mouth as he gazed at the scene out the window. "Looks like the weekend is going to be pretty nice. I was thinking about taking John Pelmar's sailboat out. Are you interested?"

"No!" she said, rather too sharply. "Oh, maybe. I've got a lot to think about right now."

"And you can't think while sailing? I actually find

I do some of my best ..."

"Not now, Erik, please."

"All right then," he said. "Jack, you want to go sailing?"

Jack's tail went thump, whack, thump against the tile floor.

"Jack wants to go, and you know he isn't a very good swimmer. He might fall overboard if you don't come along. That water is cold, you know."

"Okay!" Rhyjl acquiesced, letting the spoon fall clattering into the empty bowl. "For Jack's sake, I'll go."

Jack's tail doubled its tattoo just as Rhyjl's phone rang.

Erik couldn't hear much of the conversation. Rhyjl had stepped out of the room, leaving him and the dog to take care of the dishes. There was no doubt that Jack was more than willing to give them a tongue washing, but since there was still a chocolate coating, Erik declined the offer. "Sorry, boy. Chocolate isn't good for dogs."

Erik knew it was Alice on the phone by the ringtone. Probably confirming their plans for the get-together over at Vinney's Pizza tonight. It had become a standing date for Thursday nights since the first of the year. Sometimes the girls went alone. Mostly they made it a foursome. Tonight Tanner would be there. He and the detective had come a long way since their first meeting. Tanner had saved Rhyjl's life, for which Erik was extremely grateful. It was harder to forgive the man's bullheaded refusal to accept her innocence in the beginning, which resulted in her being vulnerable to the real killer. That was something he was still working on. Still, they did the man up thing and tolerated each other for only one reason: to accompany two incredible women, Alice and Rhyjl.

"Good thing we had those huge splits," Rhyjl said, returning from the living room. She looked tired and drawn. Even the soft honey-colored curls, which she'd begun wearing loosely about her shoulders because he liked it that way, looked limp. "Alice says they may be a bit late meeting us."

"Oh? Nothing serious, I hope." Erik rinsed and stacked the bowls on the counter, opened the dishwasher, paused and closed it again.

"Well actually, they have a multiple murder on their hands." Realizing her oversight, she added, "Erik, I'm sorry. I forgot to put the dishes away. I guess I'm still not used to having a dishwasher. You know, out of sight out of mind?" She half smiled.

"No problem." He shrugged. "Not nearly as earth-shattering as... did you say a double murder?"

"No, I said multiple. Four guys I guess. And get this. They've been there for a while, because all that was left were bones."

Erik blanched, making his rusty red beard look deeper auburn by comparison.

"No, Rhyjl. Please! Not again! You are an archaeologist and I'm an engineering professor. We are not detectives. Let's leave it to the professionals this time."

Her smile got that crooked edge to it he'd come to know so well. Half-closing her dreamy eyes, she moved closer. "But Erik, we solved the murder and had fun doing it. Didn't we?"

"Fun? You call that fun? Then you've got a bad case of amnesia!" He made to walk past her. Her arm snaked around his waist.

She didn't have amnesia. And, he was correct: It hadn't been all fun. But it had brought both Alice and him into her life. For once, she felt a sense of freedom because she could say and be who she really was. They knew her secret and they didn't care or think she was crazy. That alone was the best silver lining to the black cloud that murder created.

She'd known from the tone of Alice's voice, and the brief description of the remains, that her friend was baiting her. They were so different, yet so alike. Give Alice a fresh body and she was in her element. Throw some bare bones in her direction and her comfort zone was stretched. For Rhyjl it was just the opposite: The longer they'd been buried, the more at ease she felt. In either case, it was the story lying there waiting to unfold that had a solid hook in both women.

She liked to tease Erik. He so often took things too seriously, too literally, but the look on his face as she sidled up to him changed her course. "I understand your concern, Erik, and I appreciate it. You are good for me. Good to me, in spite of the fact I forget the dishes." She winked. "But you can't make my decisions for me. If Alice wants help with those bones, I'll give it to her."

"You do have amnesia!" He pushed her arm away, neatly did a side step, and stalked out of the kitchen to the living room with her trailing. He stood looking out the bank of floor-to-ceiling windows framing the wide expanse of the Atlantic. This was the view that had sold him on this house. The place was too big for a single man with no pretensions of becoming anything but single. That had been his prime argument with himself when he'd first looked at it. He couldn't pass up this view, though. Then Rhyjl had walked into his life. "You almost died. I don't want to live through that again. You shouldn't either! All those months of your body working to put itself back together."

"I'm not forgetting that, but this is different. The

last time, I *was* personally involved. I *knew* the killer. I'm not involved in this. I don't know the victims or the person responsible. It's really not that much different than a regular dig."

He turned from the expansive Atlantic and folded her into his arms. "What about the episodes? Those drain you, haunt you. And don't tell me they don't. The first time Alice saw you having one, she was ready to call 911. Those don't happen with archaeological specimens. That happens only with recently deceased individuals. Whatever you feel, sense, it's much stronger."

She couldn't deny that. She would never forget what it was like to live through another's death as if it was personally happening to her. Yet ... yet, if she hadn't, would they have caught the killer? Tanner was good and Alice was great, but ... "It's about bringing justice, Erik. It's about seeing that the right thing is done for those who have passed, whether it is last week, last year or four thousand years ago! Why is that so hard for people to understand?"

She turned to push him away. He stood rooted. Watched as she walked over to the dark leather sofa to sink down and hold her head in her hands. This was more than just the case Alice had called about. It had to do with her thesis. "Marc shut you down, didn't he?"

"Yes!" Her voice was almost a sob. "He shut me down. Welcome to the world of politics!" She threw her hands up, then collapsed again into herself.

Jack, who had stood at a distance, now ambled over to Rhyjl and pushed his big head between her arms and against her face. She wrapped her arms around him, burying her head, and cried. "It's not fair!" her voice mumbled through his fur. "It's just not fair."

It wasn't fair, but rarely in life was that not the

case. It wasn't fair, to his way of thinking, that she was still more comfortable accepting love from Jack than she was from him. Except Jack was safe. Well, so was he! It would just take more time for her to accept that. He could wait.

Chapter 2

Strange Bedfellows

Alice Merks had been rooted in her lab for hours, attempting to articulate the bones of the four men. Even with the careful work of the CSI crew, there had been several mixed and many missing. "Damn rodents!" she said, moving from table to table trying to figure out who the L-3 vertebra she held belonged to. It had been placed in the bag with number 3; however, on closer examination it wasn't a match. True, John Doe 3 didn't have an L-3 once she removed it, but it never had belonged with him. She was pretty sure it was John Doe 4. He was the most advanced in decomposition thanks to the acidic Maine soil. Still, she needed to be sure, because whichever man it belonged to had suffered severe crushing to the lumbar region at one time or another. Her guess was at the time of death but again, with the amount of deterioration, she couldn't afford to guess.

Rhyjl would know. She'd use that special talent of hers and not only know what belonged to whom but how they had come to be here. She'd already run it past her boss. He didn't see any problem as long as Rhyjl was qualified and the university vouched for her. The problem was Mike. She remembered his reluctance before, but that had been under different circumstances. At one time, Rhyjl had been a suspect. This wasn't the same. Why couldn't he see that? And that flimsy excuse about her age...

Glancing at her watch, she placed the glass dish holding the L-3 on the table with John Doe 4. He'd have to wait, but what was a few hours or days more when he'd already been waiting for over a year. Rhyjl would have a better take on that as well, so it was a waste of time for her to keep spinning her wheels and getting nowhere.

~~

Mike, true to his word, was waiting outside the lab for her. "How's it going?" he asked as she closed and locked the door.

The evening air as they stood under the security light still held a hint of winter. Unlike her, in her Irish cable knit sweater, he looked more suited to the chill in his LL Bean parka. It also made him look more rugged. That this appealed to her was always a surprise. "Going. I'll know a lot more tomorrow."

"Is there anything you can tell me now so I have something to start working with?" He opened the blue sedan's door for her and then went around to the driver's side.

She waited for him to start the car, thankful for the retained warmth of the vehicle. Mike's parka was looking better and better. "Not a whole lot more than I had from the scene earlier. Four men around the same age. Three were Caucasian, one black. One guy was a big man. I mean from the measurements, I'd say six-six. He wouldn't have been easy for someone to take down."

"A bullet doesn't care about size," Tanner said, pulling onto the highway heading east. It wasn't much past six in the evening, but already pitch black except for the occasional glow of a street lamp. As spring progressed, the days were already getting longer, but still too slowly as far as he was concerned. He didn't much care for the long winter nights. Too much could be concealed under the cover of darkness.

"Well, that would be true, but I haven't come across any signs of gun violence. CSI didn't find any evidence of it either. If it was a shot that took him down, the bullet didn't come close to any bone and exited the body. While the latter could be likely, to take a man down of that size quickly would have taken an expert chest or head shot. For a bullet to enter and exit either of those areas without leaving evidence is highly unlikely. Possible, of course." Her shoulders gave a brief shrug. "Well, not the head shot for sure, but the chest cavity. Of course this is still early on and I'm mostly guessing right now. Knowing how you hate to guess, I can still safely say they were each killed differently. Take the big fellow: I think his back was crushed. The black man appears to have a head trauma consistent with the use of a blunt force object like a bat."

"Could the bat, or whatever, have been used to cause the crushing injury to the back?"

"Possibly, but my gut instinct tells me no. I haven't found all the pieces at this time, but I'm thinking something more along the line of hit and run. In fact," she pulled out her notebook and a penlight, "I had something similar to this about a month ago. Yeah, here it is. A hit and run where the front tire ran over the guy's back."

"So four guys in a shallow, unmarked grave …"

"Graves," she corrected. "They were all buried at different times."

"Graves," he continued, "with no apparent MO other than the site where they were buried. How about dental?"

"Do I look like Superwoman here?" She slipped the notes and penlight back into her purse. "I'm still trying to reassemble these guys. I've only had them for what—three, maybe four hours?"

She caught his smile in the blue glow of the

dashboard, just before he reached over and gave her leg a gentle squeeze. "You're pretty remarkable. Plus, I have the utmost confidence in your abilities. Anything else you can tell me about the others?"

So like Tanner. Give a lovely compliment followed by a swift kick back into reality.

"The black fellow with the skull fracture was five-eleven. He'd taken extensive damage at different times, including a patellofemoral arthroplasty, or kneecap replacement. I'm working on getting identification from the serial number on the implant. The third, right at six foot, appears to have sustained numerous breaks to his metacarpal bones which are commonly called boxer's fracture. I'd say they were all athletic, or at least had been. The fourth, and more recent victim, had sustained several old fractures to his left side. The femur, humerus, clavicle, all consistent with a vehicular accident. What's wrong?"

Tanner felt the cold prickling run down his spine. Long ago, in the field, they'd called him Spidey after the comic book hero. It was uncanny how he knew something was up before it even happened. The accident that had left Carson half-dead, his whole left side smashed like the Humvee they'd pulled him from. He'd felt it then, just before the landmine sent their armored transport flying across Afghanistan sand. "What?"

"I asked if there was something wrong. You look like you've seen a ghost."

A black man, a giant—that's what they'd called Bass—and a man with a busted-up left side. What were the odds? "Nothing. Just wondering what the connection might be."

She knew he wasn't being honest. It wasn't that he'd ever full-out lied to her, but he was good at half-truths and evasions. Somehow he had gotten something from their conversation that she hadn't. But what? And why not share? They were partners in this, weren't they?

~~

Erik was still pouting when he and Rhyjl entered the parking lot of Vinney's. His beard did nothing to hide the rigidity of his jaw. He'd hardly spoken two sentences in a row since her ultimatum and their leaving the house. His pet rock had come out of his pocket several times during the drive to be polished between his fingers. When all else failed the stone appeared to calm him. She'd asked him once about it. He'd looked almost surprised to see it in his hand. "A gift from my mother," he said, before tucking it away.

While he never spoke of it, she knew he harbored a lot of guilt over his mother's death. That was foolish, however. There was nothing he could have done to keep his mother and her team alive. Had he been there, he would have been another victim. Still, he blamed himself and, well, his father. His father had kept him home that summer instead of letting him go on the ill-fated archaeology dig with his mother. "Grooming him for the family business," as Erik always put it. A dynasty Erik shunned.

You'd think having experienced that, he'd be more understanding of her desire to choose her own path. Apparently not. She understood his need to protect her, even though it made her feel uncomfortable. She would not be controlled, however. She was not a child. She'd listen to his concerns, both the ones that sounded rational, and those that didn't. Ultimately, it still boiled down to her decision on what path to follow. She was not going to budge. Not for him and not for Marcus.

It was with relief she spotted Alice and Tanner

getting out of Tanner's car as Erik drove his night-blue Tesla S into the packed parking lot of Vinney's. She had Alice's support on this. She also was glad to have the distraction while she figured out which direction to go with her thesis.

"Tanner," Erik said, stepping out of his car to take the detective's hand.

"Arneson."

Rhyjl thought it almost comical, the way the two men continued to study each other even after their hands had disengaged. It was believed the handshake originated as a way of extending peace and showing the participants were unarmed. Watching the posturing of these two might confirm the latter, but certainly not the former. She wasn't sure why there appeared to be subtle animosity between them, but you could feel the tense energy emanating from them.

She knew that during the investigation of the remains she'd discovered in the bone lab, Erik had done some investigating into Tanner. He didn't know she knew, but that's what comes of sharing a computer. Your privacy isn't what you might think. Oh sure, Erik had files that he had locks on, but his browsing history for Tanner wasn't one of them. She probably shouldn't have snooped. However, Tanner's competence in that case was important to her. Especially when she was Tanner's favored suspect for a while.

The detective was about as squeaky clean as his appearance suggested. He'd been a top athlete in high school. Just as she had guessed from their first meeting. Lots of awards for football and a scholarship after playing for the West when he was just 17, in the US Army All-American Bowl. He had been a strong contender for the Glen Davis Army Award. He never attended college, choosing instead to enlist in the army the spring of that year. As expected, there wasn't much information to be had for the eight years he'd spent serving his country, other than mention of being awarded the Silver Star and the Distinguished Service Medal for the conflict in Afghanistan. Rhyjl was sure that's why Alice often referred to him as her Sir Gallant during those girl talks they had whenever time allowed. She'd never confirmed it with Alice, though, because that would have meant she'd been prying.

"Well, have you decided to assist me with these individuals?" Alice grasped her by the arm, urging her toward the light and warmth promised by the pizza parlor.

"Yes, but Erik isn't very happy about it. We had a bit of a row before coming here."

"Men! Mike isn't too keen on it either, but what do they know? We make a great team and right now, I need you."

Vinney's was an assault to the senses. Music pumping over several large speakers competed with laughter and the general raucousness of the many university students. Oregano, garlic, basil and too many other scents blended to tantalize the appetite. Rhyjl's mouth was already anticipating chicken parmesan, in spite of the large banana split she'd had earlier. While Vinney's was best known for pizza, Rhyjl was of the opinion that the second page of the menu was where the true jewels were located.

They wove their way toward the back, where a table with a small folded piece of white cardboard declared "RESERVED," and sat.

Tammy, one of Rhyjl's undergrads in bio-archaeology, came out with a cute red apron tied over her jeans that matched her Vinney's red shirt, and clashed with her red hair. "What can I get all of you?" she asked, her emerald eyes taking them all in but lingering the longest on Tanner.

This was a common reaction from any waitress within Mike Tanner's sphere. Not necessarily because of his good looks, though he wasn't short on those, but because of his legendary generosity when it came to tips. "Mike's Groupies," Alice called them.

Across the table, Alice winked when Rhyjl looked up from her menu to show they'd been thinking the same thing. Tanner, after conferring with Alice, ordered a Hawaiian pizza with extra cheese to share. Rhyjl ordered the chicken, and Erik the calamari ripieni.

"Don't think you are going to get a kiss from me tonight after eating squid," Rhyjl said, and shuddered.

"What? But Vinney's is the only place within a hundred miles that serves it. You would deny me?"

"Unlike some people, I won't tell you what to do with your own life, or in this case, stomach. I'm just letting you know I don't want squid kisses."

Tammy arrived with two frosty mugs of Samuel Adams, a house pink zinfandel, and Alice's traditional merlot.

"As a detective," Tanner said, before taking a good-sized swallow of his beer, "I get the impression there is something happening here I don't quite get."

"It's nothing, Mike." Alice played with the edges of the napkin under her glass. "Erik just doesn't want Rhyjl to be involved with our case."

"Glad to hear it. But I suppose it's not going to dissuade either of you from proceeding, no matter what common sense demands?"

"Well, I am not a detective, but it doesn't take much to see you two have had this conversation as well,"

Erik said.

"Yes, had it this morning but it didn't sink in, obviously." Tanner looked at Alice, who was now tearing tiny pieces of the napkin off with her long, silver-polished nail.

"Do we have to discuss this?" Alice said. "It's not really suitable dinner conversation. Stressful topics are not conducive for good digestion."

"And bones are? And before you offer an objection, don't you dare tell me you weren't going to bring them up tonight."

"There's nothing to discuss." Rhyjl glared around the table. "Alice asked me to assist her. HER boss said I could. That's that. Now we can talk about the bones or the weather or football, whatever."

"Rhyjl." Erik patted her hand, which was putting so much pressure on the table it was threatening to tip in her direction. "You don't care anything about football."

"So Mike can teach me. He used to play."

Silence descended, except for the strains of the male lead singer of One Republic singing, *"I I I I I I I I feel something so wrong doing the right thinggggg. I could lie, could lie, could lie, everything that drowns meeee... makes me want to fly..."*

How appropriate. Guilt is a powerful emotion. The look on Erik's face, she imagined, matched her own. Alice looked utterly confused and Tanner's eyes narrowed and became steel.

"Well you did, didn't you?" She stumbled, trying to find solid ground in the quagmire she'd suddenly made. "I mean it's obvious, isn't it?"

"Obvious?" The steel didn't soften as his left eyebrow arched.

"Well, that's what I thought the first time you came

to my door. You just looked like a jock and while you are tall, you aren't lanky enough for basketball. So what's the big deal? Lots of guys play ball."

"I trust her instincts. You played football, huh?" Alice smiled and batted long dark eyelashes.

"Yeah, back in high school. Long time ago. I don't talk about it much."

"Mike, news flash! *You* don't talk about much."

His eyes softened toward Alice. "You learn more that way."

The hard lines of his mouth softened almost to the point of a grin. Maybe for Tanner, it was. Rhyjl'd never seen a genuine smile light the man's face. He came the closest to it when Alice was with him.

"So what have we learned tonight?" Alice said. "Um, let's see." She extended her finger toward Erik on her right. "You like to eat squid. You, Rhyjl," Alice's finger pointed across the table, "are confessing that Erik's and your relationship has moved from friendship to kissing. And, you don't like squid. Mike." Her finger pointing subsided into a gentle caress of his arm. "You have hidden your athletic past from me all these years. How's that for listening?"

Rhyjl shifted in her seat. Her grandmother would have chastised her for wriggling. It only happened when she was attempting to hold something back, usually associated with guilt. So she'd been wrong. Alice didn't know about Tanner's past. Was she as clueless about his military service as well? Perhaps the reason she called him Sir Gallant had nothing to do with his Silver Star. *If he's hidden that from you, Alice, there's probably a lot more.* That thought bothered her more than she cared to admit. Rhyjl feigned a laugh. "So tell me, Tanner, which football team do you like the most? The Phillies or the Lakers?"

Her three companions answered with a collective moan.

"What? Did I say something wrong? We could always revert to bones."

And much to the men's dismay, they did.

~~

"That wasn't so awful, was it?" Rhyjl asked, as they got into the Tesla to head home.

"I've had a few students tell me that piercings aren't that painful either, but it doesn't mean I want any."

"Really? I'm kind of disappointed. I thought a gold earring in your ear would be very striking."

"You've kind of had a thing going for pirates ever since that old man showed you where his treasure was hidden."

"True, and I'm the wealthier for it, thanks to you. Seriously, our conversation wasn't that awful. Admit it, four men buried together, but at different times, piqued your curiosity. It had to."

"I don't have to admit anything unless you rescind your earlier statement about not kissing me tonight."

The Tesla moved from the parking lot with the whisper of the wind. She still found that a bit unnerving. She preferred her vehicles to purr or even roar like a strong beast, ready to take on the world. Erik's car was sleek, cat-like. It fit his personality well.

Tanner was right about one thing tonight. When you listen, you learn more. Both men seemed to be very adept at that. She could sense the wheels in their heads grinding and meshing away, looking for any slip or nuance that might give them a clue as to what the others were *not* saying. It was a skill she'd never honed. Even when, as a child, it could have saved her a lot of grief. She preferred openness. Say what you mean. The earlier guilt of the evening slipped back. She'd gone behind Tanner's back to research him. So why hadn't she just been open and told him she'd done a background check at the same time she knew he was running one on her? She had her secrets, too. Nothing big or terrible, but ones she'd just as soon didn't surface.

Chapter 3

Too Many Questions

Mike Tanner didn't like the direction this case was going. His Spidey sense was working overtime. First the disclosure about the four individuals who sounded unerringly like his old companions. Then the slip by Rhyjl at dinner. She wasn't fooling him with her dumb act. She was one smart cookie, and often maybe a little too smart for her own good. Rhyjl was an enigma and he was uncomfortable with the unknown.

He let that thought roll around in his head as he walked up the two flights of the old apartment building and unlocked the door to his small apartment, nodding as a snippet of paper fell to the floor. Yeah, she was smart and observant, but there was something more he couldn't quite put in place.

He wouldn't have put it past her to do a little research. If someone did Google him, his life wasn't exactly a closed book, except for those parts the government had chosen to redact. She'd put her researching skills to good use, and if not her, then that rich engineer boyfriend, Erik. He'd seen the look on both their faces before she pulled that explanation out of her nimble brain. It was plausible she had seen him as the jock type when they'd first met. He'd been asked numerous times by other less intuitive individuals if he played football in high school or college. It certainly wasn't beyond her abilities to size people up using her anthropological training. He'd hung around enough of her and Alice's conversations to know that Rhyjl had an eye for looking at a person and telling you what they most likely did for hobbies or work. If he were honest with himself, he'd admit that her talents could be very useful. She was undisciplined, however. She ran on her gut and emotions. Harnessed, that could be good. Unbridled? People like that got themselves or others hurt.

The old bulb in the light over his bathroom sink cast a yellow glow. Who knew how long it had been there. His wasn't the kind of apartment people spent a lot of time in. It wasn't really much more than a place to flop for the night, grab a quick shower and maybe a drink. Tonight he'd do all three, but in a different order.

That hadn't been his plan, but plans had a way of not working out. All afternoon, since he'd spent time at the investigation site, he planned to cozy up to Alice after dinner at her place. A little wine, some chat. He liked the way she smelled. It was reminiscent of that old child's rhyme: *Sugar and spice and everything nice*. Yeah, that's what Alice was made of.

Stripping down, he looked in the mirror. He'd kept in good shape. Never knew when it might come in handy taking down some jerk. He had a few scars. Nothing bad, which was remarkable considering what he'd been through. Alice had once commented on them. He'd told her he'd gotten them in a mortar attack when he was serving in the army. She'd gently pushed him for more details. He'd changed the subject in a way she didn't find unacceptable. She was correct. He didn't like talking.

Then there was Rhyjl. Alice's insistence that she be part of the investigation just rubbed him wrong in every way. Alice said she needed her. But why? Alice was one of the best in her field. Sure these victims were nothing but bone, but Alice could handle it. It didn't make sense.

He turned on the water and was waiting for it to

reach full heat before stepping in. A cold shower might have been advisable, but he wanted the heat to bake the chill out of his bones more than cold to dampen his sexual desires. Turning, he glimpsed the blue-inked sketch high on his left arm just below the shoulder. The intricate tattoo of the Norse hammer was the last remnant of his connection with five men who had been closer to him than brothers. After the "incident," they'd all gone their separate ways. It was better that way.

Stepping into the shower, he heard a replay of Alice's description of the skeletons. "Four men around the same age. One guy was a big man ... say six-six." Bass? "The black fellow with the skull fracture was five-eleven. He'd taken extensive damage at different times, including a patellofemoral arthroplasty, or kneecap replacement." Keys? "The other, right at six foot ... sustained numerous breaks to his metacarpal bones which are commonly called boxer's fracture." Boomer? "One fellow... sustained several old fractures to his left side. The femur, humerus, clavicle, all consistent with a vehicular accident." Carson?

Quite a coincidence. Only one problem. He didn't believe in coincidences.

He mulled over the questions as he let hot water pound him until his skin glowed red. If these men were his old comrades, who the hell was taking them out and how? These weren't run-of-the-mill-men. They were professionals trained to be America's finest fighting machines and carry out covert missions. Whomever, they had to be good. No, better than good.

Spetsnaz? Possible. They'd had more than a few tense situations arise with their supposed Russian allies in Afghanistan. Like that time they had both been hunting the same Taliban assassin. His team had orders to bring him in alive. Volk, aka the Black Wolf, and his Spetsnaz team were supposed to take the target out. Slight conflict of interests. Spetsnaz aren't good losers. In the end, he hadn't needed an interpreter to know that some disparaging comments were made about his birth status. That had been a long time ago, though. It didn't make sense for Volk or one of his team to hold this kind of grudge, bad losers or not.

Rummaging through his mind for other possibilities, one that kept coming to the top made him the most uncomfortable: Someone from his own government? If so, why dispose of the bodies in his area? A warning?

Last time he'd checked, his department hadn't been able to trace the number of the anonymous caller. "Suspicious behavior," the caller had reported that morning to dispatch. They knew it had pinged off a tower in the Augusta area. Suspicions were that it was made from a burner phone. In the crime shows, that was always a dead giveaway for guilt. In real life, burner phones were popular. Especially by those people who couldn't afford regular cell service. There was no shortage of those in rural Maine.

Perhaps he was being paranoid. Not likely. There were four dead men too close to home. Men who he had possibly served with. Men he had fought with, survived with. Men he had called friends. He'd sleep lightly tonight, if at all.

~~

Rhyjl wasn't getting much sleep. She and Erik had made up. That he was sawing logs on the pillow next to her attested to that. He still wasn't happy with her choice, even after she'd accepted squid kisses. The case had her in its talons and there was only one way to cut herself free.

Solve the mystery.

One question kept revolving around in her mind. These men were connected, but how? All around the same age. All about the same height except for the big guy. They were athletic, according to Alice. A serial killer taking out macho men? That hardly seemed likely. Alice had also mentioned that they all appeared to have led tough lives, from the numerous remodeled fractures they had all sustained. The word "warriors" kept insinuating itself into her thoughts. So what if she followed that tack?

If she'd been on a dig in Europe from the early to Middle Ages, and come across four men like Alice was describing, she wouldn't have thought it unusual. Life was a battle back then. If men weren't practicing for war, they were living or dying in one. The age bracket was pretty close as well. Early thirties was Alice's preliminary assessment. Erik's and Tanner's age. That fact hadn't seemed to faze Erik. Tanner, however, had appeared to get more introspective as the night progressed. Probably contemplating what course of action he'd run with on the information, and yet. Something didn't quite feel right. She just had this niggling hunch there was something else going on with him.

She decided it was most likely her own guilt coming back into play. She didn't really believe he'd bought her act. Even Alice had pulled her aside later in the ladies and said she knew Rhyjl knew more about sports teams than to lump the Phillies and Lakers together.

Well, she'd get her hands on the bones tomorrow, and many of her questions would be answered. That excited her, while at the same time causing her stomach to clench. Erik was correct! There was a strong chance touching them might prove more taxing than she could handle. She didn't really know what to expect. It was true that most of her experiences had been with the long departed. The visions were faint, distant. Sometimes they got intense but it was like getting involved with a good movie: your pulse hammered, your breathing grew rapid, you experienced all the sensations of fear and grief, but you didn't experience the actual pain. Her one and only experience with a more recent death had been the one last fall. She'd experienced everything just as if it were happening to her in real time. Hopefully, that wouldn't be the case this time. In that, Erik was wrong. Her memories of that trauma were very clear.

Erik mumbled something and rolled to his side, reaching to pull her closer to him. His body was like a radiant heater. She preferred to sleep cool. How had they gotten this far? Why had she let it happen? Had it been born out of the security he provided when she'd been injured and spent months recuperating? Did she feel obligated? She'd paid him back for all her hospital expenses that had accrued. At one time, she might have been accused of fortune hunting by those who didn't know her. Erik Arneson of the Boston Arnesons was a very wealthy man. But that had changed when she had come into her own fortune. Was it possible this was love? She slammed that thought down hard. Love was for fools. She was no fool.

~~

Cigarette smoke, stale and choking, clung to everything in Rick's Americana Club, including him. The lights were just enough so people at a distance weren't much more than shadows. The Six Man Band had drawn quite a crowd tonight. Or were they just mere background, like the posters and lights for the bump and grind of Paris nightlife?

Taking a sip of water—he wished it was a stout beer—he waited for their next set to begin. She was late. They had expected her an hour ago, after the café closed. Shortly after, his stomach had begun to clench. The electricity spiking along every hair on his torso was making them stand up like quills on a porcupine. Still the band played on. There was nothing else they could do.

Aeisha was one of their best assets. She was also an asset that he wished they had never turned. He wasn't going to say that out loud. They'd all think he was going soft. Soft wasn't allowed in their profession. He'd had that drilled, pumped and pummeled into both his body and brain. He and the team had many assets over the years. They'd lost some. Collateral damage. Expected, acceptable. Aeisha wasn't acceptable as a loss. She'd already lost so much and had given when others would have pulled back. She also had her son, Dani, to live for.

Soft. Maybe it was time for him to pull out. He took another gulp of water. It did nothing to dismiss the feeling of dry cotton forming in his mouth.

Perhaps it had taken longer to close down the café, being a Saturday night. Perhaps the men frequenting it had stayed longer than usual. That could be a good thing. It might mean something was up and she'd have pertinent info.

Bass gave him a concerned look and tapped him on the shoulder. "You got that look, Spidey."

Yeah, I've got that feeling. I...

Aeisha appeared at the edge of the stage curtain. Everything about her was screaming tense. He'd seen that look in the eyes of both men and beasts just before death caught them. Sometimes he'd been the reason. Shit! Something was wrong! She glanced furtively over her *shoulder, then turned and ran toward the backstage door.*

Grabbing his stomach as though he was going to hurl, he ran after her to the accompanying laughter of those who assumed he'd had too much to drink.

He woke! Gun in hand. A cool breeze drifting through his bedroom window. A window he hadn't left—never would leave—open. A window two stories up with no easy access.

Chapter 4

Shattered Lives

This is where death came, Rhyjl thought, as she followed Alice through the sterile hallway. No pictures hung of colorful landscapes. No bright calming colors or lovely patterned wallpaper. The dead didn't require them, and neither did the people working with them. There were no ghosts here. The individuals in residence had ceased to exist somewhere else. There would be images when she saw the remains, but they did not walk these halls.

A stringent smell of Isopropyl alcohol and pine permeated the air. Not exactly pine but pine-scented, like that cleaner her grandmother used to mop the floors. She'd expected to detect formaldehyde, but maybe that was only used in funeral homes. Morgues, after all, were only short-term, not long-term facilities. If the ME and her assistant did their jobs right, it was a quick in and out. At least, that was Alice's explanation as Rhyjl followed her down the hall.

"The bodies are only here as long as it takes to establish time and cause of death. We are a small facility and many will pass through this door this week. Some are pretty straightforward. Car fatalities." Alice took a deep breath and a moment of sadness thinned her pretty, full lips before she continued. "The elderly who die in their sleep, or by accident, or from some kind of fall where there was no one present who saw what happened. Then we get the suicides. Sad, that in a time where there is so much affluence, we have so many unhappy people. I can understand the elderly who can fall into depression because of failing health or loneliness. We see a lot of those. It's the young: teens, even children, that break my heart," Alice said, shaking her head as she rummaged through her purse to find her keys. "The national average is 12.9 per hundred thousand. In Maine, it is over 17. Then we get the ones that met their end in any suspicious or unusual manner."

Once through the double doors, the room was cold. Sterile white tiles covered both the floor and walls. Stainless steel tables with sinks were lined up in the center. Again, Rhyjl wasn't sure what she'd been expecting, but it wasn't this. Her lab was warm. If Alice worked here all day, then she was either part Eskimo or had become immune to hypothermia. "Why so cold?"

"We keep the room around 50 degrees or below, for what should be apparent reasons. It's not necessary with these." Alice pointed at the closest table with the skeletal remains laid out. "But with the more traditional."

"Decomp. Gotcha."

"I told you to wear something warm. This won't help much but it's required in here." Alice pulled a white lab coat from a hanger by the door and offered it to Rhyjl.

Rhyjl moved closer to the table and steadied herself against what she was afraid might be an onslaught of emotional energies. Nothing. It might as well have been a resin skeleton used for teaching biology in high school. "Do you usually leave the bodies out?"

Alice shrugged. "No, Gene usually puts them away when we are finished. I worked late last night, as you know. Gene is my eight to four assistant. Or Forensic Tech as he likes to call himself. However," Alice moved to the table and picked up the small glass dish holding the vertebra she'd been struggling with the night before, "these guys are not going to decompose any more than they already have. Refrigeration is not necessary. And, I knew we would be in here early."

Rhyjl moved around to the other tables. At the third table she felt the familiar electrical current in the air. Strange the other two had no feeling. Tentatively she reached out to touch the radius.

"Don't!" Alice grabbed Rhyjl's hand. "We don't know anything about this guy. We don't know what kind of bacteria is still present. Gloves, Rhyjl, gloves."

"Yes, I'm sorry. I know better. It's just that..." She took the gloves absently from Alice, never averting her eyes from the big man on the table.

"What?" Alice's voice held an edge of excitement. "Are you picking up something?"

"Well, if the dead could bury themselves, I'd say this guy was a good candidate for your suicide stats. I'm getting a strong feeling of depression."

"That's not as crazy as it sounds, Rhyjl. I've actually heard of cases where relatives or friends of a suicide would dispose of the person, hoping no one would ever find out. Not often, but it does happen."

"So these guys all commit suicide and some friend disposes of the bodies?" Rhyjl winced. "Don't think so. Unless..."

The contact jolted her body with such force her legs almost collapsed from under her. Still she couldn't pull away.

Sand and metal flew like stinging insects against his skin. Intense heat washed over him like a blow dryer gone haywire. If he had any eyebrows left after all this, it would be a fucking miracle. He was screaming, or was he? The sound was there in his head but... Someone was pulling on the ragged tatters of his uniform. The guy's mouth was moving. He was trying to tell him something.

God, the guy was a bloodied zombie. The zombie was one of his own. Yes, there, there was the tattoo still visible.

Rhyjl pulled away. Visions of flames and blood still seared her senses. "This guy was in an explosion."

"Is that what you think killed him?" Alice reached out to steady Rhyjl, who was wavering on her feet.

"No, it's an old memory. He was military. I could see the remnants of a uniform, on him and on his companion."

"Well, that's a start. Any particular branch?"

Rhyjl shook her head in wonder. "Alice, do I look like an expert in military dress? I don't know. Army maybe. It looked like that desert camouflage you see a lot of them wearing these days."

"Well, was there anything distinctive you can remember about it? An insignia? If I can get some idea..."

"A tattoo. The tattoo was important to the guy. He felt relief when he saw it." Rhyjl closed her eyes and looked back into the vision.

"A tattoo on him?"

"No, the guy trying to help him. It somehow was a bond. I don't know. Just seeing it made him feel better."

"Great!" Alice said, turning to pace the room. "A guy who was once in an explosion, wearing camo and had a friend with a tattoo. This ought to be simple to find. Not!"

Seeing the expression on Rhyjl's face, she quickly amended, "Look, I'm sorry. I invite you here to help and well, I was hoping to get something more solid. More recent. It's not your fault."

"I can't control what I see, Alice. You should know that. I just see whatever the vibration is. Usually it has to do with some trauma. You have to admit being blown up is a bit traumatic. Maybe this time the guy died instantly. No trauma. So all I'm going to get is something from his past. I don't know. This is all still relatively new territory for me. Sorry I can't give you more. Maybe one of the other guys?"

Alice let what Rhyjl said play around in her mind. Perhaps, Rhyjl had given them more than she'd first thought. Okay, so the guy was military. He was big. He had been in an explosion and … "Rhyjl, could you draw the tattoo? It might be something I could use. Maybe the guy who has it is still out there."

"Yeah, I can probably do a rough sketch. Art was never one of my stronger talents. Let's see what this fourth guy will tell me, if anything."

It was much the same for the fourth man—an old memory of being surrounded by bare hospital walls. His anger and loathing was directed inward, twisted blackness. It encased him like the wrappings he was swathed in, a python crushing out his very life. Again, there was the sense of huge depression, suppressed, denied. Not even the extreme physical pain on his entire left side could supplant it. *"I should have died in the explosion. I shouldn't be here."* These were his recurring thoughts.

Rhyjl recognized the pain. She'd felt much the same after her fall. Never had she felt the anger he was expressing. Not toward the person who had tried to murder her, and especially not inwardly.

If this man had been in the same explosion as the other, it didn't appear that he remembered it. That wouldn't have been so much out of the normal. She didn't remember much of anything about her fall. Still, it was uncomfortable to be in this man's mind. To be almost one with him. She wished she could use it to gain more information by searching through the room for clues. Instead, she was limited to what the energy emanated. But this wasn't here and now. She was only experiencing the past. His past. In a way, she was a ghost.

"Rhyjl? Are you okay?" Alice asked.

"Oh, yes. I was..."

The door opened and in strutted a dowdy-looking fellow with tousled mouse-brown hair, a sad-looking goatee, and darting eyes. It was obvious he hadn't expected to see them. His jaunty strut had faltered and now was almost cautious, like a trapped animal deciding if it should run.

"Dr. Merks," he said. "I wasn't expecting you so early." His eyes darted toward Rhyjl and then back to his boss.

"Gene, I've called in some help with these new arrivals. Please meet Rhyjl Martin. She works at the University. Forensic Archaeology. Rhyjl, this is my tech, Gene Haverty."

Rhyjl smiled at her use of the word tech, when in private she'd called him her assistant. She reached out to take his hand in greeting, saw his hesitancy and realized her gaffe. She removed the purple non-latex gloves Alice had insisted she wear and repeated her offer of a handshake. He paused a moment, as if taking her measure, before accepting it. She wasn't sure why, but expected something mild. His hand gripped hers like a vise grip.

"So now you think these aren't recent victims?" he said, releasing the blood flow back into Rhyjl's hand.

"No, why would you think that?"

"Well, she's an archaeologist. Why else would you have her here?" he said, shrugging his coat off to exchange it for the lab coat that had a pocket protector and several pens sticking out.

"She is a specialist in skeletal remains, Gene. That's why I have her here."

He gave Rhyjl the once over, then turned his

attention back to Alice. "I see. So will you be wanting my help, or should I do something else?"

There was no comradery here. The temperature of the room had dropped not less than 10 degrees by the feel of it.

"Gene, yesterday's auto crash. The parents are coming in around noon. Perhaps you could see what can be done to make the boy look more presentable." Alice turned her attention to Rhyjl. "You were saying?"

"This one was in an explosion as well. I..." She walked over to his left side to examine the bones. The trauma was massive. "Extensive remodeling to both the posterior and anterior of the femur. By the looks, he was fortunate the femoral artery wasn't severed. You saw the pins used, of course."

As soon as the door shut between them and Gene, Alice whispered, "Yeah, I know. I'll get them run through the database today for a match, but what else can YOU tell me?"

"Soldier. I think probably the same explosion, but I can't be sure. Again, this guy was deeply depressed, or at least he was at the time of these injuries. I suppose that's to be expected and could have changed. He seems to have recovered very well."

"What makes you say that? Those injuries look as if they could have been quite debilitating. I was thinking possibly even wheelchair bound."

"No, look at this break on the right ulna."

Alice leaned in closer to look at the fine fracture line Rhyjl was pointing to.

"This is a classic defense wound and occurred much later," Rhyjl said. "I'd say several years later."

"A fall?"

"I suppose, but most people when falling use their

arm to break a fall this way." Rhyjl threw out her arm with the palm out and down. "If unable to do that, they often land on the ulna's proximal or Olecranon process. I see no evidence of fracturing there." She knocked her elbow on the table as if breaking a fall. "This, however," she held up the ulna, "is a break consistent with throwing the arm out like this in a defensive blocking action." Fist up, Rhyjl's arm moved in front of her body.

"So you think our guy went back to fighting after the extensive injuries to his left side?"

"That's my take. There's one other thing." She lowered her voice. "There's something wrong with some of these guys. I'm not getting a lot of energies off them. It's like something is blocking them or me. I've never experienced anything like it."

Rhyjl identified which victim the third lumbar vertebra belonged to. It was as Alice had surmised, and did indeed belong to the man whose back had been crushed. She didn't agree with Alice's assessment of possible hit and run. "How wide is a tire, unless we are talking about big machinery here?"

"I'm not sure. Six inches, maybe more?"

Rhyjl pictured the heavy tread of the tires on her new Jeep. "Um, I'm going to say at least six if not more like nine. We could go out to the parking lot and check. But for the sake of argument, we make it nine inches or twenty-three centimeters," she said, holding her hands out and across from each other, then adjusting them until she was close to what she thought would be the right spacing. "Now how wide is the crush pattern?"

Alice pulled out the small tape measure she carried on her belt. "Well, it starts at the second lumbar, possibly the very proximal edge of the third, and runs up the column to the first thoracic. Roughly a little over thirty centimeters."

"So we are looking for something a little over a foot wide. I suppose it could be a tire. Look, the third lumbar and the first thoracic are damaged, but less than the third through the twelfth thoracic. Think of the shape of a tire. Yes, I think you may be right. Whatever did this was carrying a lot of force but was also slightly curved." Rhyjl paused. Something wasn't setting right.

"Something is still bothering you though, isn't it?" Placing her hand on Rhyjl's shoulder and gently squeezing, Alice said, "I was hoping you could do that magic thing and work this out. Maybe Mike is right. I'm looking for an easy solution and being lazy."

"There's a number of things bothering me. So we can see by the way the ribs appear to have been spread and by these fractures here, that we have avulsion. Again, it indicates that the force was more of a rolling force than direct. These ribs," Rhyjl pointed to the victim's right side, "were rolled under while the ones on his left side would have splayed out. We have compression fractures of the thoracic vertebrae but no other indicators of violence." Wrinkling her nose and squinting her eyes, she tried to envision how the murder scene would have looked and played out. Again, it didn't make sense. This man didn't just lie down placidly and let someone run over him. Yet, that's what it looked like.

"Alice, have you done a toxicology screen on these?"

"No. In each case, it is pretty obvious the cause of death. I just haven't figured out exactly how. Why? What are you thinking?"

"Just a thought. I'm not sure I can put it completely together at this point." Rhyjl bent closer to the table and picked up one of the ribs that had been torn from the sternum. *Why isn't it speaking to me? Am I trying too hard or not hard enough?*

"Give me a try." Alice leaned in over Rhyjl's shoulder. "Is it something in general, or specific to that rib?"

"I get the distinct feeling this individual wasn't aware of his death." Rhyjl set the rib down and reached for the left humerus. "Did you see any indication of damage to the extremities? I mean look at this. No trauma. I didn't notice any on the other arm either. There are none on the legs, only the wide pattern across the back. If he was run over, why..."

"Rhyjl? Rhyjl!"

The alley was dark. There was no telling which way to go. Spidey had chased after her like he was on fire. Where was she? Where was he?

A scream rang out. He turned to the left and plunged on through the fog and shadows. This was the old part of the city. It was a potent brew of decaying vegetation, petrol fumes and the cloying perfume of the flowering vines and assorted flowers in pots and window boxes. A few lights from curtained windows cast pale puddles of light on the wet pavement.

She was no more than a dark puddle against the gray stones. Spidey was cradling her against his chest. A dark stain ran between his fingers and down his forearm to pool at his side. She reached up with a trembling hand toward his face, then went limp. There was no cry, no sound of sorrow. Spidey just pulled her closer. A study in contrast: light against dark, good against evil. Tonight the innocent paid the price. She would not be the last.

Rhyjl shook herself free. She'd seen a woman murdered! Or rather this man had. She'd felt his sorrow and yet, oddly, his acceptance, as if this was just part and parcel of a normal day. She'd heard his thoughts. No, for just a few moments it was more: she'd been him! She closed her eyes to bring forward the landscape and the scene before her. A city, narrow streets, old, wet. The woman was swathed all in black from head to toe. The man holding her. Had he been her killer? Suddenly, she realized what she was seeing. The black shirt he wore had both sleeves torn away at the shoulder. Deja vu? Again, there was the tattoo, faintly resembling an anchor. Yet not. Something in the back of her mind stirred. Not an anchor but...

"Rhyjl?" Alice said. She was bracing her friend from behind, attempting to keep her from collapsing. "Rhyjl?"

"I'm okay. You can let go."

"Yeah, right. Next time, can you give me a bit more warning?" Alice went over to a desk and pulled out a chair. She offered it to Rhyjl, who just shook her head, then Alice sank into the cushion herself. "I know I wanted you to work your magic. I just..." She took a deep breath and closed her eyes. "It's scary as hell what you do."

"What do I do?" Rhyjl leaned against the table for strength that was slowly seeping back into her. She wanted to leave. Find somewhere warm. Find Erik. Yes, that too. While Alice had become everything an awesome girlfriend should be, Erik was her rock. For better or worse.

"Well." Alice opened her eyes. "You... it's hard to explain. First it's as if you've been hit. You jerk or shake. Then, you look like you have gone into shock. All the blood and warmth drain from you. It's like … Well, it's like you become, uh, like them." She motioned toward the tables' occupants.

"Lovely." She and Erik had never broached the subject in much detail. She knew her episodes scared him.

Truth? She thought they terrified him. He'd never gone into detail past that. The scientist researcher part of her kicked in. Was she leaving her body? Alice's description almost made it sound something like that. She'd always just assumed she went into a trance. Out-to-lunch sort of thing. A dream. Yes, a dream. But while you might toss, turn or even walk in a dream, your body didn't change.

"I'm sorry it scared you, Alice."

"Yes, well, I did ask for it. So what did you see?"

"A murder, Alice."

"So this guy did relive his death, after all?"

"No, he—I—saw the death of a Muslim woman in some city in Europe. I'm not sure exactly. Most of those old cities' alleyways look pretty much the same."

"I'd make light of that and tease you about why you were hanging out in old alleyways, but I think I'll leave it for now."

Rhyjl grinned. "I just bet you will. That's a topic for another girls' night. This guy was chasing after the woman and the other man. By the time he caught up with them, the woman was dying in the arms of the other."

"Wow! Did the other guy kill her?"

"Maybe. It was hard to tell."

"So what aren't you telling me?"

"How do you know I'm not telling you something?" Rhyjl unbuttoned the lab coat Alice had loaned her as she walked toward the door. Peeling off the gloves, she threw them in a stainless steel can with a red biohazard bag. "I'll see you later. You may have resistance to this icebox, but my teeth are beginning to chatter."

Alice reached out and touched her arm. "Go get warm. We can talk later. And don't forget to draw that tattoo, if you remember what it looks like, please."

Rhyjl doubted she could forget, even if she wanted

to. Some things just burn themselves into your memory.

Chapter 5

A Game of Clues

Rhyjl sat at the computer. Google was great when it came to finding photos of things. She'd found plenty! The last hour had been spent looking at tattoos of anchors. The victims had been military. Anchors made sense, especially when it came to the Navy and even Marines. None of them had come close to what she'd seen. Then she played her hunch from earlier and it paid off on her first search. The tattoo on the man's arm was of Thor's Hammer.

She was familiar with the symbol because of her Norse studies. The Norse god, Thor, had a hammer which in Germanic mythology was called Mjollnir, meaning "crusher." This magical hammer name could be etymologically linked as well to words for "lightning." Thor being the god of thunder and lightning, after all.

As a military tattoo, it very well could be emblematic. Thor had fought against chaos so that creation could continue. Wasn't that what all wars were about: good versus evil? That the line could sometimes be blurred as to which side was which, well, it wasn't as clear-cut as it often appeared, to her way of thinking. Did anyone ever really fight for evil? She and Erik had run this discourse through many evenings. Especially after he had been listening to news of the Middle East. She could see his point. Religious zealots had killed his mother and her archaeological team. But had those individuals really seen themselves as fighting for evil? Probably not. They had most likely seen it as being a force of good. History was full of it. When Rome spread out across much of Europe, and parts of Asia and Africa, had they seen themselves as evil? You'd better believe those they conquered and subjugated had. Yes, Rome had brought many technological advances, safe roads for trading, etcetera, but took away in other ways, that which was cherished or believed, as well as bringing death. Didn't Merriam Webster define evil as "causing harm or injury to someone?"

She thought of the two times she'd seen the man with the tattoo. He had been in the middle of what could be called chaos: an explosion, and a woman dying. Had he chosen to mark himself as the crusher of chaos?

The scenes played over and over in her mind. Who was he? She'd thought in the first scenario that the face covered in blood and filth looked familiar. Or was it that he just looked like so many generic photos of soldiers in war? In the second, his face was turned mostly away, and what was visible was cloaked in shadow.

Jack stirred at her feet, lifting his massive head to stare at her with soulful eyes. She glanced at the clock on the screen and was amazed at how much time she'd spent looking at men's arms covered in ink. "I bet you need to go out, don't you?"

Jack's tail thumped his reply. His big body stretched, then rose to nudge her elbow, which was now at nose height for him.

Looking out the windows, she saw the wind that had been battering the coast all morning had subsided. Instead of bending the trees surrounding the New England Cape, it only tickled the smaller branches. It was a good time for her to take Jack out for a stroll along the cliff trail. Her head felt muddled. Possibly a hangover from the morning's activities. A brisk walk in the cool salty air, hopefully would clear it.

The walk along the cliff was stark at this time of the year, while at the same time having an incredible rugged beauty. The Atlantic was pewter. White pointed caps still rode the waves, even though the wind had died to barely a whisper. In the distance, she could see the islands that had always reminded her of a family of turtles. Today, even though the clouds still hung low on the horizon, she could see all the way across to Mount Desert Island.

Jack, bouncing along beside her, would occasionally tear off ahead to find a stick to give her as a gift. She had tried numerous times to teach him to fetch. It wasn't that he didn't know how. He just seemed to get bored of the game quickly. Still, he loved to find sticks to place at her feet and look expectantly for her to acknowledge his efforts. It was almost as if when she threw it away from herself, he would follow it with his eyes just as a person might and then move on to other interests. She imagined him thinking, *If she doesn't like it, I'll find a better one later*. He usually did, or he'd bring her a rock. One day, just out of curiosity to prove her theory, she'd kept the stick, tucking it away in the pouch of her hoodie. He didn't bring her any more treasures. She could have sworn Jack also carried a smile on his face for the rest of the day.

Today they'd only wandered a quarter of the way when Jack spied Erik and raced to join him. Rhyjl, being focused on the distant shores, would have missed him entirely if not for the impetuous canine. Erik was standing on the sweeping lawn that spread like a carpet from the base of the massive three-story stone building that was the heart of Down East University, down to the cliff and path.

The mansion, including many of the surrounding

buildings, had been built around the 1890's. The original owner, while not as prominent as the Fords, Astors, Vanderbilts, and Rockefellers, was nevertheless one of the wealthy segment of society known as Rusticators. Drawn to the incredible beauty of the third largest island on the east coast through the works of painters such as Thomas Cole and Frederick Church, the wealthy had flocked to Mount Desert Island and the surrounding areas.

Rustic, however, was not their true nature and soon the "camps," as they affectionately called their homes, evolved into huge estates, or "cottages", that rivaled any aristocrat's home in Europe. Many of those homes were later destroyed when the fire of 1947 devastated much of the island, ending a lavish era. While Acadia National Park had been established in 1919 — the first National Park east of the Mississippi River— it wasn't until after the fire, that the island was later transformed, with the help of the Rockefellers, and became better known as the Acadia National Park of today. During the island's heyday, however, DEU's original owners had bemoaned the fact that their home required a short sail to the social activities. In the end, they were grateful their camp had escaped the devastation.

As he stood gazing out upon the stormy Atlantic, Erik looked for all the world as if he was an apparition lingering from that time. Sometimes she wondered if he was out of a past time. Although his focus was in the future, that wasn't true of his physical appearance: full beard, combed-back curls that sometimes tumbled across his brow when he was immersed in whatever he was doing. His daily conduct and strong sense of right and wrong also invoked a sense of the past. He was intense. Passionate about his work, his students and her.

It was the last that was disconcerting. She didn't

believe in love. She'd seen it ruin lives. People claiming to be in love, with nothing else in common, was a recipe for disaster. Look at her mother and father. For that matter, how could Erik believe in it? He'd admitted there was no love between his parents. Lust on his father's part, perhaps. His mother had been what others might have called a gold digger. She was accomplished and brilliant in her field of archaeology, but starting out? Digs took money. Research took money. Erik's dad had the money. Lust and need do not make a comfortable bed.

If she married, it would be to someone with the same passions. They'd build a relationship on common goals.

Alerted to her close proximity by Jack's excited bark, Erik waved, then proceeded down the sloping lawn in a half-run toward her. Jack met him halfway in a bounding circular dance. His laughter and Jack's animation warmed her. But seeing any person and dog enjoying themselves in such a fashion would do the same. It had no more meaning than that.

~~

"You're cold," he said, wrapping his arms around her.

"A little. How was your day?" She turned from his arms and began to walk the trail leading to the point. She knew he hated to go there. It reminded him of almost losing her. He couldn't forget. She had done her best to put it behind her. It was a beautiful promontory. What Erik didn't understand was there was probably no single place on earth that didn't have a connection with death. It was all around them, inescapable.

"As expected. I gave a test on integrative circuitry

today. I'd had better hopes for the outcome. Maybe it's just me, but it seems like too many of the students want it spoon fed to them."

"It's not you. I see it too. I imagine it's how they are used to learning. Perhaps it's just that most of them either don't want to put out the effort, or don't have whatever it is that makes them want to understand."

They walked along in silence. Erik picked up a stick and threw it several times for Jack to recover. Of course, Jack was eager to please. Jack fetched for him. It must have something to do with male bonding, she thought. The wind had blown the clouds away. It was looking like Erik's prediction for a nice weekend was realistic. "Still planning on sailing tomorrow?"

"Have you changed your mind? Will you be coming along with Jack?"

"I had thought about it."

Erik touched her arm, then pulled her close once he knew she wouldn't move away. "Look, I'm sorry. I'm not trying to run your life, I..."

She leaned in, embracing his warmth. "You just worry about me. I know."

He laughed, while tipping her chin up so he could search her eyes. "Are you going to tell me that ever since we met, our lives haven't been a little on the dangerous side?"

"Hasn't been boring, has it?" She gave him a little poke in the side. He was extremely ticklish and she didn't want serious. This time, however, it didn't work. Rather than jumping back and away, his grip strengthened.

"I'd like to try boring for a while. Wouldn't you?"

"Erik, if what I'm doing is too stressful for you, perhaps it's time I get a place of my own again." Her jab hadn't worked, but her words cleaved them like precision steel.

He fell back a step, his arms dropping to his sides. "Is that what you really want?"

"No... maybe. I just don't want you to be so stressed out."

"And you think that moving out wouldn't be stressful?" His arms flew up in the air as he turned to the sea. "We are good together, Rhyjl! We've been good together since we first bumped into each other. I can assure you that your moving out would not relieve any stress. It would only create more. If having you in my life means danger and adventure, and yes, stress, then bring it on." He turned and trod the path back toward their house, leaving Jack distressed and confused.

The giant canine looked at Erik's retreating back and began to trail him, until he realized Rhyjl wasn't following. Stopping, he whined and lay down, resting his nose between his forepaws.

"Go!" she commanded. "Seek Erik."

The dog lifted his head, turned to look for Erik, then placed his head back down and looked at her with worry. "Great! Like master like dog. It's not like I'm going to fall off the face of the earth, you know." And yet, in a way, only a few months prior, she had. It had been Jack's love that had found her and Erik's that had saved her.

Sighing, she turned back toward the house, with Jack traipsing merrily beside her.

~~

Alice spent the day poring over the bones. She hadn't even stopped for lunch. Her only break had been when the parents of the seventeen-year-old auto victim arrived to claim his body. She'd done the ritual. Offered her condolences for their loss, answered their questions. "Yes, he died instantly. No, he never suffered." The parents hadn't asked "Why" like so many others did. They had already been told the "why" by the State Police. They'd offered their son a stick of dynamite in the form of a sporty new car. Then they had added the match, a fancy iPhone. Had he looked up from his cell phone screen long enough to see the truck coming toward him? Or as Rhyjl suspected in the case of the mysterious skeletal remains: he hadn't had a clue what was about to happen? State Trooper Burke had said the boy was texting to his girlfriend at the time. Alice hadn't been told what the boy's text had said. She hoped it was a happy thought.

The door to her private office opened after a brief rap. Tanner walked in, looking a little drained.

"Tough day? You look a little wiped," Alice said, getting up from her chair and walking around to the front of her desk.

"Day was fine. Rough night. You have anything more on those skeletons?" He moved closer, looked around, then pecked her on the cheek.

"Must have been a doozy of a night. Either that or I'm starting to rub off on you. Imagine, Mike Tanner showing affection in public." She smiled, her arms circling around his neck.

He broke the moment by stepping back. "I need something on those remains. Was Rhyjl any help?"

She sighed, while at the same time gritting her teeth. If he was going for this argument again... "She was." *I'm just not sure how to tell you.* "She asked me to have a tox screen done on the bones."

"That's highly unusual and a little on the pricey side. Has Jim Ackerman agreed to that?"

Her boss hadn't. Probably because, at this time, she

hadn't come up with a good enough reason to convince him. "I haven't spoken with him yet," she said, returning to her chair and folding herself into the black leather confines. "She... I... we felt that the way the bones were broken in the man who had been run over, was suspicious."

"How?" He stood with his legs slightly apart, his hands grasped behind his back.

"Usually in a hit and run there are injuries to the extremities. Fractured legs from being hit by a bumper. Fracturing in the arms. In this case it was like the guy laid down with his arms over his head and just waited."

"So you are thinking he might have been unconscious prior?"

"Yes, I think that is fair to say. But why was he unconscious? Rhyjl suspects drugs might have been involved."

"Can they get a good toxicology reading on the presence of drugs from bones, especially ones this old?"

"Well, we've known for some time that bones will retain toxins such as heavy metals. New research has found a way to detect opiates, cocaine, and a few others. We don't have that kind of equipment here. I'm looking into the forensics lab in Sudbury, Massachusetts."

"So until then, what else do you have?"

"We are pretty sure the one fellow was run over."

"You told me that last night. What's different about today?"

"Mike, I might be able to tell you if you'd stop interrupting." When he nodded without a verbal response, she continued. "It looked like a hit and run last night as I suggested, but I was tired and hadn't had much time. Today we examined the body more closely. The guy wasn't hit. Run over yes, but not hit. He was lying face down and probably already dead or unconscious when the vehicle ran over him. The other thing, it was an unusual tire. It was big, at least thirty centimeters. I thought a truck, but..."

"A tractor?"

She cleared her throat and glared at him. "Possibly. I haven't had a chance to look into the specifics as yet. I just know if it was a car, it was probably more like the off-road type. Besides, who drives around on a tractor?"

"Farmers. Did you forget where we found the bodies?"

"Um, you are right, of course. Maybe CSI should go back to the farm and check the machinery. Not that there's likely be much evidence after this amount of time. There might be traces of blood, but I doubt it. If nothing else, we could compare the tire width to that found on the bones. Death by tractor. That will be a new one for me. Have you found out who the owners of the property are? Could they be involved?"

"Not likely. Older couple. Actually the husband just passed away. The wife is down in South Carolina with their daughter. No one has been at the farm for the last two years. I guess they've been talking about selling it. Hard, though. It's been in the family for six generations."

"Yes, I can see where it would be, but if no family members want to live on it..." She let it go. It was an old story. Families didn't stay in one place any longer. Jobs and physical preference often took them away from their home towns. If she thought about it, she didn't really know any of her friends who weren't from "away," as the old-time Mainers would say. Once, a conversation had come up with a crusty old fellow who had informed her that even if someone had been born in Maine, but their parents were from "away," they still couldn't call themselves Mainers. As he'd put it, "Just 'cause kittens aw bon in the oven, don't make um biscuits!"

Tanner phoned in the request to CSI, helped her into her coat, and held the door open. He offered to take her to lunch. Who was she to turn it down? Did it matter that it was almost four in the afternoon? "How about if we swing by my place? I can change into something a little nicer and we could go to Jackson's in Bucksport."

She didn't have to ask twice.

~~

At five in the evening, Jackson's was starting to fill with the dinner crowd. Any later, seating would have required a reservation or a long wait. The decor was done in colors of the Atlantic. Mostly blues, grays and white. Accents were weathered pylons and heavy hemp rope that looked like they had been looted from an old dock. On a few, glassy-eyed wooden seagulls perched. It was adjacent to one of these that a handsome young waiter, dressed in white shirt and black pants, seated them. He asked if they would like anything from the bar, then left two menus, promising to return as soon as they were ready.

Alice picked up the wine menu before opening the dinner one. She already knew what she wanted. The shrimp scampi was especially good here.

"Merlot?"

"I shouldn't," Mike answered, closing his menu and giving a nod to their waiter, who was standing by the bar carrying on a conversation—or possibly flirtation—with a pretty brunette bartender. "Technically, I'm still on duty."

Tanner scanned the other patrons around them. No one was paying particular attention. An older couple to his left were discussing a forthcoming trip to Florida to find a new home. A younger couple directly behind him were planning an evening out. The two well-dressed suits on his right were agonizing over the not-so-robust economy, despite what the government was claiming. First rule he'd learned was not to discuss business in a restaurant. You never knew who might be listening. Still, any information Alice might have on the newest residents in the morgue was like an itch screaming to be scratched.

Alice, however, was evasive while they dined. The more he probed, the more she changed the subject. She and her sidekick knew something about the remains she wasn't telling. To distract him from his questions, she kept returning to her favorite topic of the evening, the evil of cell phones. He got it. No, he didn't see the mangled bodies like the first responders or Alice.

"I don't know what can be done, Alice. We have laws. If our troopers see someone on a cell phone they pull them over. It's not like we can outlaw the phones."

"Why the H-E double-hockey-sticks not? We outlaw everything else. Kids can't buy booze underage. Can't buy a gun. Why should they have phones underage? I know all the arguments." She flipped her left hand dismissively. "I've heard them over and over again. We have all these concerned parents pushing for gun control, yet they hand over a cell phone and a car without thinking twice. You know I'm not a Second Amendment freak, but do you know how many shootings I saw this last year versus death by texting and driving? Zero! Not one teen dead from a gun. I saw twenty-six kids and nine adults come across my table thanks to cell use while driving. That doesn't begin to count the number tally for the state. Eleven kids a day, Mike! Eleven kids a day is the national average! And some unlucky individuals like Trooper Burke are the ones that do the cleanup. You know he kept saying how his kid was a friend of the boy he helped untangle from that car crash the other night. The other two kids in the car are in serious condition. I'm thankful neither of them ended up on my table. It's not the blood and gore, Mike. It's not even the victim. That boy likely never knew what hit him. It's the senseless wreckage they leave behind in other people's lives."

He reached across the table to cup his hand over hers. "I do know, Alice." He knew better than most the toll senseless deaths could wrack up on a person. You had to walk away from it or end up with the barrel of a gun in your mouth or death at the end of a needle or a bottle. "We can only bring closure. We can't change people. You've said that a time or two, right?" He squeezed her hand and smiled. "So back to the case at hand. Did you get anything back on dental records?"

Alice pulled her hand away, picked up her fork and began stirring the remnants of the shrimp scampi she'd ordered. "Not yet. Either these guys didn't go to dentists or they don't exist. The men, I mean, not the teeth. Well, of course if the men didn't exist, the teeth... Stop looking at me that way! These guys are like ghosts. Even Rhyjl said as much. Even the guy with metal implants can't be found in a database."

"So you aren't getting very far with identification. How about cause of death? I know you said ..."

"Well, that's kind of a pain as well. It looks like these guys were all killed randomly. I'm not seeing any specific MO. If we can't link how the victims were connected, it doesn't give me much to give you. Rhyjl has given me the best lead so far. She..." Alice laid her fork down, took a long pull from her wine glass, looked Mike in the eye and dropped her voice to a whisper. "Mike, could these guys be something like special ops or CIA?"

A couple centipedes moved up his spine. "What could Rhyjl have possibly found that would suggest something like that?"

"She said, if they were skeletons from the past, she would have noted them as warriors. They are covered in remodeled fractures, Mike. And while it is true that the one guy looks to have had a rough go in an accident, it also looks as if he went back to some kind of activity that required defensive moves."

Mike shook his head and busied himself fiddling with the napkin he'd laid beside his plate. "You've been watching too many action movies, lady. They could be just plain veterans. You do realize we've been involved in some kind of foreign conflict for as long as you and I have been alive."

"Perhaps, but why do I keep hitting all the dead ends? That's not normal, Mike."

She was right. She was probably right in all of it, if those remains were who he thought they might be. He'd been doing a little checking on his own. Nothing official. He couldn't and wouldn't be able to explain his reasoning to his superiors at this point, but he still had connections in strange places. Sans Granger. Only if H-E double-hockey-sticks froze over, as Alice would say, would he ask or have anything to do with that son-of-a-bitch.

Chapter 6

Riddle Me This

Erik hoisted the main, his breath catching, then working the rudder so they glided away from the small bottle-shaped bay toward the islands. It was bittersweet every time he heard the sound of the canvas rising. The *Windcatcher* was a lovely little sloop out of Ontario. With an overall length of twenty-nine feet and a waterline of twenty-one, she was sleek and responsive. Her hull was sunset red. Her sails white except for a wide trim of blue on the mainsail.

On the water, he never felt alone. Even if Rhyjl and Jack hadn't come, his mother was always with him in the salty air when the wind moved the craft along. She had loved her work as an archaeologist. All the digs in dry arid places were her addiction. But sailing was her passion. On the water, she had been free. Freedom. That had been what she named her forty-five-foot schooner, the *Eleutheria*. The *Eleutheria* had always been manned. Her crew of four, which included a cook, was at his mother's beck and call anywhere on the Mediterranean. She'd been his mother's pride, and where she'd spent every spare moment away from her digs. It was during these times that Erik was the closest to his mother. She'd always told him the *Eleutheria* would be his someday. After his mother's death, his father had sold her. Just one more betrayal heaped upon the rest. He felt the tightness in his chest and breathed deep to release the old pangs. He couldn't change yesterday. He could make new tomorrows. He could start today.

Rhyjl fidgeted with the strings of her hoodie. It

might be a bright, clear day, but the sun was still being stingy with its warmth. That didn't appear to bother either Erik or Jack. Erik was very much at home with a sailboat's rudder in his hand, the sails seemingly shifting by magic to take full advantage of the wind. Jack stood at the bow barking as if he were calling out "Bring it on! Bring it on!" Rhyjl, snuggling deeper inside her hood, had found that Erik had been correct once more. Sailing did allow for good thinking time.

There was something that kept nagging at the back of her mind. Something she knew should connect but kept escaping her. Two of the four men had been silent on their own deaths, but had retained substantial energy about their past. Somehow, it was tied back to the man with the tattoo. One man had seen a savior who brought him comfort. The other had seen a death connected to the mystery man. Her mind kept playing back the scene from the darkened streets of the old city. The woman draped in black, not much more than a silhouette against the sheen off the rain-soaked pavement. Who was she? What was her connection to these men? His thoughts had also identified the one who held the woman as Spidey. Had Spidey been her killer? It was all a tangled and dark web. She felt it clinging to her, but at the same time, she didn't want to be free of it. She wanted more than ever to return to the morgue and see if he would tell her more. But Erik had been right about that as well. Contact with the dead sucked the life out of her. As much as she wanted to, she knew she didn't have the energy or strength.

She needed to somehow stop the fraying of the fabric that was her and Erik's relationship. Their evening together had been as silent as death. Erik had shut himself away in the room that had once been hers, but was now the guest room. He'd taken a laptop with him. She didn't think it had anything to do with his students or even the invention he'd been working on for the past year. As the night wore on and he didn't come to bed, it brought home how much he was either hurting or trying to hurt. She hated his silences. They were rare, but that made them more disturbing when he did have one. The only thing that was worse was his polite detachment, as if she were one of his female students who was attempting to be overtly friendly. This morning he'd been the latter, and had been more solicitous toward the dog and the picnic basket than her. She was amazed how deeply that cut. She'd wanted to reach out and touch him, to feel the warmth that always spread between them. Instead, they'd both remained reserved, only connecting with Jack, who appeared out of spirits as well.

These thoughts took her back to the scene in that distant city. She let her mind sink into the vision. The man with the tattoo holding the woman. Her ghostly hand reaching for his face as if caressing a lover. The warmth and life draining out of her into a puddle even mighty Thor could not stanch.

"Too cold?" The voice intruded into her dark thoughts.

"No." She smiled up at Erik. "Just thinking."

"Must not have been pleasant thoughts."

"Not particularly."

"About the four dead guys?" he said, taking a seat next to her.

"That and other things. Shouldn't you be at the tiller?"

"Wow, you really were deep in thought. We've hove-to. I thought some hot tea and a snack might be nice before we head back." He extended his hand more as a courtesy than to help her up.

She accepted the familiar heat. He pulled her close. She melted into his embrace. "I'm so sorry, Erik. You're always right. I can't do this without you. But I need to do it. Can you understand?"

Erik squeezed her tighter. "I'm not always right, just mostly." He felt her familiar move to poke him in the ribs, and clamped her arms closer to his sides. "I spent a lot of time last night thinking about you, this, us. The truth is, I'd like to hide you away and keep you safe, but I can't. Because if I were successful, then you would cease to be you, the woman I fell in love with. However, that doesn't mean I'm always going to be happy about it. Can you accept that?"

Rhyjl buried her face deeper into his shoulder. Could she? Should she? Was it right for one person to struggle in a relationship just so the other person could be happy? Isn't that what her mother had done? Always giving up herself for her undeserving husband. How great had that turned out? "I don't want you to sacrifice yourself for me."

"That's not your choice." He gently eased her away until he was holding her at arm's length and looking into those bewitching hazel eyes. "It's mine. And understand this. I don't consider my time with you, even when it's difficult, a sacrifice. What we have is magic, Rhyjl. To quote from the *Shannara Chronicles*, 'Magic always comes with a price.'"

~~

"Give me flesh!" Alice said, looking with dismay at the skeleton lying on the exam table before her. "If I had flesh," she glared at Tanner, "I'd know that the tractor tire was or was not the cause of death, with or without blood residue. Mottling could give me an excellent idea of tire tread, but this?" She pointed at the bones and then turned away to go back to her desk, expecting he would follow. "Mike, I just don't know. It's the right size, but..."

"Is this another plug for Rhyjl?"

She whirled around to face him. "Dammit, Mike, will you *please* get past this hang-up of yours? I don't know if Rhyjl could make this call any better than I at this point. It's just too hard to tell. Bones don't tell all. If it were skin, well, skin is laden with information right on the surface. Puncture marks or unusual coloring to indicate poisoning. A fingerprint, so to speak, of bruising in the pattern of the weapon or in this case, the possible weapon. All the bones can tell me at this point is it was probably a very large tire. Not the type."

"Okay, I've got it. I'm just anxious to get going on this and so far, I don't have that much to go on." He began pacing the floor of the examination room, going from victim to victim. "We shouldn't even be in working this today. It's Saturday! I should be watching a football game or spending my time with a special lady somewhere other than this." His arm waved in a one-eighty. "But this case has me missing sleep at night."

"And why exactly is this case so much different than any of the others we've worked on? Mike, in all the years I've known and worked with you, I've never seen you so wound up."

"I don't know." He did, of course, but he wasn't ready to share his thoughts with her or anyone at this point. What could he say? *I think that I know these guys and someone is out to make me a fifth victim.* "I just don't like the feel of this case. It's too convoluted."

After dropping Alice off the night before, he'd gone over his apartment with a fine-tooth comb. He'd learned to be cautious, almost to the point of paranoia. Just part and parcel with his former job. Those who weren't ended up dead. Old habits were hard to change. Like putting the tiny wisp of paper inconspicuously at the side of his door each time he went out. Just small enough so unless you were looking for it, you wouldn't see it when it fell.

Two hours of diligence had turned up nothing. Nothing was out of place. There was no evidence of surveillance or bugs other than the spider he'd disturbed. There had been no marks or unusual scratches on the windowsill. He'd thought about looking for fingerprints to run through the Integrated Automated Fingerprint Identification System of the FBI, but doubted anything would come out of it. Hell, if it was who he thought it might be, not even Interpol would have what he needed to confirm his suspicions. What had Alice said? "Ghosts." Yet someone had opened his window, and done it with such stealth, he hadn't heard them. That, in itself, was an incredible feat considering how lightly he slept. But to what end? If they'd wanted to kill him, they could have. It was like they wanted him to know he was an easy target. Toying with him. There was another possibility. Someone was trying to warn him. Was he meant to be another victim? But who? Why? His mind flashed back over the past twelve years. One didn't do what he'd done without some people getting their noses bent out of shape, or broken, as the case may be. Only a few names surfaced that met the criteria. But business was business. Your opponents expected loss and defeat, just as you did. There was no room for petty grudges. They might not like it but...

"I agree with you there." Alice's voice intruded into his musings. "This case is a nightmare: skeletal remains in unmarked graves, with nothing in common that's visible at the moment. I'm just a small-town medical examiner. This is the kind of case the big labs in the cities should be dealing with."

"Humph! Don't underestimate yourself. You're far from the local doc with no forensic training."

"Training I've got. Equipment and personnel are what's missing. Speaking of that little troll, he should have been in an hour ago."

Mike's response was well rehearsed, since they'd had this discussion many times. "Why do you put up with him, Alice? You are his superior. Fire him."

"Not that simple, Mike. When he does his job, he is good at it. He's also got a family. His wife is expecting a baby next month."

"Yeah, and you just don't have the heart. We've discussed this too many times. If you can't work with him, then let him go. There's got to be others out there who have families and need jobs."

"That's part of the problem. There are probably lots of qualified technicians out there that are flipping burgers right now. If I let him go, I don't know if he will be able to find another job."

"Sure he will! He can have the burger flipping job of the new tech you hire."

Mike wiggled his eyebrows up and down, his closed-mouth grin stretching from ear to ear as he made a flipping motion with his right arm.

For the first time in two days, Alice laughed.

~~

"I need your help, Erik. I just got off the phone with Alice. She is hitting dead ends with all her inquiries about these four guys."

"What kind of help?" Erik asked, swiveling his chair away from his main computer screen to watch her approach. She was dressed in a long T-shirt she called a maxi something. It was casual and oh so unbelievably sexy.

She recognized the look on his face. It both annoyed and flattered her. Since they had started sleeping together, it seemed his appetite was insatiable. "Not that kind." She winked. "I need you to try some of your magic and see if you can break through to get some information that... ah, let's say might be a bit confidential."

"Are you asking me to do something illegal?"

"I'm asking you to just break through a few firewalls."

"You are asking me to do something illegal."

"Here's the thing. Those four guys are military. I think I might even have a link with this tattoo." She flipped open her leather-bound journal and showed him the sketch she had made of the tattoo. "The problem is, every time Alice tries to run a search for dental or metal implants, she comes up empty..."

"Stop right there, Rhyjl. I don't do illegal. Not for Alice and not even for you." He swung back to his computer screen and tried in vain to focus on the circuit board he'd been working on for the past month. Damn!

The fact that she was still standing there with an expectant look on her face—a look she must have learned from Jack when he was a puppy—was his undoing when he glanced up. "Do you have any idea what would happen if I was caught hacking into government records? Especially records that for some reason have been closed that securely? Let me tell you, all hell could break loose. Our home would look like something out of 'Call to Duty.'"

"So are you refusing to help me out of a sense of ethics or fear?"

"Both, and I'm proud of the first and not ashamed of the other. Look Rhyjl, I want to help. If I'm honest, you have my curiosity more than just a little piqued, but government records? Suspicious corporations, gang operations, maybe even individuals whom I suspect might be guilty of a crime—you didn't hear me say that last bit—but the military?"

She exhaled a long heavy sigh and slumped into the big overstuffed chair. "I know you are right. It's just so frustrating. It's like they are ghosts, Erik."

"That's your specialty, love. Haven't you been able to get their vibes?"

"No... well... yes and no. I did get something from their past. That's one of the reasons we know they are military. I have the tattoo. But I've no idea of even where to begin to gather more info on that. At one time they were in Europe. Or at least two of them were. But see, I'm not even sure about that. There's this mystery man. He keeps showing up in their memories. But I don't know if he is one of them or not. I even had this crazy idea that he might be the one killing them."

His circuit board would have to wait. She'd roped him in. There was no hope of evading this now. "What makes you think this mystery man might be the killer?"

"I don't know. He's just a common link. The only one we have so far. But I don't think he is one of the victims. I'm sure I would feel that if he were. He's not dead. He's alive. Somewhere."

"So why does that make him a suspect? I'm failing to see your reasoning."

"I don't know. Maybe because he is still alive and not dead like the others."

"Or maybe he just hasn't been killed yet. Perhaps your mystery man is the next victim." He saw his mistake as soon as the words were out of his mouth.

"Then if that's the case, it's even more important for us to find the link before he does join the others in death."

Erik did a palm plant. "Ugh. I can't even believe I fell into that. What kind of information do you ladies need?"

"Oh, Erik, you are awesome!" She did a little dance around the room before landing in his lap, almost sending the two of them and the well-padded executive chair over backward.

"There's still a limit to how far I'll go. So what do you need that hopefully won't land me in a federal prison for the rest of my life?"

"There were several implants. A knee replacement and the guy who was in the explosion..."

"Explosion?" The pressure was building behind his temples. He didn't like drugs, even the over-the-counter kind, but after this, he might just succumb to a Tylenol or two.

"Yeah. Anyway, he was kind of pieced back together with several pins and plates. All of those have ID numbers and manufacturers. But where Alice would normally be able to get the numbers from the company and then trace them to the hospital, etc., she runs into a block. The companies must have some kind of records. If you could start there. Then if we could find the hospitals..."

"Then even if you couldn't find the direct recipient, you could get a list of patients? Then trace the whereabouts of the surgery patients? Is that what you are thinking?"

"Well, yes, that was kind of my train of thought."

He looked into those pleading eyes and felt what

little reserve he had left fail him. "Then get me the numbers and get off my lap. This is going to take a lot of time and effort."

~~

"Where did you get that tattoo?" Alice said, as she stroked her fingers lazily down Tanner's arm. Her bedroom was dark except for the blue glow seeping from the nightlight in her bathroom. She didn't need to see the tattoo beneath her touch. She knew it well.

"Why?" He pulled her closer, liking the way her body conformed to fit him.

"Just wondering. How long have you had it?"

"A lifetime ago in a small town called Fayetteville—a grungy little place. It's a wonder I didn't end up with a nasty infection. But then, at that age, we all think we are invincible. Why all the interest in a tattoo that you've seen numerous times?"

"We?"

"The collective, as in all young people. Alice, what's this all about?" He propped himself up on his elbow while he stroked her tousled hair back from her face. He loved this quiet intimate time more than the act of lovemaking, and that was saying something, since the latter was spectacular.

"I was just thinking of the things people put the human body through. Do they keep records in those places?"

Her hand drifted from his arm to his face, a caress as warm as the sun. This time it failed to warm him as it usually did. "I don't normally have a tough time tracking where your thoughts are going and why. You're losing me on this one, however." He wasn't going to admit that the direction their conversation was taking was making him uncomfortable. And why should it? The answer was simple. Four murder victims he was becoming more sure every day were his old comrades. Now out of the blue, Alice was bringing up tattoos. What had she said earlier? "...skin is laden with information right on the surface." But in this case, there was no skin. So again, why the sudden interest in tattoos?

"If someone did get a tattoo, would you be able to trace that? If someone committed a crime, let's say, and the only information you had was an eyewitness description of a tattoo?"

"A needle in a haystack, Alice. The only thing the tattoo would be good for is once you caught the suspect. Then you could use it just as you would any other identifying mark such as a scar, mole or some other kind of mark a person might get in their life such as an unusual piercing."

The florescent numerals of her bedside clock glowed the excuse he needed. "Wow, almost midnight. I need to be on my way home."

"Mike, stay, please." She reached for him even as he disentangled himself from her and the bedding. "It's late."

"Exactly. I have things I need to attend to tomorrow. I need to get some sleep." *I also don't want to risk placing you in danger if I'm being stalked.*

"But you can sleep here. It's a forty-minute drive to your place. You could be sleeping all that time instead of driving."

She stretched out, covering the spot he'd just abandoned like a cat reveling in the warmth. He wanted to stay. He wanted to wrap her around him like a second skin. "Because, with you looking like that, I don't think I'd get much sleep."

Alice listened to the sound of his car starting up and heading down her driveway. The temptation to think that she was nothing more than a stop-off comfort station for him was strong. That wasn't Mike, though. There was something else and it wasn't his need of sleep, albeit, he was correct in thinking that sleep wouldn't have been forthcoming. "One of these days, Detective Tanner, I'll plumb those deep waters you keep so well hidden," she said, laying her head down on the pillow he'd abandoned and breathing in the scent of him.

Chapter 7

On the Trail

Why did it seem her life was always complicated? She'd almost been able to put aside her thesis while puzzling on the four skeletons. Then this morning she'd checked the messages on the cell phone Erik insisted she carry. The message was left on Saturday and was short: "Monday. My office at eight."

Rhyjl had been dreading the talk with Marcus about her thesis ever since their argument. What was there left to say? He'd already made it quite clear what his intentions and thoughts were toward her project. The meeting tomorrow was like a case of food poisoning roiling around her middle. She knew in so many ways he was correct. To push through would be suicide. She might as well take all her diligent work of the last eight years and toss it in the fire. And a fire it would be. She didn't need him to go over everything again. Yes, First Nations status would be threatened. Yes, the government would be on her back like a tick on a dog.

When all was said and done, if she were lucky, she might be able to get a job as a waitress. In the case of that scenario, she might become one of Tanner's groupies. She often wondered if the waitresses got into hair pulling and fist fights when he walked in the door. How often did someone give out a tip that was a match for the meal they had ordered?

Still, it wasn't as if she couldn't afford to lose her work. That she would have to turn to being a waitress, even one of the "groupies" was a moot point. Erik had already shown her how the small fortune she'd taken home from the pirate booty could be invested and allow her to live quite comfortably for years, if not the rest of her life. Then, of course, she could become Mrs. Erik Arneson and never have to worry about money again.

It wasn't like he had proposed or anything. Still, she always had the feeling that's where he was headed, and he was only waiting until he felt she might agree. Fair enough. If she were honest with herself, it had become a constant battle that lay just under the surface of her daily routines. If she let her heart get a say, she was lost. Erik was handsome, though not movie-star quality. He still turned more than his fair share of women's heads. A fact that had often brought out the green-eyed cat in her. He was wealthy. Again, not that she was in need as she once had been.

No, what was most fatal to all her resolve to steer clear of him was simple: She was happier with him in her life than she was without him.

Just like what he was doing now, crunching away on his computer. She knew it went against his core. He said he wasn't doing it for her so much as to sate his own curiosity and possibly save a life. The truth still remained: he would be happy working on his circuits if she hadn't brought him into her obsession. But why had she lured him in? Because she thought better and worked better with his input. He asked the questions she very often needed to hear. He played Devil's advocate when she needed to think things out more clearly. Most importantly, he made her smile when she was being too serious or laugh when she was struggling. He helped her to see possibilities when she only saw roadblocks.

"I've got the lists for you. You'll have to take it from here and weed through it," Erik said, breaking into her musings.

She reached up from her chair where she'd been doodling with the tattoo drawing and took the sheets of paper from him. She scanned the list in seconds. There were four hospitals. Two stuck out like flashing neon. Walter Reed and Bethesda Naval. She looked up at him with an unspoken question.

"You got it. They are all military hospitals. However, Walter Reed and Bethesda merged in 2011. I'm playing a hunch here, but I'd say start with Walter Reed records."

"Why's that?" She scanned the dozen or so names listed under Walter Reed.

"Because that's where I ran into the most trouble and the files I found were heavily redacted. However, it's also where I found a series of serial numbers in sequential order except for gaps. Those gaps in the order just happen to match the ones you gave me."

"Clever, clever man," she said, smiling and holding her hand up to receive a high five. "How did you reduce the number of names? I mean, there's got to be thousands of patients that go through..."

"You want all my secrets?" He winked. "Let's just say I did a lot of cross referencing. Possible year or years for those surgeries, the type of surgeries, the manufacturing dates on those parts. It all flows like reading the currents and wind direction when sailing."

"Well, thanks, sailor! How about I text Alice and see what she can make of all this," she said, holding the papers he'd given her along with the drawing she'd sketched. "Then we can take a break for lunch."

"You cooking or buying?" Erik asked, reaching his hand down to take hers as she untangled shapely legs from beneath her to rise.

"I thought I might fix us a sandwich," she said, accepting his offer.

"Okay, I'll buy. You..." He was cut off as she pulled him down rather than allowing him to pull her up.

"You'll pay for that," she said, poking him in the ribs with her free hand, then smacking a big kiss on his lips. "Vinney's and no squid!"

~~

Sunday was his day off. Saturday he was on call, but didn't have to go into work. Sunday, however, was all his. Unless some important murder or mayhem popped up. Since this particular part of the world wasn't exactly known as a high crime center, he was probably safe.

After spending half the night digging through numbers to find people who might give him some answers, he'd spent the better part of the morning calling around. By the fourth call, he'd caught an old friend just as he was heading off to play a round of golf. Half an hour later, he had what he wanted. An hour after that, he'd received a call from Augusta.

His next priority for the day had been setting a series of traps around his apartment on the chance he had a visitor again. His Spidey senses were off the wall. Once he'd finished that, he had set his sights for Alice's. He'd only made one stop at the florist to pick out two dozen long-stem roses, the aroma of which was filling this vehicle with a sweet, spicy-fruit scent reminiscent of sangria. Throwing a glance in their direction, he hoped for the umpteenth time he'd made the right choice, picking the yellow over the red. In the movies, it was always red. Yellow, he knew, was Alice's favorite color.

Her home sat at the top of an open rise with a view

of the ocean flanking thick-growth conifers whose stature had been stunted by the harsh Maine winters. People on this side of the continent were often not cognizant of how short the largest trees were here, unless they had spent time on the west coast where he'd grown up. California's redwoods and the spruce and cedars of the Pacific Northwest dwarfed these eastern cousins.

He swung through the wrought-iron gate, following the paved drive up to the stately home. It was turn of the last century, built probably around the late eighteen or early nineteen hundreds. It was white with black shutters, typical of other homes of that period, and had an inviting wrap-around porch that he and Alice had spent many long summer evenings enjoying. Brown mounds and strips of flower beds surrounding the house were sleeping now. Come June they would be a riot of colors, shapes, and sizes. Alice loved her flowers.

She greeted him at the door with a kiss that promised a lot more. Her hair, down the way he'd left it last night, invited his hands to tangle themselves in it. He gave in to the temptation and pulled her closer.

"I thought you were working today." She nibbled at his lower lip.

"I had some private things that I needed to get accomplished. Finances and such." Like security and setting booby traps. "It didn't take me as long as I thought."

"It's cold out here. I've got a fire on and we can take up where we left off last night." She grasped his hand, leading him through the front door.

"Ah, wait." He pulled away. "I've got to get something out in the car I forgot."

"Can't it wait?"

"No, it'll just take a second." He bounded down the

steps to the driver's side of the blue sedan and pulled an armful of yellow blooms out.

In the language of flowers, yellow roses were a sign of joy and friendship. She and Mike definitely had that. Red was for love. She hoped he felt the latter. Mike probably didn't have a clue what they symbolized, so she would take them just the way they were. "Beautiful!"

He was pleased with her smile and acceptance. He'd made the right choice. His day was looking up.

Once inside, Alice abandoned him in the foyer to go to her kitchen. Moments later, she returned with the flowers nicely arranged in a soft green fluted vase, and a lined paper with what looked like names written in her flowing script. As she set the bouquet on the dining table, Tanner looked over the names Alice handed him. "How did you find these?"

"A little legwork. They're only possibilities, but I thought you might be able to look into them," she answered, making a few more adjustments to the flower arrangement.

Where seconds before he was calm and relaxed, he now felt stretched like a bow string. Every muscle feeling the strain of not letting go. He didn't need to look into the names she'd given him. He had already come up with three of them himself, thanks to the help of his very high-placed friend who owed him favors. A friend who had access to files no one other than personnel with the highest clearance should have been able to get. Alice didn't have that kind of clearance, friends, nor the talent. He had a good idea who she knew that might. Arneson's face flashed in his mind, setting his jaw to tighten until his teeth cried for mercy.

"What's wrong?" Alice placed a gentle hand on his arm. "I thought you wanted me to get these names? Now you look like you want to snap my head off."

"Not yours." His words pressed between the tight gaps in his teeth. He placed his hand over hers and forced himself to calm. "Look, I think it would be best if you let me take this from here."

Like a contagion, his stress had leapt over to her. She abruptly pulled away. "You're asking me to do what, exactly? Not do my job?"

He reached with both hands toward her shoulders. She countered by placing several more steps between them.

"Mike, something is wrong. There's something you are not telling me. Now you want..." She took another step back as he made to advance and her slender, well-manicured hand resolutely became a wall between them. "As I was saying, you want me to..."

"Do your job. Only your job. Don't go getting in this any deeper then you have to, and that includes dragging in your friends. Dammit, I know where you got this list." Arneson's interference was probably what had set off some alarms. If she'd just let him follow his own investigations. "Arneson has no business being in this, Alice."

"That's what you said about Rhyjl."

"Rhyjl? Well, okay, I gave in on that, but..."

"You did no such thing, Mike Tanner!" Stiff-arming him, she pushed past. Her trajectory was set on a course for the entry door. All the secrecy she'd allowed during their relationship was suddenly like coarse slivers, painful with infection, covering her heart. "Don't let it hit you on the way out, Detective," she said, opening it for him.

"You're being unreasonable, Alice. I'm just trying to protect you."

"From what, Tanner? From what! From doing what I'm supposed to do? My job description is pretty simple. Find cause and time of death and identity of deceased individual or individuals if unknown. What part of my job don't you understand?"

"Look," he said, closing the door after a slight tussle. "There are things about this case that are not like any other case you have ever worked on. If I had the authority to transfer it to someone else, I would."

"Now you've stepped over the line. By what authority do you have the right to take my case?" She reached for the door handle once more. His fist slammed against the door inches above the knob.

"I think this is an investigation that belongs in different sectors all the way around, Alice. Not just yours, but mine. These guys were military. I think there are others more qualified to deal with it. I also thought it would be a relief to you. Weren't you the one complaining yesterday that someone with larger facilities, staff and equipment should be handling it?"

"Mike!" She held her index finger just under his nose, her eyes squinting as if she hoped to crack into his brain to pry the information loose if he wasn't forthcoming. "What is it that you know that you aren't telling me? No, don't prevaricate. Not this time."

Pit Bull came to mind as he looked at his tenacious partner. She had her teeth into this bone, or bones, as the case may be. She wasn't going to let go, no matter what he said or did. "These names are all names of servicemen. Three of them I know or used to know. I haven't seen them in several years. I've been trying to find them. I was following a hunch after your description of the past injuries. I'm concerned that inquiries, mine or more likely Arneson's, have possibly set off some alarms. Word came down from the higher echelon this morning that I should be prepared to turn the case over to someone else. And that's fine. I'm done with it. That's all there is to tell. Not mine. Not yours. Not ours, and I AM glad."

"Bull," she said, walking away. "You can't say it's over. It's not over for you."

Following, he shook his head. *Pit Bull. Yep, understatement.* "Didn't you just hear what I said? Why do you think I'm lying?"

She crossed the room to a vintage liquor cart holding several pear-shaped glasses and a crystal decanter half-filled with a warm caramel-colored liqueur. Picking up the container, she held it up toward him. "Interested?" When he nodded, she poured two snifters half full. She handed him one on her way to the sofa near the fireplace. Maybe a drink would help. What she really wanted right now was for him to leave.

The sofa was big, beige, and covered with decorative throws and pillows in a myriad of floral patterns. It was her favorite spot in her home. Kicking off her slippers and curling her feet under her, she sank deep into its comfort and watched the flames as she tried to let go of the tension she felt mounting. Blue propane flames crawled over fake wood, absent the popping and crackling sound of a real fire. She missed the richness of that, but she didn't miss the mess of hauling wood or cleaning out ashes. The fire was doing little at the moment to keep her mind from going over the information Rhyjl had sent to her, especially the drawing of the tattoo. "Oh, I don't think you are lying about someone taking this case over. I don't even think you were lying about being relieved about it. But if you are telling me the truth about having known these guys, it's not over for you. You may not have authority, but you won't drop it."

"My hands are tied. And I might add, I wouldn't be surprised if they don't show up Monday to take those bones off your hands. That means that your hands might not be tied, but they will soon be empty."

She sprang to her feet, snatched his drink from his hand. "Mike, I really think it is time for you to go." She headed back toward the front entry, only stopping long enough to put the barely touched brandies back on the cart.

He scrambled, almost leaping over the sofa to meet her there. His arms once again reached out to her. He needed her to listen. He needed her to understand. "What can I say? What can I do?"

"We can start telling the truth. We can place some trust into this equation. Then, Detective, we might have this case solved before we lose our chance."

"By Monday? Alice, that's less then twenty-four hours."

"Then we will just have to see what more we can learn before then, won't we? I'm calling Rhyjl. And you're going to start talking."

"Alice." But he knew, just as sure as he was standing there, he had lost this battle even before it had started.

"And you can start by telling me about that tattoo."

"My tattoo?" Her interest from last night came flashing back to him. "What does that have to do with anything?" he said, realizing that his hand had involuntarily traveled to where the mark was on his shoulder.

Alice smiled and turned away from him. "Rhyjl?" She spoke into her cell. "Hey, I hate to bother you, but could you meet us over at my lab? Yes, Tanner and I are headed over there now. Yes, now. Oh? Well, bring a pizza with you. I still haven't had lunch."

Chapter 8

Shot In the Dark

Lukewarm pizza in the cold, sterile environment of Alice's lab was not quite what Mike had in mind. He'd been thinking something more like potato salad, BBQ ribs and baked beans while curled up on the couch with his favorite lady. Somehow, the aroma of garlic and tomato mixed with antiseptic wasn't conducive to appetite stimulus.

Alice wasn't fazed in the least. She took a nibble between every other word as she paced the room, laying out the details of the current situation. "We need to figure out how these guys died, and where and when, and we need it all done by tomorrow morning. Erik, you were great in finding the names. Between you and Mike..." She glared at Mike when she saw his surly grimace. They had already argued about Erik's involvement. An involvement that wouldn't have been necessary if Mike had been more forthcoming. "...we now know who. We need to know the why, where and when."

Tanner rolled his eyes. "Alice, we have less then twenty-four hours," he repeated, for who-knows-how-many-times. "We are neither gods, nor magicians. There's no way..."

"There is, and that's where Rhyjl comes in."

Erik, eyes closed, lowered his head and shook it slowly while massaging his temples with his right hand. Why hadn't he picked up that Tylenol?

Tanner, in complete contrast, cast his face heavenward, looking for Divine guidance.

"I can't, Alice," said Rhyjl. "I don't know what you think I can do that I haven't already."

"You can and you already have. You gave us Mike's tattoo."

All three faces now focused on Mike.

"You!" Rhyjl said. "You are the one I saw?"

"Saw? What are you talking about?"

"Well, you see, Mike, you aren't the only one with secrets. Rhyjl has one that only a few people know about. Rhyjl sees images from the past."

"That's it! I'm outa here. You're saying she is some kind of physic?" He leapt up, grabbing the coat he'd thrown over the stool. "I deal in facts, not fantasy!"

"See, this is just what I mean, Alice." Rhyjl got up as well and headed for the door. "This is why I don't tell people. And now, you've violated my trust."

Rhyjl was surprised that the threat of tears was stinging the corners of her eyes. What did she care what Mike Tanner thought?

"Stop." Alice's voice was heavy with authority. "Mike, you asked me why I needed Rhyjl. Rhyjl sees parts of people's lives, especially their deaths. She touched the bones on the closest table. The first victim." The giant of a man she knew now knew was Bass. "Rhyjl saw that this man was in an explosion. She saw, and felt that he was burned. She saw another guy trying to pull him to safety. The man helping him had this tat on his arm, Mike." She held up Rhyjl's drawing and explanation of the image of Thor's hammer. "Your tat."

Tanner looked from the drawing to Rhyjl, who stood with her hand paused on the door handle. "You saw that? How is that even possible?"

"I don't know," she said, still trying to push back the tears. "But I'm not some sideshow freak, Tanner."

"Rhyjl's gifted, Mike. But it's hard on her. That's why I wanted Erik here. He's good at figuring things out, but more importantly, he seems to stabilize Rhyjl."

Tanner dropped to the stool. He searched the faces of the others in the room. Erik was grim. His eyes narrowed, as if willing to take up the gauntlet if Mike said one more damning word involving Rhyjl. Alice was firm. She had her no-nonsense look: tight lips that were slightly turned down at the corners, her eyes cool ice. She'd never been one for flights of fancy. She must understand where he was coming from? Yet, she wasn't going to accept his attitude and was challenging him to do the same. Rhyjl was now leaning against the door as if she no longer had the strength to remain upright without it. Her teeth worried her bottom lip. Her eyes darted in every direction except his.

"I don't understand this." He shrugged his shoulders. "I'm not even going to pretend that I do." Taking a deep breath, he continued, "But I'm willing to listen. So," he gestured for Rhyjl to join the group by taking the chair she'd abandoned moments before. "You saw Bass in an explosion. You saw me dragging him away. You saw my tattoo. No insult here, but how do I know you and your boyfriend didn't piece things together from information you've dug up? You've both been busy researching."

Erik stiffened. Alice intercepted. "Rhyjl can tell you details that there is no way they could know no matter how much they researched. Tell him, Rhyjl. Tell him what Bass was feeling. Tell..."

"Alice, I'm not some dog trained to perform tricks. If he doesn't want to believe ..." Rhyjl shrugged.

"No," Tanner said. "I don't want you to tell me things like that. I want to know how. How do you do this? Show me. Humor me."

"Fine!" Rhyjl walked over to the table closest to her, which happened to belong to the black man whose name Alice said was Leander Duba. She snatched up the upper bone of his arm and brandished the humerus before her like a sword ready for battle. Duba was one of the victims that had remained strangely silent when she last examined him. She didn't want to prove anything to Tanner or put on a show. Duba was safe, she thought. "I do this," she said, confronting Tanner. Then, turning to her friend, "Alice, this plan of yours isn't going to work..."

His surroundings were dark except for a ribbon of light coming from under two rough wood closed doors. It stank of mold, piss and dust. The sharp edges of the plastic zip ties were cutting into his flesh and causing his hands and feet to lose feeling. The chair was hard metal. No chance of breaking it to free himself like he did that one time outside Nuristan. Think. Think. What was the last thing he could remember? His brain was cotton candy, his thoughts sticky. His throat coarse grit.

Footsteps approaching on the other side of the door. Not one, but two sets. One was a heavier tread than the other. A click. Bright light punctured his eyes like flying needles. Blinded. Red curtains where his eyelids should be.

"There's no escape this time, Keys. You should have minded your own business."

That voice! Damn. But why? What...

Crack! The blow sent a burning wave through his head, turning his brains to mush that threatened to explode his eyes out of his skull.

Erik swept Rhyjl up as she collapsed. Her eyes were open, yet unfocused. At least on anything they could

see. She was growing colder even as he pulled her against
his warmth. Panic seized him. Would this be the time she
didn't come back? He hadn't told her about his nightmare.
The one where she got swept away into the death of
someone and couldn't find her way back. Couldn't
reconnect to herself. Alice's voice was distant, soothing,
yet with that edge that said she expected to be obeyed. She
was talking to him, Tanner, and most of all Rhyjl.

"I'll take that humerus now, honey," she said,
removing the bone from Rhyjl's grip. "Come back to us,
now, Rhyjl. Come back. Erik, bring her into my office. It's
warmer there. Tanner, open some doors and stop gaping,
please."

It was a lot warmer in Alice's office. Not only in
physical temperature, but decor. Where the lab had been
cold stainless steel and white tile, Alice's office was a
miniature of her home. One wall consisted of floor to
ceiling shelving and cabinets. The upper shelves, burdened
heavily with books, were divided from the cabinets below
by what looked like a gray marble or granite counter. Two
antique glass canning jars, with clamp-on lids, held little
colored packets. A third was filled with what appeared to
be chocolate powder. A painting of a path bordered by a
riot of wildflowers was behind Alice's desk. Two leather
chairs flanked it. Big splashy floral prints covered the other
walls. A large overstuffed chair with dreams of becoming
a loveseat sat wedged in the corner. It was this chair Alice
directed him to place Rhyjl in, while she grabbed a sea-
green knit throw off the back.

"Tanner, fill my electric pot and get some water
heating. She'll need something to drink if she isn't too
woozy."

"Did she do this last time?" Erik's heart was
constricting. The pressure behind his eyes was growing.

He was breaking out in a sweat, even though his veins were ice floes.

"No," Alice replied. "Not to this extreme. I mean, she got weak and wobbly but..."

Tanner picked up the pot. "Can someone please explain what this little show is all about?"

Erik's fist connected with Tanner's jaw before he'd even thought about the consequences. It was against the law to strike an officer. Right now? He could care less. "This is no show. We could lose her!"

None of them had anticipated the blow. Tanner stood solid. An immoveable rock, his right hand still holding the kettle.

"Erik! What the... what do you mean, 'lose' her?"

"I... I don't know. Just a feeling."

"Well, don't go there. Look, her color is already improving."

All three turned back to the chair. Rhyjl's eyes had closed. She appeared to have snuggled deeper into the cushions and the blanket covering her.

Tanner remained anchored in place, rubbing his free hand over the red patch that spread from his chin to just below his left ear. Alice knelt beside the chair and moved the blanket just enough to take Rhyjl's wrist between her thumb and three fingers. Focusing on Rhyjl, she appeared to be mouthing something, then nodded. "Her pulse is strong and normal, Erik. There's nothing to fear."

"Says the lady who once wanted to call 911," he replied, crowding Alice to the side and lifting Rhyjl's hand to his face.

"If I can comment now without connecting with your fist, Arneson, I'd like to know what just happened."

"We attempted to tell you, Mike. You aren't a very

good listener at times. So, Rhyjl can see into people's lives. It's not easy for her, and sometimes it takes its toll on her. This time seems to have hit her particularly hard."

"Ah, I don't know. This seems a little too woo-woo for me. I'd almost believe it's some kind of con, but can't see any reason..."

"It's no con!" Erik jumped to his feet. What was one more hit? He'd been wanting to wipe the smug attitude off...

Tanner, reading his intentions, braced himself for the attack.

"Stop! If you two cannot get control and stop acting like pubescent miscreants, I will kick you both out."

Rhyjl moaned. Her eyes fluttered, then opened to take in the scene. "Erik?"

"Here," he said, dropping to his knees beside the chair. He reached for her hand.

She pulled it away and moved it to the back of her head. The pain was still there. It felt like having the air knocked out of her: numbing. Like being caught in a vise grip. "He didn't die instantly, Alice. He knew."

"Knew what?" Alice and Erik asked in unison.

"Keys. He knew his killer. He felt the blow. He knew he was a dead man."

It was Tanner's turn to sit, or rather collapse into the office chair next to Alice's desk. "What did you call him?"

"Keys. His murderer called him Keys. It was a name he was comfortable with. Can I get some water?" Rhyjl looked hopefully at Alice.

"Water's hot. Would you rather have tea? I have some of your favorite."

"Not right now. My throat is just so..."

"Water coming right up." Alice went to the bank of

built-in cabinets and shelves, swung open two cabinet doors to reveal a small motel-like refrigerator. She grabbed a bottle of water, handed it to Rhyjl and then grabbed Tanner. "Let's fill that kettle."

Outside her office, Alice turned to Tanner. "Erik got a good shot on you." She reached two fingers to his jaw. He pushed them away.

"Yeah, let my guard down. I'd never have pegged him for the violent type."

"Haven't you figured out by now that Erik would move heaven and earth, as well as bend every law of physics if it meant protecting Rhyjl?"

"From what? I wasn't attacking her."

Alice shook her head as she turned. "People skills, Mike. You're sadly lacking. Let's get some ice for that bruising."

He'd begun following her until the last comment. Stopping abruptly, he said, "This isn't ice that has been around corpses, is it?"

"Don't be absurd. Of course it isn't."

"Well, with the mood you've been in lately, I wouldn't put it past you to do something like that."

Alice turned back to him, giving him a wink that was far from reassuring. "Well, to quote Agatha Christie, 'Revenge is a dish best served cold.' Now, do you want that ice or not?"

~~

Tanner sat as far across the room as possible from Erik and Rhyjl. A towel with a handful of ice was pressed against his jaw. The kettle Alice had filled was emitting a low rumbling as it heated.

"No one in here is contagious, people. We could

move a little closer so voices don't have to be raised for this conversation." Alice gave Tanner a hard stare.

No one moved.

"Okay," Alice said, pulling her chair around the desk to ease the gaping gap between her friends. "What did you see, Rhyjl? No, on second thought, any idea of why you saw something this time and not last?"

"I can answer the first. I'm still not sure about the second." Rhyjl propped herself up. Erik had tucked himself in beside her. The chair was very accommodating. Perhaps, she thought, she should get one for their home.

"So Duba was in a room. It was dark. I had the feeling it was like in a basement. Concrete walls maybe but that doesn't quite feel right. Stone? It was cold. No, chilled like a cellar. You know?"

Alice nodded, and crossed over to the cabinets to fill a cup from the kettle that had beeped twice. "Go on."

"He'd been asleep. No that isn't right either. He'd been out of it but not naturally. His head was fuzzy like he'd been drinking or drugged. His thinking was slow. He went to move. Couldn't because he was tied. When he did move, it was painful. The ties bit into him. He also felt that his hands and feet were falling asleep, or were asleep, because he couldn't really feel them."

"What was he tied with?" Tanner was now leaning a little closer.

"I didn't see them, of course, but he thought they were zip ties."

"What difference does that make?" Erik asked.

"Premeditation." Tanner said. "Whoever did this was prepared. They weren't just grabbing something out of the blue like a scarf or belt."

"You said 'keys' earlier," Tanner continued. "Could it have been handcuffs and he was thinking about

..."
...

"No!" Rhyjl struggled out of the chair. She was slipping back into the scene, feeling trapped. She walked toward the kettle, thought about making herself tea, then turned. "It was my...his name. "The man called him Keys. Said something like "You won't get yourself out of this one, Keys."

"What man? Can you describe him?" Tanner slid closer to the edge of his seat as if planning to get up.

Alice stretched out her hand and pushed it down signaling him he should remain where he was. "Patience, Mike. Just let her feel her way through this."

Rhyjl closed her eyes, took a long inhale and then slowly exhaled. The breath was laced with numerous scents. Alice's jasmine perfume. Steeping Earl Grey tea. A hint of the same pine-scented cleaner that was so prevalent in the lab. Her thoughts also conjured a musty dank flavor.

"The room was dark. The only light was coming from under the doors. It was quiet except for his breathing. Then he heard muffled steps. A light flashed on. A really bright light. But it wasn't like an overhead one. It was like it was pointed at him. It blinded him. He heard the other man's voice. He knew who it was, but I didn't get any impression except strong dislike. The man said he wouldn't get out like before. Oh, and Duba, just prior to this, had been thinking that he wouldn't escape his bonds by breaking the chair like he did some other time in a foreign-sounding place called... Nuri..."

"Nuristan?" Tanner said.

"Yes! That was the name."

"That's in Afghanistan," Erik said. "I spent several weeks there with my mother and her team a long time ago."

"Is that where you learned to fight, Erik?" Tanner put the ice back on his chin.

"No, Iraq, actually." Erik glared back.

"Boys!" Alice stood to block their view of each other.

"What more can you tell us about the man?" asked Tanner. "Was he alone? What did his voice sound like?"

"I don't think he was alone. There was someone else, but I didn't know, I mean..."

"Yes, we understand what you mean," Alice said, sitting once again.

Rhyjl nodded, taking another deep breath before continuing. "Keys didn't know who the guy was. But he did think it was a guy. The man speaking, however, *was* different. Keys knew him. Disliked him. It was an educated voice. I didn't get the accent. Kind of British but not really. It wasn't deep. I just can't pin it down."

"You don't think you'd recognize it again if you heard it?"

"No, Tanner, I didn't say that. I would recognize it. I just don't know how to describe it."

Tanner's mind was doing the Indy 500: laps and speed. How many people would know about Keys' escape from Nuristan? The six members of their team. Their handler, Jason Granger. Jason's boss. And the men who had tied Keys up.

"Could the voice have had a touch of Russian?"

"I'm sorry, Tanner. I just don't know. You have to understand I'm hearing something through another person's experience. It doesn't always make sense. You know if it were me, I'd probably be analyzing it as the person spoke. But your friend? He just recognized it and didn't give it much thought other than wondering why the person was there."

"Anything else?" Alice prompted.

"Then he felt the explosion on the back of his head and knew, if only for a second, he was a dead man."

There was a long stretch of silence. Tanner's footfalls eventually broke it as he left his seat to walk around Alice's desk to stare at the painting there.

No one in the room believed for a moment that the picture was of interest. Alice could only imagine what he was thinking. He knew this man, Keys or Duba, whatever his name was. They had been close. She knew that because she knew Mike. He didn't get close to people or let them in his life unless they were special. Someone he could trust.

It was Tanner who eventually broke the well of silence. "I don't know how you do it, Rhyjl. You've given me a lot to think about. I need to go and sort it all out. My time here is done. Alice, can I give you a lift home?"

Erik stood and approached Tanner. "Hey, man, I'm sorry." He held out his hand.

Tanner looked at the offered hand but didn't accept it. "I'll accept your apology, but next time you swing on a cop, you are going to jail."

Erik responded by letting his arm fall to his side. "You're all heart, Tanner."

They gathered up their belongings, tossed the pizza no one felt like finishing, and left using the back door.

Outside, the cool evening air was softening into spring. Gone was the bite of winter. The evening star was just barely visible on the horizon. In the distance, a gathering of peepers was starting its serenade.

How very bucolic, Alice thought.

Boom! Tanner's body slammed her to the asphalt. She couldn't breathe! To her right, she could just barely make out Rhyjl's and Erik's crouched figures on the other side of Tanner's sedan.

"When I say 'three,' see if you can make it to the other side where Rhyjl is. Okay?" Tanner whispered, or was he shouting? She couldn't tell over the ringing in her ears.

She didn't have time to respond.

"Two ... Three!" He catapulted off her like a loaded spring.

Chapter 9

Shake It Up

"I don't want police protection," Tanner said, for the eighth or ninth time. Alice had stopped counting as she became more involved with her own argument with the EMT who was being pretty adamant about transporting her to be thoroughly checked. She wasn't surprised, when he took the blood pressure cuff off, that her blood pressure was skyrocketing.

She agreed with Tanner. No one could have stopped the episode they'd just gone through. They'd had no warning. They could have had twenty cops surrounding them and the result would have been the same.

Detective Devners was short, rounding, and losing what had once been a thick mane of hair. She'd only met him once in an official capacity. He was tough, play by the book, and biding his time to retirement. She didn't like him. Tanner never talked much about his associates, but it was apparent that he was most likely of the same opinion as she.

Tanner continued to fill Devners in on what he'd already deduced. The sniper had used the rooftop of a building blocks away. He explained that after the tire was blown out, he'd done his own rounds to search for the shooter before the police or ambulance crew had arrived. When the detective asked how he knew where to look, Tanner explained angle and clearance. There were only two buildings tall enough to get that angle. Only one had a clear line of shot.

From the tone of the senior detective, she knew he

was skeptical. "That's a helluva long distance, Tanner. You're talking sniper here."

"I know what I'm saying, Devners. I also know when you find that bullet, it's going to be a 30 caliber. The guy was quick, professional," Tanner explained. "No traces. Not even shell casings."

But he'd wanted Tanner to know he'd been there. "Too easy, Tanner," was all the note said. Typed, of course. Tanner hadn't turned it over as evidence to the techs who were scouring the place. He'd check for fingerprints himself, but knew there weren't likely to be any.

She finished signing the papers the EMT had given her: the HIPPA paper stating her privacy rights—sure— and the disclaimer that she was refusing transport, which amounted to the other side of the block. It was all standard procedure, but annoying as hell after what she'd just been through. After handing the clipboard back to the tech, she reached her fingers to the dressing covering the slice over her eye and winced. Another half-inch lower and the flying steel-belted chunk of tire rubber could have put her eye out.

Being shot at was a strong heady mixed cocktail: part exhilaration and part numbing fear. There were probably a few other emotions mixed in as well. They just hadn't come to the surface.

Rhyjl and Erik approached. Rhyjl looked as if she'd either been crying or was about to. Erik was grim. Other than a few bruises they might discover tomorrow or later tonight from pavement diving, they were fine. Tanner? Well, he wouldn't say anything, would he. Her father would have called it stoic. And there was nothing worse, in her father's mind, than a stoic patient. You couldn't treat or know where to begin treating if your patient wasn't communicating. Unless it was all-out obvious. There was nothing about Tanner that was all-out obvious, and the revelations of the last couple days had really brought that home.

Watching him sprint away after the rifle shot had been almost surreal, like watching something out of a spy thriller. In fact, this whole thing was like something out of a thriller. He seemed to know exactly where to go, while managing to keep as much cover as possible. She'd felt her heart almost stop with an expectation of seeing him dropped by another shot at any moment.

"You okay, Alice?" Rhyjl asked, taking her in a strong embrace.

"About as good as can be expected for being shot at and tackled to the ground by a hundred-eighty-pound gorilla. How about you?"

"Scared. That kind of adrenalin rush is still too fresh in my mind. Maybe a little PTSD."

"Maybe."

"The cops are through with us. I'd like to get headed back home. Can we give you a ride?" Erik asked.

"Thanks, Erik, but I think I'll stick with Mike."

"Do you think that's wise? Someone's gunning for him. He's taking risks." Erik shot a look in Tanner's direction that was brittle cold.

Alice felt a stinging heat building in her chest that wanted to spew out in a hot stream of abuse. Yes, Tanner was a target. But it wasn't as if he'd known and had intentionally placed himself or them in danger. Her sizzling indignation suddenly took a hit of icy slivers. Or, had he? Melting through the ice, she was more subdued. "Let me speak with Mike first. Can you wait?"

When Alice was out of close range, Rhyjl turned on Erik. "What was that? She's hurting. Is hurt. A lot more than any of us, and you are throwing out cheap shots at her man."

"Don't start on me. I told you we should stay out of this."

"Yeah, you did and by that admission, we are equally as guilty as Tanner. Tanner faces danger every day. Every cop out there does. Shouldn't he have friends? Should we wrap ourselves in bubble wrap, Erik, because the world can be a dangerous place?"

"You know what I mean."

"No, I don't think I do." Her own adrenalin was still running on high volume. When she'd first opened her eyes to see Alice crawling across the pavement towards her, her heart had skipped a beat, fearing the worst. There wasn't any blood that she could see, but that didn't mean Alice wasn't wounded. Once the two women consoled each other and came to the understanding that there were nothing more than minor abrasions, it was like a dam breaking. She couldn't hold back the tears.

"I'm scared, Rhyjl," Erik said. "I don't like admitting it. It makes me feel weak and ineffectual. If we are to believe what Tanner says, this guy or person wasn't out to hit us or we'd be dead. That means this person is either trying to warn us away—and I for one am willing to heed his warning—or, he's playing with Tanner until the right time and moment. He obviously doesn't care who's around. It's like a damn game of Russian roulette."

Rhyjl reached for him and pulled him closer until her head was buried in his chest. His heartbeat was sprinting at top speed. He was scared. That made her more so. She hadn't realized until this moment how much she needed Erik to be her rock.

She tilted her head back to look up into those deep Atlantic-colored eyes. "Alice needs Mike like I need you.

Don't discount that, Erik. Not now, not ever. Like you quoted, 'Magic comes with a price.'"

He did his boa constrictor embrace. The one that always took her breath away.

"Okay, boss. For better or worse."

She would have laughed at the way he'd said it, if her heart wasn't puddling with gratitude.

"Hate to break up this tender moment, but Alice and I could use a lift if you wouldn't mind."

In the background, Mike's sedan was being hauled up on the flat bed of the red Hank's Towing truck. Rhyjl still didn't understand why the whole car was being treated as a crime scene, when it was only the tire that had been targeted and destroyed. But then, there wasn't a lot in her experience that she did understand about the way the law worked. She'd watched as the crime investigation crew had packaged every little piece of evidence they could sweep up. They'd inspected the walls of the building and at one time, she wasn't sure that she and Erik weren't going to be asked to strip down.

"Are you going to be without wheels long?" she asked Tanner.

"No, they'll get through it pretty quick. I'll probably have it back by Tuesday. Not that I'll need it."

"Why not?"

Alice answered for Mike. "They've put him on leave until this mess is cleared up. Devners was more than happy to pass that information on."

"Ah. Well, maybe this time it is for the best. Maybe we should sit this one out," Rhyjl said, knowing full well even as the words left her mouth that none of them could or would.

"So, back to Alice's?"

The idea of stopping someplace to eat was bantered

around for an awkward few minutes. They agreed no one was really interested in food.

"Can we just go?" Alice said. "I think I want to put my feet up with a soothing drink in hand."

When Tanner and Erik both opened the opposite front doors of the silver Rubicon, Rhyjl stepped up to take the driver's seat. "Thanks for being gentlemen and opening the doors for us." She smiled. "You guys are going to have to sit in back. I don't let anyone drive my Jeep. I want Alice up front. My ride. My rules."

The two men looked at each other, nodded, then moved to the rear doors. It was obvious from the tightening in both their bodies, it was going to be a fun trip back. Ah, well, it was only forty minutes. They'd survive.

Chapter 10

Misty Memories

"We need to talk, Mike," Alice said, unlocking her door, then quickly moving inside to punch in the security code. She knew most of her local friends and neighbors didn't lock doors, let alone have a security system. It was a pretty crime-free area, but Alice's roots were deep within the beltway of Boston. No one left their doors unlocked where she'd grown up. Out of habit, she checked the phone for messages. Only one call. Her dad. She'd get back with him later when she could trust herself not to break down.

"I'm sorry this happened tonight. I'm sorry you and the others got involved. I don't know what else you want me to say, Alice."

She could tell by the way he moved he was listening and checking out every shadow. Obviously, they hadn't left the spy thriller back at her office. "I want you to tell me who those men really were, their connection with you and why you think that sniper didn't take you out tonight. That's what I want you to tell me."

"Alice, I don't know that I can. It's..."

"It almost got us killed tonight." She grabbed the decanter from its trolley and poured two snifters half full. Pausing, she looked at how much was still in the decanter and added more to their glasses.

"No, not killed. Scared. There's a big difference. As I told you before, this guy knows what he's doing. To take a shot like that from that distance..."

"Are you sure he didn't just miss? For God's sake, Mike, how do you know he wasn't aiming for you and missed?"

"The set-up. The distance. Someone doesn't go out over twelve hundred yards and not know they will hit what they intend to. There's a whole lot of confidence involved in a long shot like that." He took the offered glass and followed her to the living room.

Going to the wall, she switched on the gas fireplace. He pulled the curtains. She was about to ask why when it hit her again they were on a movie set. You always close the curtains so the killers outside can't see what's going on. She took a hit of brandy, focusing on the trail of heat it left in her throat. She took a second when the first didn't have much effect.

"I need more than that. A whole lot more." She curled into the sofa pillows, tucking her feet under her. "It won't go past us. Past this room. But I've got to know. Otherwise, you'd better walk out that door and not come back, Mike Tanner. Ever!"

He settled on the couch next to her, but his body was stiff, alert, as if he expected something more to happen at any moment.

"I reset the alarm, Mike. The curtains are closed. Should we have gotten police protection like Devners suggested?"

"No. Old habits." He attempted a smile. Failed. "These people, the ones in your lab, my friends, were more than friends."

"That's a good start. Keep going." She took another sip of the brandy and frowned because her glass was now only half as full as his.

"I met Bass at boot camp. He was a moose of a man even then. He'd come straight out of high school just like me, but that's pretty much where our similarities ended. I'd been a high school football jock with dreams of becoming an All American. Rhyjl was right about that. Bass, he was more of an All American than I could ever be." He looked at his snifter, wanted a drink more than he could say, but put it down. He wouldn't have his instincts dulled. Not tonight.

"Bass had been working his parents' farm in the Appalachian Mountains not far from Boone's Cumberland Gap from the time he was 'big enough to pick up a hoe,' as he liked to tell it. He was proud of his Kentucky heritage in a way that I never did feel for my home state of Washington. But then Bass's family had lived and worked that farm for close to a hundred and fifty years. My parents had escaped from California in the late seventies to the Seattle area, not long before I was born. Bass was looking to serve his country. I was looking for an escape."

"Escape from what?" Alice shifted, took another drink, and was wondering if she were ready for this conversation on top of all the other trauma of the day.

"Well, I was well on my way to my dream. After playing for the West in the Army All-American Bowl, I'd even won a scholarship. Then I was cut adrift in one quick brush with death. My parents were on their way home from one of my games. It was raining. It's always raining in Seattle—at least that time of the year. Some guy who had been drinking a hot Starbucks spilled it, and ended up swerving over the line into the path of my parents' car. They were killed instantly."

She reached out to touch him. "I'm so sorry, Mike. What happened then?"

"My folks were typical of a lot of couples. They owed more than they had hopes of paying off. Dad's life insurance was minimal. Mom didn't have any. By the time the estate was settled, there was nothing left. I tried flipping burgers and a few other dead-end jobs. Stayed with friends' families long enough to finish high school. Then one day, as I was trying to figure out what step to take next, I saw a recruitment center. I enlisted in the army.

"Bass and I wanted adventure. The farm boy wanted to see the world, and I wanted to forget. That's when we met the others. We were all lone wolves, you might say, but somehow we had to form a pack. We did."

"So you formed a pack and went to some little joint to get matching tattoos."

"More or less." He shrugged. "That was Carson's idea. He was of Norwegian descent. Tall, blond, icy blue eyes. Put a horned helmet on his head and he had the look of a Viking. Of course, he would have cringed at the horned helmet part, since he'd corrected me a dozen times that Vikings did *not* have horned helmets." Tanner's lips drew together in a tight smile. "He was big into Norse mythology. Said he had warrior blood in him. He'd been big into SCA reenactments, too. Had a necklace with a silver Thor's hammer. He said we were all like Thor, fighting Chaos. A few beers later and it all sounded good."

"And the others?" She got up to refill her glass. "Are you going to drink that?" she said, pointing to the untouched snifter.

"Nope. I think I'd better not."

"Staying sober in case we have visitors?" The idea sent creepy crawlies skittering throughout her. She took his glass and folded herself back onto the sofa.

"I don't think so, but I'll play it cautious anyway."

"So the others. How many of you were there in this pack?"

"Six total. Keys, Jamie, Carson, Boomer, Bass, and me."

"So you were all in the military, right?" Between the drama and the alcohol, she was feeling more than a little off balance. It wasn't something that happened often. That's because Alice Merks didn't like being out of control. Tonight, she was making an exception. "Continue," she said, waving her arm about.

"Are you sure you want to continue?" Tanner asked. "Maybe a nice soak in the bath, I'll wash your back and you wash mine..."

"No chance, mister. I want the truth and nothing but the truth."

Mike Tanner scrubbed his hands over his face. He didn't like talking about this. He really shouldn't be talking about this. At the same time, Alice was the best thing in his life. He'd play it close to the line. Giving her enough without too much. After all, what did it matter anymore? There were just two of them left.

"We weren't just military, we were..."

"Ghosts? Spooks? Isn't that what they call them?"

"You've been watching too much TV, Alice." Tanner smiled. "Nothing quite so romantic. We were special ops. The guys who are called to carry out missions that require unconventional methods and resources. Sometimes we worked alone as a unit, and other times along with the regular troops."

"So what happened to you all? One day you're all doing special ops and the next Mike Tanner is a cop. What about the others?"

"Our last mission was undercover in Paris."

"Oh, that must have been tough."

She had no idea. "We were there keeping an eye on a known terrorist cell we had been hunting for over two years. It started out in Afghanistan. We were posing as a band working at a nightclub. Called ourselves the Six Man

Band. We had an informant. Her name was Aeisha. Her brother was part of the cell. After Aeisha's husband was killed, her brother took over their restaurant. We needed someone on the inside. Someone who wouldn't be suspected. We turned Aeisha by telling her that her brother had killed her husband."

"That's filthy, Mike! Was it true?"

"Yes, it was true. Aeisha's brother was about as heartless and cruel as they come. He was a radical Muslim. Aeisha and her husband weren't. In Aamir's eyes, killing Aeisha's infidel husband and taking over the business was doing Allah's will."

"Did she believe that?"

"Aeisha was a beautiful and highly intelligent woman. A lot like you. She'd been educated at private schools in Switzerland. No, she didn't believe like her brother. Neither had her parents. She also didn't want her son to be like that."

"She had a child?"

"Yes. It was for him she endured, and was only biding her time until she could stash enough money away to escape."

"Mike, you keep talking about her in the past tense. What happened to her? Did she and her son escape?" Alice felt ribbons of tears welling up in her eyes. She wasn't the teary kind. Maybe it was the booze. Maybe it was just the adrenalin letdown... Or, maybe the drained look in Mike's eyes and the way he gnawed at the corner of his mouth told her his answer wasn't going to be one she liked.

"We eventually got Dani, her son, out. But no, she died in my arms on a dreary night in a dark street. She'd come to the club to tell me something. I pretended to be sick and left to follow her. She was terrified. I was pretty sure her brother or one of his companions had caught her out. It was only a matter of time. I kept trying to tell our handler, Granger, that we needed to get her and the boy out. I even went above his head to his superiors. Not for the first time, I might add. Granger, the ass that he was and still is, convinced them everything was under control and that we needed to give it just a little longer."

"You were the one Rhyjl saw!"

"What?"

"Rhyjl saw a man with the tattoo holding a dying woman on a back street in some European city. She didn't know where. She couldn't see you clearly. She was watching you through the eyes of the big man, Bass. She thought you might have killed the woman."

Tanner planted his face in his hands. "Christ, Alice. Don't ever repeat that story to anyone else! Do you hear?" he said, raising his eyes to lock with hers. "If that sort of information about her ability got out... do you have any idea what the government would do? What people like Granger would do?"

She HAD been spending too much time on TV shows and movies. In response to his question, visions of X-Men and Professor Xavier flashed through her mind.

"Or... they would just think I'm crazy, the same way you did until you saw it for yourself."

"Yeah, or that. Either way, I think it stays between us."

"I think I'll get another drink. You still staying sober?"

He placed his hand over her arm as she went to rise. "I think we should have something to eat before any more of that." He nodded to her empty glass.

"I'm a big girl, Mike." She pulled her arm away but didn't try to rise.

"I know you are. And I'm a big boy. I'd like

something to eat and I'd enjoy eating with you."

She rolled her eyes and flashed him a crooked smile. "Smooth move. Okay." She rose a little unsteadily. "Food... I think I have some smoked salmon and enough greens and tomatoes for a salad. Would that tame that hunger of yours? You can come out to the kitchen and we will finish this talk."

"And I'll handle any sharp implements, I think."

Chapter 11

The People You Meet

The silence was thick as chowder for the first fifteen minutes after they'd dropped Tanner and Alice off. Rhyjl turned on the radio to offset the chill coming from the front passenger seat. It was fruitless.

"Erik, please, can't we talk? A lot happened this afternoon. For one, I was both surprised and pleased when you apologized to Tanner for hitting him."

"I wasn't sorry for hitting him. I'd do it again in a moment. Cop or no cop, what he accused you of..."

"I don't want to go there. But face it. My... uh... ability is a little hard to believe. Mike wasn't reacting that much different than anyone else would. You can't go around hitting everyone in the world." Her hand reached toward him. His met hers halfway, and gave it a squeeze.

"I don't want to hit everyone in the world. Just Tanner."

"Then what were you apologizing for?"

"You don't know what it's like for those watching, when you are in one of your trance-like episodes."

"No, but you and Alice have given me a pretty good idea."

"Yeah, perhaps, but for Tanner, he wasn't just seeing and hearing something about some person he didn't know. Your vision was of the last moments of his friend's life. It was a worse punch than the one I gave him; an old-fashioned one-two punch. First, the shock of seeing what you could do threw him way off balance. His friend's death took him down."

"So I should be the one apologizing?"

"Nope. You were just doing your natural thing. Hopefully it will help us find whomever is doing this."

"Erik, you confuse me. One minute you are upset we got involved in this. The next, you are using the word 'us' in conjunction with the apprehension of this jerk."

"Yeah, I confuse myself," he said, as they turned into the driveway of their home.

They could hear the Jack alarm as soon as they got out of the vehicle. Erik slammed the Jeep's door a little harder than Rhyjl thought necessary.

"I'm taking Jack out for a walk. We'll probably be gone awhile."

"Erik?" She knew the time for talking was on hold. Erik needed space. If she were honest with herself, she did, too.

Jack greeted her with leaps and bounds. His little happy dance. If it was possible for a dog to smile, Jack wasn't just smiling, he was radiant. He always was when they came home. Erik gave a sharp command to "sit." Sharper than his usual when Jack's boundless energy didn't make it easy to slip his leash on. Jack sank to the floor, nose between his paws.

"Maybe I should take Jack out?" Jack's tail thump-whacked on the floor.

"Rhyjl!"

"Don't expect me to drop and bury my head in my hands, Erik."

"Look, I'm sorry," he said, looking from Rhyjl to the dog and back again. "We'll be fine. Jack will be fine. Just let us get out of here and work off some energy."

She nodded and watched as they went to the glass sliders at the back of the living room. Jack paused as the door opened and looked expectantly back at her before he followed Erik out into the last vestiges of the day.

A tear cut a hot trail down her cheek. Such devotion and love. What had she done to deserve it?

The day's events had left her feeling like an old worn shirt cuff—tattered and stained. The remembered fear of thinking Alice had been hit was still like vinegar in her mouth. Then there was Tanner's reaction to her ability. Secretly she was glad, real glad, when Erik knocked that look off Tanner's face. She wasn't about to tell Erik that. Had Tanner run by the book, Erik would be in jail and she'd be walking Jack. She couldn't picture Erik in jail and yet, because of her, he'd been placed in the realm of that happening twice in the last two days.

Going to the refrigerator, she opened the door and stood looking. She really wasn't hungry, but supposed she should come up with something for Erik when he returned with Jack. There were a couple of Samuel Adams standing stoically under the cold light, a half-finished bottle of zinfandel from last night, some sour cream, a wrinkled tomato, a quart of whole milk, a small block of white cheddar and a sad head of lettuce. Hardly exciting fare. Right about now, the remnants of the pizza they had unceremoniously dumped in the trash back at Alice's lab would have been nice. But who knew? They had all lost their appetites. The others had been thinking along the same line as she, that they would pick up a nice meal after they were finished. Well, that had gone well, hadn't it.

Beep. Beep. Beep. The refrigerator objected to being left open for so long.

"Yeah, yeah, yeah. Nag, nag, nag," she said, shutting the door. Perhaps there was something in the freezer?

She found a package of hamburger, and three freezer-burned buns left over from a BBQ they had last fall when her grandmother had been staying with them. She put them each, in turn, into the microwave on defrost mode. She sliced the tomato, cheese and lettuce and arranged them on a plate, then stood back. It might not be uptown, but washed down with the Samuel Adams, she didn't think Erik would mind too much.

When nine rolled around and she still hadn't heard anything from him, she put all the food into containers and plastic food storage bags. She left the wine out. She was on her second glass by then and there was only enough for one more. Might as well finish it.

~~

At first, Erik had been too pumped up to be aware of much more than the impending eruption he felt building. Seventeen years! Seventeen years come May since he'd felt this confused and angry. This scared. This helpless. He'd come close when Rhyjl danced with death last fall. That had been different. It was quick. What they were enduring now was protracted. Yes, even four days was beginning to feel like an eternity. Another difference was they hadn't felt targeted last time. Again, he'd been concerned for Rhyjl, but it had never touched the rest of them. Tanner least of all.

Tanner. He was part of this. A lot more than any of them knew. He doubted even Alice had an inkling of how deep this went, but he could bet that Alice, being Alice, was going to get to the bottom of it tonight.

Erik realized that even as short as his fingernails were, they kept biting into his palms every time Tanner came to the forefront of his thoughts. At this rate, his palms were likely to be bloody by the time he got back from the walk.

He wasn't quite sure what brought him out of autopilot. A turn in his thoughts or a turn in the path. It could be either. It also could have been the gnawing of his stomach or that the path was becoming more difficult to see. The evening light when he'd left the house with Jack had been a muted glow to the west. A half-moon had made its way over the rooftop of the house. He'd been able to see clearly enough for a short walk without bringing a flashlight. Now, he glanced at his cell phone. He'd been gone almost an hour and was at the twist that meandered down to the promontory where Rhyjl had come that fateful day. He knew it was still one of her favorite places, but he would never enjoy the view so long as her broken body lying at the edge of the surf remained burned in his memory.

He turned back. The trees' canopy was tightly woven here. The moon looked less pleasant as its light filtered through the skeletal bare branches. A little chill prickled at the back of his neck. The bare bones of the trees turned his thoughts back to Alice's lab. He pushed them aside to focus on his footing. Jack pulled against the leash, more sure-footed than he, but just as uncomfortable and eager to leave. They'd both be glad to reach the wide expanse of lawn flowing down from the campus proper.

When they reached the moon-bathed grassy expanse, Jack kept nudging his hand, wanting and waiting for the leash to come off. This was Jack's favorite part of the walk, when he was allowed to run along the path looking for squirrels, or in this instance, investigate those strange "re-deep" sounds permeating the night air.

Erik eventually gave in and let Jack have his head. He even allowed himself a chuckle when Jack bounded after the spring peepers, only to have their chorus suddenly still as if someone had flipped a switch. Jack's head swiveled to and fro, then zeroed in accusingly at Erik as if he was the one who had silenced them.

The moon was just a little less than half. It was still light enough to cast a pencil-line path upon the cold Atlantic below and give the trees somber shadows. A few clouds teased the calling frogs' hopes for rain. Erik knew the amphibians would be disappointed. The forecast for tonight was clear with possibly a light frost. Still, he enjoyed watching liquid mercury clouds ride across the sky, playing games with the moon and stars. His foreboding lifted. His mood became lighter as he scanned the heavens. The big dipper, or Ursa Major, looked especially clear. Perhaps because the moon was somewhat subdued. Ursa Minor, the little bear, also seemed brighter with the tip of its long tail, the North Star, forever guiding sailors home. Once he'd thought of becoming an astronomer. When he was nine and would lie out on the boat deck with his mother gazing at the stars. She would point out certain constellations and tell him their names in Greek. Happier times. Happier memories. He'd loved visiting and exploring the different countries she took him to, but, until he met Rhyjl, his adventures aboard the *Eleutheria* were the highlights of his life.

Jack bounded toward the bank of trees that were the boundary between the campus and their home. He stopped abruptly, his body still as a statue. Erik smiled, thinking Jack had finally found his squirrel, and knowing if he approached, it would spoil Jack's fun. But such was life and they needed to get home.

A twig snapped. Jack sprang, positioning himself between Erik and the intruder. This was no squirrel. His hackles were raised. A low growl resided deep in his throat. It was not loud. Not menacing. A warning to Erik more than the shadow that slipped out of the tree line.

"Evening, Professor," said the man. "Nice night for a stroll."

It was too dark for Erik to make out the man's features. Cold tendrils of fear constricted his lungs, making it hard to breathe. How did the man know it was him? Because of Jack? Possibly. He fought down the rising panic. One deep breath. Two. "Yes, it is," he answered, his voice surprisingly calm considering the pounding of his heart.

"Nice dog."

"He usually is." Jack pressed closer to Erik, creating a shield as the man drew nearer.

"Well, enjoy your evening." The man strolled past in the direction Erik had just come from.

"You, too." Was it just his imagination, or had the fellow intentionally kept his face in the shadows by looking down?

He stood for what seemed like an interminable time, watching the man slip in and out of the cloud shadows and moonlight along the cliff path. Jack never moved, frozen in a blocking stance. His ears alert. Even when the frogs began their song, Jack remained vigilant with Erik rather than playing. When no further evidence of their encounter remained, they turned for home.

The house was silent. Only the glow of the table lamp and a dying fire testified that the house had been recently inhabited. A tight fist of fear clenched his heart. The man he'd spoken to had been coming from the direction of the house. Had someone been waiting for him to leave? They hadn't followed. No, too much time had elapsed for that. They'd remained behind. Waiting until he'd left. They might even have followed from Alice's lab. Rhyjl's name wanted to tear from his throat.

Jack pushed past, knocking him into the doorjamb

on his way to the kitchen. No hesitation. No growl. There was nothing disturbing him except the lack of water in his dish. A fact that was made apparent by the metallic clang. Obviously, there was nothing out of the ordinary. Still, he moved silently toward the bedroom, where the door was slightly ajar. Peeking in, he was just able to make out Rhyjl's sleeping form. Pulling the door closed with a muffled click, he shook his head. He was letting his imagination run rampant. Being shot at would do that to a guy—or at least, this guy.

On his way to the kitchen, niggling guilt replaced apprehension. Next to Rhyjl's chair, he spotted the single wine glass and the empty bottle sitting on the end table. He glanced at his watch. Was it really nine-forty? He'd left at what? Seven-thirty? Eight? It had probably been closer to eight by the time they'd dropped Tanner and Alice off and gotten home. It hadn't seemed that long.

In the kitchen he found evidence of a dinner that hadn't happened. Hamburger buns sat on the counter. The cast-iron pan waited patiently on the stove top. Opening the fridge, he saw the cut tomato, grabbed a beer, took a seat at the table, and looked out at the dark. Where did they go from here?

After the second Adams, he locked the doors. Double-checked the window locks. He'd have to talk to Rhyjl about keeping the doors and windows locked when she was home alone.

After making sure everything was secure, he went to the bedroom. Rhyjl appeared to be asleep just as when he'd first come in, but he knew she wasn't. He didn't know what to say. Didn't know if he had the energy to say anything. Jack settled at the end of the bed on his doggy mattress. They'd long since given up trying to crate him at night. Erik stripped down to his boxers and crawled beneath the covers. The bed seemed especially cold, and got colder still when she didn't move to seek him out. Was she still upset about the conversation on the way home, or that he'd been gone so long? Or maybe one had been compounded by the other.

Without warning the bed jolted. A flying missile of muscle and fur exploded onto the covers between him and Rhyjl. Jack whined and pushed his cold nose against Erik's cheek. The massive head then turned to shove under Rhyjl's arm, coming to rest on her chest.

An unusual silence followed when neither Rhyjl nor Erik ordered the big dog back to his bed.

Perhaps it was best that Jack had chosen that moment to join them, Rhyjl thought. There were no words left in her. She'd heard Erik come in. Well, the clatter of Jack's dish had woken her. She might have rallied to join Erik if he had called her name or come to wake her. He hadn't. Just the click of the bedroom door as if he wanted his privacy. In all fairness, he might have been acting out of consideration, figuring she needed her sleep, she tried to reason. But as so often was the case, her reason battled with her emotions.

Sleep remained elusive, it seemed, forever. Eventually, Erik's breathing slowed like the outgoing tide. Jack shifted and whimpered, caught in a dream. An endless parade of minutes mocked her from the blue light of the clock. She made note of it when the time turned to a line of threes. Closing her eyes, she focused on Erik's breath, matching each inhale and exhale with her own. The sound of a soft scratching against the glass French doors to their room played at the edge of a dream. Jack growled ever so softly. From under sleep-laden eyelids she could just make out that the clock had slipped to fives and a two. She moved to sit up, but a hand stayed her.

"Don't," Erik whispered.

The soft scratching sound came again. There was a shooosh of wood sliding against wood. Erik's nightstand drawer opening sounded unreasonably loud. So did the unmistakable metallic slide-click of a semi-automatic. Slowly, slowly, Erik pulled himself up.

Silhouetted against the pale glow of the waning moon, the masked prowler froze.

Chapter 12

Ghosts

Alice gazed into the fire. The flames danced in wild abandon over the glowing faux logs. "So you wouldn't stay here with me before this, because you didn't want to put me in danger. What's changed? Why is it okay now?"

"What's changed is that I was foolish enough to think whomever is stalking me was only willing to take me out. If I kept my distance... but that didn't work, did it," Tanner said, lifting her feet off his lap to get up from the sofa. He paced the room, again, looking for any hints that they might be observed.

"So you think he isn't just after you at this point. That he might go after any of us?"

Tanner stopped and looked at her with sad resignation. "I don't know what to think, Alice. That he shot at us in public, could mean anything. I just don't know. Up to this point it's been covert and singular. "

"Shouldn't we warn Rhyjl and Erik?"

Tanner paused. *Should he have taken Erik off to the side and warned him of a possibility?* "No. I may not care for Arneson, but I don't think he's taking this lightly. He'll be more on guard. I think Rhyjl will be more vigilant as well. Having someone stalk and almost kill you once tends to heighten one's awareness."

"So you've known for a while someone is after you." Her voice was sharper than she had intended it. He was doing everything he could, it seemed, to make her feel better. He'd apologized several times. Still, she felt a hot coal of resentment kindling in her stomach.

"I suspected, yes. But I didn't have anything other than circumstantial evidence to go on. To be honest, I was also confused. This guy could have taken me out," he said, flashing back to the night his bedroom window had been opened. "He had ample opportunity, I'm embarrassed to say. After all this time, I chastised myself for getting complacent. I surmised it might have something to do with the bodies we found, but couldn't be certain. Not at first, at least."

"When did that change?" Her hands twisted and turned around each other, trying to untangle fear, anger, sadness.

"When you gave me more accurate descriptions of the victims. I started making inquiries. I was discreet. I didn't even go through the usual channels. I used some back doors, so to speak. I started with Bass. One, because there aren't many guys over six foot six. I suppose the other was that I was probably the closest to him. I'd been out to his folks' farm. They're good people. They treated me like family. Bass said that's just the way people down in that neck of the woods were. But I didn't quite believe it. You know, they talk about people being the salt of the earth. Bass's parents, well, they are."

"So, you called them?"

"Yeah, I called them. They were thrilled to hear from me. Asked if I was in the area and if so, invited me to dinner. I explained I was hanging out with the Yankees up here in Maine, but was looking for Bass. Bass's dad hung back a moment, then told me they hadn't heard from him in several months. They were a little sad to hear I wasn't with him, or at least knew where he was. But then, that was the case for close on to ten years."

"So they didn't know or suspect something was a little strange?" She always wondered how someone could go missing for long periods of time and not have parents or family searching every nook and cranny for them. Unless they were orphaned, like Tanner. Her parents called several times a week. They might be five hours away, but if they thought for an instant something... This thought reminded her of the message left on her phone earlier. She'd better call back first thing in the morning or her dad would cancel his appointments and drive up to check on her.

"Bass was always kind of a wanderer. 'Restless' is what his mom called him. She'd look at him with such love and pride and say, 'My boy was born on a windy night. Whenever the wind came back this way, I knew he'd be off with it.'"

A vision of a weathered woman in worn clothes came to mind. A woman who would be equally happy standing at a stove fixing food grown by her hand, as she would be fixing a broken fence. It was probably stereotypical, but she'd met a few of them in her travels and especially up here in the more remote areas of Maine.

"She said Bass had come home about two years ago. She thought he might stay that time. He'd started working the farm during the days and put together a little bluegrass band that played a few local taverns on weekends and nights. Then one night he came home from working a gig. His dad said he seemed anxious. The next morning he'd packed a few things and was gone."

"And they weren't just a bit suspicious that something was wrong?"

"They just assumed it had something to do with government work. They didn't really know what Bass did. It's not something you talk about. But after years of Bass being gone for long stretches at a time with no word, they took to heart 'No news is good news.' They did say they had received a message saying he was in Syria about four months ago."

"But he couldn't have been. I mean the man..."

"No, he never was. After speaking with them, I had a glimmer of hope. I checked. Bass never left the States. Not as a civilian. Not as an operative."

"So someone was deflecting any inquiries."

"That's my take. Someone didn't want to set off any alarms. Anyway, that's when I started looking into the others."

Tanner sat back down on the sofa as she sprang up. The earlier soothing effects of the brandy were wearing thin. "Don't tell me. Same scenario." She walked toward the kitchen. She was sure there was a bottle of merlot there.

Mike's voice raised a little in volume to make up for the distance. "Yes and no. Keys never knew his dad. He'd been close to his mom. His mother died of cancer while he was in Afghanistan. She didn't tell him. Guess she didn't want him to be worried. Growing up, she had supported them by giving piano lessons. Keys was one of her best students. She'd always hoped he could make it in the music industry. Keys wasn't the type. He didn't cope well with civilian life before he joined the army, and even less when he mustered out. He drifted for a while, then went into private security, and I'm not talking alarm systems. He'd hired himself out to the owner of a big construction outfit that works all over the world. My source says the boss man is suspected by the FBI and other agencies of being involved with moving drugs and illegal arms. Keys' last known whereabouts was out in Phoenix, Arizona. Rumors were that Keys and another guy were taken out by the competition. No bodies. No evidence."

Alice returned from the kitchen with a steaming mug in her hand, just as Tanner made this last statement.

He raised an eyebrow in question.

"Tea. Chamomile, to be exact. I need a store run. No wine." She plumped a pillow with her free hand, then settled back into the sofa.

"You're probably better off."

"Uh huh." She wrinkled her nose at him while the tip of her tongue parted her lips. "So do you think this other guy could have been Bass? Could Keys have gotten himself in a little deeper than he should have and called on an old buddy?"

"The thought occurred to me. But I don't think it is likely. Bass and Keys were close. I can't see Bass getting involved in something like that, though. Keys, he'd grown up in a tough area of New Orleans. Skirting around the edges of the law wasn't exactly new territory for him. Bass was, as I told you, Mr. All-American."

"So somewhere out there, there's another body? And if so, why not just bury it along with our guys?"

"I've given that a lot of thought, too."

"Yeah, I bet. No wonder you haven't been sleeping nights."

"Exactly," he said, glancing at the big golden sunburst clock on the wall. It was already going on midnight and the night was looking at quickly becoming another long sleepless one.

"Your theory?" she said, bringing his attention back to the conversation.

"This burial. It's symbolic. Whomever is doing this is making a statement. A statement about us. About our group specifically. Bass and Keys both worked with other ops groups after I left. So did Boomer. Jamie, Carson and I left field work at the same time. I got out completely and went into law enforcement. Carson continued for a while in the military here at home, working with returning vets.

Jamie went into the family insurance business. Whatever this guy wants, it goes back to the six of us."

Alice sipped her tea and hoped it would calm her nerves, which were becoming more frayed as the evening and topic of conversation wore on. Her mind could run rampant with thoughts if she let it. One recurring scenario was Tanner ending up on her lab table. Four people were dead. Possibly a fifth, if it was true about the one who went missing along the same timeframe and place as Keys. Tonight they'd all been shot at. Or had it just been Tanner? Maybe it wasn't just a warning, as he was so cavalierly suggesting. Maybe the shot had missed. Maybe she could lose him. And that bothered her more than she thought imaginable.

She and Tanner were good together as colleagues and friends. The sex was better than good. She liked his little idiosyncrasies. Some of them showed in a subdued way, like how very kind and generous he was behind that rough cop exterior. Rhyjl's visions of the last couple days had revealed something else, too. Mike held people and things together even when the going got tough. He was someone they trusted. Someone they could get behind. Someone—her mind went back to Rhyjl's description of the woman dying in the alley—they might love. Mike's words came back. Aeisha had worked in a restaurant. She'd been saving up money so she and her son could escape. Was she why Tanner tipped waitresses so generously? Was it his way of paying tribute to a woman he'd loved? She felt her muscles tense. Opposing emotions locked in a death battle. She could love him for that kind of devotion. She could hate him that it was for someone other than her. The latter rocked her to her roots. She'd never felt this way—didn't think it was possible. Was she in love?

"I'm sorry, Mike. What did you just say?"

"I think maybe we should retire for the night. You're falling asleep on me."

He had no idea of how far from sleep she was at the moment. "No, I want to know what you just said. I wasn't sleeping, really. I was thinking."

"I was saying that I also dismissed the thought of it being Bass who might be the second person involved with Keys after I discovered Boomer's sudden disappearance."

"Missing without a trace, right?"

"Yeah. Boomer was out in California in a small bedroom community outside LA called Inglewood. He had opened a dojo out there. He was actually doing pretty well. Not enough to support his lifestyle, however. Fast women and faster cars. Didn't take a lot of searching to discover he was in debt way over his head and was behind in both his bills and taxes. One day, about seven months ago, a sign shows up on the door of the dojo. It says he has been called away on family matters and will be back in two weeks. He never shows."

"Did you contact his family?"

"That's just it. Like me, he was orphaned."

"What about tracing his car or credit cards?"

"Dead ends. According to my sources, when he didn't show up after two months, his landlady called the police. The investigation yielded almost nothing to go on. His fancy new Corvette and a few personal items were missing. His bank account shows three large cash withdrawals from different ATMs over three days, then nothing. His credit cards were all topped out. Officially, they think he has gone underground to avoid creditors and tax collectors."

"Oh, he went underground. But I don't think it was intentionally, to avoid anything," Alice said. "Which brings us to Carson."

"Not much there. He left Veterans' Affairs and was doing charity work with homeless vets. Kept pretty much to himself. One day he was there, the next day he wasn't. The people he worked with just figured he'd moved on. The woman I spoke with said that was about six months ago. She also added that working with the homeless can be both rewarding and very draining, and more often frustrating. Burnout is common."

"No family, landlord or bank account?"

"None that I could come up with. He has a sister somewhere, but has been estranged from her as long as I can remember."

"Mike, this is really sad. With the exception of Bass, these men were invisible in so many ways. Forgotten. They drop off the face of the earth and no one thinks twice."

"It's all part of the training, Alice. Blend in. Be part of the scenery, but not connected. It's hard to come back from years of that."

"But you have." She squeezed his hand, which was lying across her leg.

He thought of his apartment, his routines. With the exception of Alice, would anyone question his disappearance? Not likely.

Chapter 13

Expect the Unexpected

Jack catapulted off the bed. "Woof roo, woof roo."

Erik's repeated, "Down, Jack!" was having little affect. Jack didn't care if there was a sheet of glass between him and their night visitor. The door shuddered as the big dog hit it. The glass bowed. Other than Rhyjl's breath, nothing broke.

The raccoon shot into the darkness.

Erik removed the magazine from the Glock, then ejected the shell. He slid them back into the drawer of the nightstand. His heart was thudding hard against his chest. Only a damn raccoon!

"How long has that," Rhyjl nodded to the gun, "been there?"

"Since tonight." Erik leaned back against the headboard. "I've had it locked up in my desk. Tonight I wanted it close by."

"You were expecting our visitor?" Rhyjl attempted to stifle a laugh.

"I had a run-in with someone while I was walking."

"What?" Her levity plummeted. Whatever laughter had bubbled earlier, popped.

Erik thought back to the encounter. "I've no proof. It might just be my imagination, fueled by our earlier event."

"What happened? Did someone confront you?"

"Give me a second. I'm trying to repeat the events in my mind so I can give you a clear picture. Okay, Jack and I were just about at the end of the walk. This guy was there in that grove of trees just below where the path takes that dip. I probably wouldn't have seen him. Jack did. He went into defensive block mode."

"Wow, that's unusual for him. He's normally Mr. Congeniality. Erik, he must have sensed something from the other guy."

"Yeah, that was my thought, too. The guy didn't make any aggressive moves. He acted quite pleasant. You know—'Hello professor. Nice night. Nice dog.'—sort of thing."

"So he knew you? Did you recognize him?"

"That's just it. It was way too dark. I couldn't make out any of his features, and when he passed me, he kept his face slightly averted."

"Erik, that's creepy. Are you sure it couldn't have been a student who knows you?"

"I tried to believe that. I tried to tell myself that even though it was dark, it was possible. I mean, it isn't that far from the house. A man with a big dog. Yeah, it could have been. But something still doesn't feel right. For one, his voice wasn't familiar. Then there was Jack's reaction. I've got to tell you, when I got home and there was no sign of you... Well, I felt my heart drop."

She reached out to embrace him. "I just was beat, Erik. The events of the day and the wine..."

"I'm sorry I missed dinner."

"Sure you are." She managed a weak smile.

"No, seriously, I'm sorry I didn't make it home sooner. Just a lot to think about."

The old grandfather clock they'd picked up at an antique shop chimed six from the living room. "I suppose there isn't much sense in going back to sleep at this hour," Rhyjl said.

He pulled her closer as she shifted to get up. "No,

but there are other things we can do at this hour."

His voice was like a hot tub after a long day: warm, inviting and oh so... "No! No! No!" She pushed away from him as if he'd turned to flame.

"What the..."

"Oh no! It's Monday!" Erupting from the bed like a tornado spawned from a cloud, she sped to the bathroom.

"Yeah." Erik shook his head. "So?"

"I've got that meeting with Marcus this morning! With everything going on, I completely forgot! I'm not ready!"

She said something else, but he couldn't make it out over the hissing beat of the shower. He thought about joining her. No, the only appetite he would get satisfied this morning was with a bowl of cereal. Yep, it was Monday.

~~

Across the campus, spring was emerging from winter's hold. Grass was morphing from brittle brown to green. Men in green jumpsuits bent over naked flower beds or raked winter's dead into piles to be carted away. Another couple of months and the campus grounds would be dressed in all their colorful finery. Rhyjl acknowledged the gardeners with a nod as she hurried along the faux brick paths. Others, whom she'd watched working around the campus for years, she spoke a hurried greeting to. This was her home three-quarters of the year. Her only away time was during dig season.

She loved Down East University. She had from the first moment she'd laid eyes on it. While she missed the open spaces of the ranch back home in Montana, there was something about the New England charm she felt drawn to. She liked how the fluorescent colors of fall died into the stark, monochromatic, skeletal grip of winter before the first snows covered the world with a shroud of white. How spring warmed the earth and turned the heaping snowbanks to rivulets of liquid spider webs across the parking lots and walkways.

Ahead of her, the Anthropology building still retained much of its turn-of-the-nineteenth-century charm. The U-shaped two-story brick building had once housed an impressive number of horses, carriages and everything equestrian. The second story had no doubt been used for storage as well as quarters for the grooms and trainers. Above the arched entry, a chiseled stone horse head with soulful eyes watched those who passed through the doors. On the paving stones in the courtyard was an oval stone basin once used to water the horses. Within the basin was an island, from which water burbled and splashed from spigots, the sound making a cheerful welcome. The top of the island supported an elegant bronze rider astride his majestic mount, no doubt a reminder to all the horses who had drunk from it what their sole purpose in life was.

The Archaeology Department office at the top of the stairs and to her left was a swarm of activity. With over half of the semester gone and finals appearing on the horizon, the usual hysteria of students who hadn't spent their time wisely was taking over. Amidst the chaos stood an oracle of wisdom. Reed-like, she seemed to bend yet never break. Her waist-length hair reminded Rhyjl of a raven's wing washed by moonlight streaks of gray. Magenta, or Mags, as everyone called the glue that had held the department together for close to twenty-five years, was up to her expressive eyebrows in panicked freshmen and sophomores. Some familiar faces of older students from the 400-level Osteo lab were present as well. She made note of them and would put forth an effort to meet with them individually when she found a few moments to spare.

Catching the older woman's eye, she lifted her own eyebrows in an understood question and got the expected reply when Mags tilted her head in the direction of the hall leading to Marcus McClellan's sanctum. She wished there was time to talk. Mine what information she could from Mags before facing her mentor. Mags had a way of knowing what was going on with people in the department, often before they themselves did. There seemed to be only one time when that had failed. Of course there had been no way Mags could have known that her desire to help out a student would turn to murder. It was a confidence held between them. Just one of many lessons they'd each taken away from the incident last fall.

Pausing at the frosted door with the occupant's name printed in gold, Rhyjl drew a deep calming breath, then raised her hand to knock. With her rap falling just short of the door's wood frame, she heard the familiar voice. "You're late, Rhyjl."

"I'm not late," she said, opening the door and walking into the book and artifact-lined office. Some people had books for looks. Marcus wasn't one of them. He turned from the view outside the large window to face her. Looking at Marcus, standing there as he was now, made her wonder why she'd ever found him attractive. His hair was grayer, especially around the temples. But it wasn't the changes to his hair. The gray actually gave him an air of sophistication. No, it was the deep lines that had etched worry around his eyes and disappointment at the corners of his mouth.

"I expected you ten minutes ago." He smiled, indicating with a wave of his hand that she should take the chair waiting for her before he took his own seat. She glanced at the Mayan clock, which looked like a radiant sun containing dots and dashes. She was right on time. Eight on the nose.

"You're always early," he answered, reading her confusion accurately. "Have a seat. I think I may have come up with something that will interest you."

"I thought we were going to talk about my dissertation?" Rhyjl took the seat, after looking at it as if it might be a trap. She knew Marcus. She knew that sly smile. The one where his lips compressed into a thin line with only a slight upturn at the corners. The one where his tongue played at his cheek. The one that always meant he had you right where he wanted you.

"We are." He remained standing, his hands clasped behind his back.

For a moment she imagined he had his fingers crossed as well. No, he knew exactly where he was going. With Marcus there was no such thing as luck. He made his reality.

"I've given your work a lot of thought. It's good, Rhyjl. Really good. I mean it, so don't give me that look like I'm about to eat you. But I don't think the time is right. I don't believe any good will come of it. No!" He pulled one hand from his back to hold it up like a cop directing traffic. "Hear me out before you let that razor tongue escape. I could be wrong about the timing, however, I've done some research of my own. There are other brave or foolish souls out there who have chosen to pursue this road that Europeans came here early on. Solutrean and the origin of America's Clovis Culture is raising its head once more. Not a new concept, but in the past, even those respected in our field had careers that faltered by following that path. Now? Well, perhaps the times have changed.

Perhaps. Time will tell."

"So you're telling me what? That you are going to back me in this?" She looked at him as if he had grown a tail.

"I've come up with a proposition. I'll back you, as you say, as long as you fulfill something for me first. And..." he held his hand up again, "after doing it, you still feel the same way you do now."

"What are you up to, Marcus? You know how long I've dreamed and worked on this. What could you possibly come up with that would make me second-guess myself? It's a waste of time." She rose slowly from the chair. There was heaviness in her heart where the momentary hopes that had risen on wings were securely chained again.

"Are you so easily defeated, Rhyjl? I'm offering you the opportunity to have exactly what you wanted. To see your work open new doors, to give voice to those long gone and see justice for them. Isn't that what you've been telling me?" He narrowed his eyes, the smile returning along with the slightest tilt of his head. He had her and they both knew it.

"What do you want?" She leaned with both hands on his desk. Her arms straight and braced as if expecting a blow.

"I have a friend. Connor Doyle. His firm does contract work. He's in need of a forensic archaeologist. He asked me if I could recommend someone. I told him about you. The pay is better than good. You would more or less be your own boss."

"Sounds very Irish. Is this work Viking period related, and in Ireland?" She'd spent one summer in a field school outside of Dublin during her junior year. The people were great, the weather was fine. She never developed a taste for Guinness, but the music and comradery in the pubs was a plus.

Marcus laughed a full body laugh. "Oh, he's Irish, with the wild red hair and temper to match. But no, the work is in the Four Corners area of the Southwest. Anasazi, to be exact."

"I don't know anything about those people or that era, other than a cursory introduction."

"You know bones. And that's what he needs. 'Bones is bones.' Isn't that another of your mantras?"

"When does this job start?"

"In three weeks. But I told him you had to finish your obligations to this institution first. You're expected by the fifteenth of May. Housing is provided. Perhaps not as nice as you've become accustomed to lately, but Conner takes good care of his people."

"Marcus! You've already accepted for me! What the..."

"Now that's my girl. Fire. I like it when your eyes light up." Marcus mirrored her pose on the other side of his desk. Their noses almost met. "Do this, Rhyjl. And when you come back, I will throw everything I've got behind your doctoral thesis. If that's what you still want."

Rhyjl swept down the hallway and through the department. She was a storm no one wanted to run afoul of. Even Mags. Once outside, she slowed her pace and stood glaring at the mounted rider posed above the water fountain, his mount strong but subjugated. Men! Be it animals or women, they always had to have the upper hand. Who the hell did Marcus think he was? Ask her, yes. Okay. But he'd already told this Doyle guy she'd take the job! She wanted to punch something. Someone. Why hadn't she just told him to shove it? What was wrong with her that she let all the men in her world run her life? She wasn't some damn helpless puppet for them to pull her strings. She was stronger than that. Marcus was right. She had fire and convictions. Why didn't she stand up for herself?

Chapter 14

Hacked

Erik closed the fridge for the third time that morning. If he were honest with himself he'd go to town to Perfection Confections and get the biggest apple fritter they had. Maybe two. He had a to-do list that was longer than his arm. He needed the energy. What he really needed was to get the last two days off his mind. Then, just maybe, he could get focused on what he should be doing.

He opened the fridge door, smacked himself on the forehead with his hand and slammed it. Maybe if he did it hard enough, it wouldn't open for him a fifth time. It was too early for beer but...

The house was quiet without Rhyjl. Not even Jack's snoring next to his food dish could make much of a dent in the emptiness he felt when she wasn't there. The way she mumbled to herself as she scribbled notes on the big yellow legal pad. The old tunes she hummed as she went about the house doing the little things. Sometimes, but not always, she'd break out into a heartfelt rendition. Songs she'd heard her mother play when she was a child. He wasn't even sure she was aware she was doing it half the time. This morning it had been a song about someone always trying to run her life. When he asked her about it, she said it was called "Sunshine." She couldn't remember the artist.

One line from the song kept running through his mind—*He can't even run his own life. I'll be damned if he'll run mine.* Was she thinking about him or Marcus? Or was he trying to read more into it than there was?

Stepping over a sleeping Jack, he made his way to his command center. The best way to get past all crap and speculation was to bury himself in his work. At his computer, he was king. He programmed his world. Be it classroom tests and assignments, or his own inventions. His fingers carried him across keystrokes to places others couldn't even imagine. His domain...

"What the hell?" Across his screen where his login should be, a message blinked. *Hello Professor.*

He pressed several keys. The message should have disappeared. It sat there mocking him. A throbbing curser inviting him. "Who are you?" he typed as he spoke.

"*A friend.*"

"Friends don't hack my computer."

"*They do if you aren't paying attention.*"

"To what?" Erik looked around the room, half expecting to see his intruder there. Was he being watched? He thought about the possibility that at this moment they were viewing him through the huge expanse of windows at his back. Was someone out there with binoculars? No, nothing so crude. The computer's eye? He glanced at the small webcam at the top of his screen. Most likely. But what could he do? He was locked out. Toss his sweater over it? He could cut the power, but his own curiosity wouldn't allow that. There was no way this should be possible. This firewall was the best of the best.

"*This is a demonstration that you should leave hacking to the pros. You left your signature all over. Yes, I know your work well enough to know your lines of code. I cleaned it up. You did set up red flags. I can't do much about them. I did keep them from tracking you. This is a high stakes game. Keep clean. Stay away. The players can get nasty.*"

The screen went blank. His login came back. His

world had been returned. But it would never be the same.

Chapter 15

If Only

Alice woke to find her bed empty. The place where Mike had slept was cold. She felt that familiar sinking in her chest. Her breath caught a little. It wasn't the first time. It was his usual. Hoping that last night had changed anything was foolish.

The Wedgewood Jasper clock on the Chippendale nightstand showed it was just past seven. The clock was a treasure she'd found only a few months back at an upscale antique store while visiting her parents in Boston. She'd never known that Wedgewood had made anything other than the traditional powder blue she'd grown up with. Blue was not her color, however, so while she was attracted to the style, she'd never thought to own any pieces. When she spotted this one in a soft sage green with the raised white decorations and a scene of a woman being visited by a cheerful cupid, it was love at first sight. Cupid had definitely paid her a visit, she thought, half rolling out of bed. Now if he'd just point that arrow in Mike's direction.

Stiff and sore muscles greeted her, making her desire a roll back between the covers. It was too late. She'd have to settle for a hot shower and some herbal tea to soothe her bruised body.

The shower was heavenly and just what the doctor had ordered for a quick fix. There were more bruises than she'd expected. A small abrasion on her right arm stung from the water, as did the larger one on her knee where she'd hit the asphalt. She'd add a pain-soothing tincture to her tea this morning. Tonight she'd relax in a good hot soaking Epsom salt bath with lavender. No complaints. She was alive and so were the others.

Piecing her day together, she was in the middle of a mental run through: Call Dad, go to the office and get the remains ready for transport, stop by the grocery and pick up some shrimp, a pint of cream for the Alfredo sauce, and asparagus if they had any. She was in the mood to eat in tonight. Then she'd...

"Is there room for two?" Mike asked, slipping his hand along her water-slicked back. He didn't wait for the answer. Sliding in behind her, his hands roved over her flesh.

"I thought you'd left," she answered. His scent—a combination of sandalwood, sweat and masculinity—the one that set her on fire, mixed with her coconut and vanilla. Deep inside she felt the primal stirring. Maybe cupid had found his target. Maybe work could wait for a while longer.

Mike's breathing was measured next to her, their legs tangled together. This, just this, was how she wanted every morning to start. The strains of "Clair de Lune" intruded into her blissful space. The phone ceased. They'd leave a message. The tone picked up at the beginning again. Groaning, she snatched it from her nightstand. "Dr. Merks."

"I thought I should tell you that some agents from the government were here. Ah, you might want to come in," her assistant said.

Glancing at the clock, she gave a deep sigh. "It's not even nine." Then something in his words reached her consciousness. "What do you mean 'were here?'"

"They just left. I couldn't call you before. They kept me down the hall in reception with an agent that kept pelting me with questions."

Sitting on the edge of the bed, her fingers kneading the sheets like a cat sharpening its claws, she would have pounced through the phone if possible. "What the hell's going on? What kind of questions? Did they take the bodies? Did they give you any kind of paperwork?"

"I think you'll have a better idea once you get here," he said, before silence took over.

"Damn! Damn, and damn again!" she said, throwing the phone on the bed and exploding toward the bathroom.

"Hey. Whoa. What's the problem, gal?"

"They've come for the remains of your buddies!" She mumbled something more, but it was indecipherable through the closed door and sink water running.

"I told you they would be showing up today," he shouted through the door, when he discovered she'd locked it.

Tanner was dressed and slipping on his shoulder harness for his gun when she came out. He had a morning shadow on his normally clean-shaven face that made her pulse jump and would have been reason enough to... but no. She had to go see what had happened at her lab.

"Should I come with you?" he asked.

"No, I'm sure it's nothing. Just our government's insensitivity when dealing with civilians." Her hands were still shaking with the adrenalin rush as she buttoned her rose-colored silk blouse. "I was planning on fixing us a nice breakfast." She grabbed the gray linen jacket off the hanger and turned to him. "Take a rain check?"

"Yeah, I'd like that." He smiled. "Since I've got the next couple of days off, I think I'll do some poking around. First, though, I've called for a ride. I've got to go home and get my bike."

A look of consternation washed over her face. He

knew she hated motorcycles since that day he'd talked her into going for a ride. He pushed on giving her no opening. "No car, remember?" He looked at her sideways, his eyebrows raised in an arch. "Then a quick run to Perfection Confections and then over to Erik's."

That stopped her. "Erik's? Why?"

"He just left me a text message. Says we need to talk."

"Are they okay? Nothing's happened..."

"Alice, slow down. It was a text message, not a 911 call. I'm sure everything is fine. He just probably has questions that are leftovers from last night. I would. Plus, he's that kind of guy. The need-to-know kind. Nothing to worry over."

"I suppose you're right." She picked up her cell and scrolled through. Nothing from Rhyjl. That was probably good.

Morning sun streamed in through the bay windows of the bright kitchen's breakfast nook. When she'd picked this home, she'd wanted light rooms that would bring the outside in. She spent so much of her day in her lab with death, that when she was away, she craved being surrounded by life.

They sat in companionable silence drinking tea, or at least she was. Mike was letting his grow cold. It could have been that he was lost in thought or that he would have preferred coffee. Beyond the glass, the chorus of birdsong gave way to the muffled purr of a car coming up her drive. His ride had arrived. He gave her a quick peck on the cheek, snatched his coat from the back of the chair and was out the front door. She watched from the window as he climbed into the trooper's car. It stung that their morning together had so quickly come to an end. Still, perhaps this was a new beginning. She would keep her mind focused on that, and if he was going to start spending the night, then coffee and a coffee machine were going to be needed additions to her kitchen.

Chapter 16

Retrospect

Gerry Greene was everything a young state trooper should be—enthusiastic, courageous, a strong sense of justice, and the right mixture of compassion and toughness. A Captain America poster child. *Someone like I used to be before combat and dubious orders tainted and corrupted my soul,* Tanner thought. He nodded to Greene, then walked around the front of the cruiser to the passenger side. He open the door and slid in. It had been a long time since he had ridden shotgun. Brought back a lot of memories. Not all good.

"Morning, Tanner," Greene said, with a slight nod.

"Gerry."

"Sorry about your incident last night. Dr. Merks? Is she doing okay?"

The way he said it made Tanner study young Greene more closely. "She's shaken, but taking it like the pro she is." Greene wouldn't be the first or last guy to set his sights on Alice. Just about any of the men she'd worked with were part of that club, including a couple of the married ones. It was more than her beauty. It was the way she worked. The way she made their jobs easier. The way she could close a case so you wouldn't have to go home with doubts you'd done the right thing one way or the other.

"That's good. She's a special lady."

On that, they could both agree.

"There's been a slight change of plans, sir," Gerry said, backing the cruiser around to leave. "Detective

Devners told me to bring you in for debriefing before taking you back to your place."

Last thing he wanted was a talk with that pompous ass, but then some things couldn't be helped. Hopefully he could get through it fast and then get on with his plans for the day.

Gerry pulled down the long drive bordered by a white-painted board fence. Right now the fields on either side were empty. The grass was just starting to grow. Come the end of June, a farmer from down the way would cut it for hay. Then his daughter would run her horses out on the grass.

Alice liked it that way. She loved watching the grass grow and sway like the waves upon the ocean. She liked watching the two gray Arabs cavorting in the mornings and then lazing in the afternoon under the shade of the big sugar maple down at the end of the drive. He'd asked her once if she wanted horses of her own. She laughed. "Not this city girl, but they do make a pretty picture." Alice loved beautiful things, which had always seemed diametrically opposed to her chosen profession. But then, Alice was no simple lady.

Several times, Tanner caught himself glancing in the side mirror. Was he hoping to see her, perhaps standing out on the porch? Up until now, he and Alice had kept their relationship low profile. Sporadic lunches or dinners out. A short evening at her place that often left them both feeling awkward when he'd get up and leave shortly after midnight. Their meals out had changed slightly since Rhyjl and Erik had come into their lives, especially with Thursday nights at Vinney's becoming a regular occurrence. Their rendezvous at home hadn't. Not until last night.

"Any ideas on who they were or whom they were

after?" Gerry asked as he pulled out onto Gibson Road, heading toward Highway 3.

Here the narrow paved road was lined on both sides by rock walls farmers had built up over a hundred years ago to keep their livestock in. Gone now were the majority of pastures like Alice's. Most of them had turned to thick copses of maple and pine. Soon these forests would turn to a mixture of variegated greens. In the fall they would transform into a patchwork of electrifying neon reds, golds, and oranges. Even the evergreens would look more vibrant. The colors that made New England famous.

Tanner had come to this part of the country because it was different than anywhere else he'd ever been. He'd come to agree with the sign that greeted travelers as they crossed the state line. "Welcome to Maine. The way life should be." Then he'd met Alice and there was no turning back for him.

"It's none of my business, sir," Greene said. "But..."

"You're correct," Tanner said, a little more harshly than necessary. "It's not." Right now he wanted to be left alone with his thoughts. He had a great deal to think about. Things that might change the life he'd built here. The few relationships he'd nurtured. But it seemed young Greene would not be put off.

"They're saying down at the station that someone was waiting to kill you. Any ideas why?"

"Why people are saying that? Or why someone would want to kill me?"

"The latter."

"Good question." Tanner fiddled with a loose thread on his jacket. "One I plan on finding out the answer to." Except he didn't think they were out for the kill. At least not yet. At this point, it felt more like a game of cat and mouse. He wasn't big on games.

"Then there's always the other scenario. You were with other people," continued Greene. "Could be one of them was the target. Dr. Merks, possibly?"

"Now why would anyone want to shoot Dr. Merks?"

"It's rumored that she's received a few threatening notes this last year."

This was news to Tanner. Of course he knew she'd had a couple of high profile cases. The nastiest one had been the hit and run case involving the teenage girl. Everyone had put it down to the jealous boyfriend. Alice had proved that it was the girl's own "grieving" father who had chased her down with his car after he'd raped her. Of course the family was angry. They wouldn't buy the father's guilt or the boyfriend's innocence. There had been a lot of screaming and insults, but she'd never mentioned threatening notes to him. Still, it could all be rumor. Law enforcement was no different than any other group when it came to speculation and gossip.

Of course all angles would have to be investigated, not just his—Alice, Rhyjl and even Erik. No one, it seemed, could just go through life without making enemies. Unless you lived in a bubble. He knew it wasn't meant for them. He had the note. But no one else knew about it. So it was only procedure for them all to be investigated.

That son-of-a-bitch who had raped and killed his daughter had been real good at covering it up. He'd even planted incriminating evidence on the boyfriend. But Alice, with her diligence, had caught him out. Yeah, he'd investigate that lead if he were in charge and...

"So is that why you stayed at Dr. Merks' last night?" Greene slipped past his musings.

"As you said before, it's none of your business, but her safety and well-being were of the highest concern to me."

They drove in silence for the next half hour, lost in their own thoughts. Tanner allowed his mind to drift back to the events and conversations of the last twelve hours. Something — no, several things — had changed last night between him and Alice. He'd opened up and shared with her in a way he didn't think he knew how to. Not since Aeisha. Aeisha, the woman he'd let down. The woman he had considered spending the rest of his life with. The woman he had held in his arms while the life drained from her body. He had failed her in life and death. It was Jamie who had taken on her son. Oh, yeah, he'd spent as much time with Dani as he could over the years. He'd helped with tuition, making sure Dani attended the best private school in Groton, Massachusetts, and had put a sizeable amount into savings for his college. But he hadn't been able to give Aeisha, or her son, the one thing they needed or wanted the most—himself. Men, in his line of work, couldn't take on a family. He couldn't provide stability. Jamie, now he was different. Bass might have been able to pull it off as well. Not the rest of the band. Look how they had all ended up—dead and lost. That point had been driven home even harder when Alice had commented on them being ghosts—invisible and alone. He could feel the same raw clenching in his chest as when he had decided to step aside so that Jamie could pursue Aeisha. He'd known that Jamie was in love with her. He was pretty sure that's why Jamie, for some time, had talked about retiring. Going back to the family business. That was the kind of security she had needed, and Jamie was a good man.

He wouldn't let that happen again. Not with Alice. Things were different now. Yeah, they were different.

Tanner pulled himself back to the present. He was used to his own detective's vehicle. Unmarked and unnoticed. It had been a long time since he'd been in a cruiser. He'd forgotten how traffic not only suddenly slowed to the speed limit, but often dropped below it.

The car they were behind now had one such driver. Tanner remembered he'd often been tempted and sometimes pulled that type of individual over to "make sure they were all right." After all, traveling 45 in a 55 zone was suspicious. Could indicate impaired abilities, car troubles. Worth checking out, but he wasn't so inclined today. Just annoyed.

Speaking of annoyed, his phone alerted him to an incoming call with a loud ring. Call him sentimental, but he still thought that a phone should sound like a phone, not the beginning of some concert. One glimpse of the caller ID set his teeth on edge.

"Tanner."

"What kinda mess are we in, Tanner?" Erik Arneson said on the other end. "Didn't you get my text? I've been hacked!"

"That sort of thing happens a lot in the computer world. I'll give you the number..."

"I don't want any damn number, Tanner! I want answers. First last night and now this. I'm being threatened, Tanner. Somebody connected with this situation is warning me off and I bet you have a good idea who."

"I'll be there in forty." He pressed disconnect and turned to Greene. "Slight change of plans. Drop me at my place. I've got something I need to do, then I'll go see Devners."

"But my orders came straight from Captain Durand."

"Well, I just changed those orders. I'll take full responsibility.

~

True to his word, Tanner pulled up to Erik's house on his black Harley right on time. Erik had been standing on the porch. A deep frown cut his face. His hands were braced on his hips. His hair tousled.

"Took you long enough!" Erik came down the four steps to the paved circular driveway. He looked like he wanted to throw a punch.

Tanner hoped he wouldn't. It would not bode well for the prof. "I said forty, and I'm here in forty."

Erik looked over the bike as Tanner laid his helmet on the seat. "Demote you to motorcycle cop?"

"Cut the crap. I'm here. Tell me what's happening."

The wide steps led up to a porch with a railing that ran across the entire front of the house. It was a classic Cape. But unlike others he'd seen dotting the New England countryside, this house was plain, almost stoic. It had probably weathered more storms than he'd been alive for and would still be standing there when he was gone. There should be flowers beds or hanging baskets. A set of rocking or Adirondack chairs. A table to set a pitcher of ice-cold lemonade or tea on in the summer. That's how Alice would have made it. But Rhyjl wasn't Alice. No adornment to soften the cold exterior of gray clapboard with white trim. No concession to frivolity, with the exception of the entry door with its ornate cut glass that took up half the door and the full matching side panels. But, perhaps he was being unfair. Rhyjl hadn't lived in this house for more than the last six months of winter, and half of those she'd spent recovering from the fall that had almost taken her life.

Erik started his recap of the evening's events before they'd reached the door. It included his encounter on the cliff trail. The man who had hung back in the shadows yet knew his name. Rhyjl had remained home. She'd gone to bed early. When he'd gotten back to the house he hadn't noticed anything strange other than the door was unlocked. The back door, he said, when he noticed Tanner looking at the front. He then admitted that in retrospect, that wouldn't have been unusual, but became an issue after his meeting on the path.

"So you came home, the door was unlocked but that's not unusual. Rhyjl had gone to bed. What about the dog?" Tanner said, as Erik opened the door to the big-eyed Saint Bernard blocking half the entry inside and looking like it had more than tripled in size since he last saw it. "I can't see anyone getting past him." He reached out the back of his hand so Jack could get a good scent without being threatened. It was a trick he'd learned long ago from his dad, who had raised Golden Retrievers as service and comfort dogs.

"Oh, sorry, I didn't say. He was with me on the walk."

"And what was his reaction to this person?" In Tanner's experience, dogs were usually a good indicator of a person's personality. "Was he cautious? Reserved? Defensive? Or mellow like he's being with me right now?"

Erik paused, looked at the way Jack was doing his leaning thing into Tanner's leg. It was a move he usually reserved for people he liked. Well, there was no accounting for the dog's taste. "He was guarded. He leaned and braced against me. His hackles were even up."

"And the man didn't make any aggressive moves?

How was his voice? Deep? Belligerent?"

"No, calm. Yeah, calm. Almost eerily so. But now that I'm thinking about it, he had just a hint of an accent. Familiar, too. I should be able to place it. Turkish, or..." Erik closed his eyes and tried to hear the voice. "Um," he said, shaking his head after a moment. "Just not placing it, but I know I've heard it before."

"The man's voice or the accent?"

"The accent. Like when I was a kid. You know I traveled and summered in a lot of different countries with my mother's team?"

Tanner did know. He knew everything there was to know about Erik Arneson. Probably more than Arneson realized. He knew some things about Arneson's father, too. Things he'd bet Mr. Boy Scout didn't even know. Like the fact that Erik's mother's death hadn't been what all it seemed, and that the young Erik hadn't just been kept home on his father's whim. "Okay, so maybe a Middle Eastern accent of some type?"

"Yeah, I think so."

"So moving ahead, when did you discover you'd been hacked?" Tanner looked around the room. There were throw pillows tossed around. Papers had been scattered off the table by the sofa as if it had been turned over. The rest of the room had been tossed as well. Not big time, but as if someone was looking for something in a hurry. He figured his coat wouldn't be out of place if he tossed it on the back of the sofa as well. "So is this," he indicated the chaos in the room, "part of what you found when you got back from your walk?"

Erik looked around, grimaced. "No, this is all my doing. I was looking for any kind of evidence the guy might have left behind." Erik gave Jack, who was still vying for Tanner's attention, a narrow-eyed stare. *Traitor,* he thought.

"So where's Rhyjl? What does she think about all this?"

"Gone."

Tanner crooked an eyebrow and gave Erik a sideways glance. "Gone?"

"No!" Erik shook his head and waved his arm in a circular motion. "Not that type of gone. She had an appointment with the head of the Archaeology Department this morning. She left about an hour ago, maybe closer to an hour and a half. She should be back any minute."

"So she wasn't upset by this hacking?"

"She doesn't know. I discovered it shortly after she left."

Tanner's arm made a broad sweeping motion. "And when did all this happen?"

"After she left. I, uh, well, just say that I'm feeling a little paranoid right now."

"So what were you expecting to find?"

Erik shrugged, walked over to his desk chair and sat, inviting Tanner to sit in the chair he'd grabbed earlier from the kitchen and placed next to his. "I don't know. Bugs maybe."

"I see. Did you find anything?" Tanner smiled. Took the offered seat and looked at the three screens that showed several different screen savers. Two of archaeological sites Erik's mother might have worked on, and one of a beautiful two-masted schooner skimming along on cerulean waters with white cliffs in the distance.

"Ha, very funny. I'm glad you find this humorous. No, I didn't."

"Nice boat," Tanner said, changing tactics. He didn't think the situation was humorous, but Arneson's overreaction and paranoia did tickle his rather perverse sense of humor.

Erik's brow wrinkled along with the bridge of his nose. If anything else crinkled it was hidden behind that full crop of beard and moustache. Then he followed Tanner's gaze and the light dawned.

"My mother's. When she wasn't digging or in her lab, she was sailing. She loved the Mediterranean." Erik's voice cracked. He discreetly tried to clear the lump that had caught in his throat. He missed the *Eleutheria* and his time on her with his mother.

"Eleutheria is Greek, isn't it?"

"Yes, it means personal liberty or freedom." Erik was surprised Tanner knew that. Perhaps there was more to the man than he'd been willing to credit.

"She's a beauty. Do you still have her?" Tanner asked.

"No." A brittle edge made its way into Erik's tone. "My father sold her soon after my mother died."

"Ah." *And it still angers you,* Tanner thought. "So, moving along, tell me what exactly happened here." He scooted the chair in closer to the desk.

"It wasn't until I'd been up for a bit. Rhyjl had already left. I was taking out the dog, wondering what to eat..."

"Cut to the chase, Erik. I don't need a complete blow by blow of your morning. What happened that made you suspect you'd been hacked?"

Erik pointed to the main screen of the three. The one with the *Eleutheria* on it. "So I sit down to do some work. The instant I turned my computer on, someone was waiting."

"Waiting?"

Erik leapt up and threw his arms wide, looking down at his computer with a look that reminded Tanner of a disgruntled mother hen seeing a dragon where a chick should have been.

"Yeah, waiting. I went to log on. The second I did, my screen was taken over. I was suddenly in some kind of chat room with only myself and the hacker." He relayed as best he could the conversation, then added, "There are programs that allow you to run one computer from another, like Remote Desk Top. But this was much more sophisticated. And that doesn't even factor in that they would need to get past my firewall, which is state-of-the-art. Shit, it's better than the one our government uses."

Tanner wasn't sure about that. There were firewalls and then there were firewalls. "First, the hacker said he was familiar with your code. Are you sure it might not be a student? He was here on the campus, knows your work, and he did refer to you as 'Professor.'"

"I'd know if one of my students was capable of this kind of work." When Tanner looked skeptical, Erik added, "Don't get me wrong. I've got some brilliant students. But this? This was professional all the way through."

"So was anything compromised? And what makes you so certain this has anything to do with last night?" He was pretty sure it did, but wanted to get Erik's thoughts first.

Erik plopped down in his chair. It was leather. Real leather. Not that stuff that they tried to pass off as leather. Ergonomically correct, of course. Probably cost more than one month's rent on his humble apartment. Erik wasn't making that much from his teaching position. It was family money. Tanner's jaw tightened every time he thought of it.

"Timing!" Erik said, his knuckles turning white as he gripped the chair's arms. "I don't believe in coincidence. The shooting. That was your warning. I'm not big fan of guns, but I don't believe someone who thought they could shoot from any distance and hit the target they were aiming for, would have missed. Second, professionalism. The shooter. The hacker. These aren't your average thugs off the street. They know exactly what they are doing. The hacker said it was a game. And Tanner, that's what I'm thinking it is. But the hacker also said I was out of my league. I'll agree with that. But I can't get rid of this nagging voice that says you aren't. You aren't, are you? That shooter? He's playing with you. Otherwise he would have taken you out."

"Oh, thanks." Tanner leaned slightly forward, his elbows resting on his knees, his hands folded, but not in prayer. In restraint.

"Now it's time for you to cut the crap. You know what I mean. The hacker could have scrubbed my files. Hell, he could have crashed my whole system or anything he wanted to. But no, he tells me it's a game. Warns me to get out because it's dangerous. Saint or sinner, Tanner? Who is this guy? I bet every last cent I own, that you have a good idea."

Tanner's grip tightened until his fingers were mottled white. His mind flashed on a small man, thin as a pole, with arctic blue eyes, olive skin, and dark curly hair. Wolf's hacker, Shadow Man. He could have retired and been as well off as Arneson if he'd had a dollar for all the times sensitive information had been pulled by Shadow Man, or Ten´ Cheloveka, as he was better known.

"Can you show me the text?" Tanner asked.

"No. Erased as soon as he left the conversation." Erik's lips compressed into a thin line as he remembered how he'd tried every trick in the book to get it back or get a trace. But it had all failed, and it made his blood boil to think his hacker knew exactly what he was trying and was sitting somewhere laughing. "I tried everything I knew to retrieve it or get a trace. Bastard had bounced it off so many servers from Australia, China, Russia, and the UK, I felt like a rat in a maze."

"So that's a dead end." If it were Ten´ Cheloveka, he would expect nothing less. "What more can you tell me about the man from last night? His height, build, coloring? You said he spoke to you? How did he phrase the words? Anything you can remember."

Erik closed his eyes and scrubbed his right hand over his face several times. "Um, it was dark. Hard to tell. He wasn't especially tall. Maybe five-ten. He was on the uphill side so that could be off. Dark clothing." Erik shook his head and looked closely at Tanner. The man was weighing everything he said against...

"How old?"

"Our age. Maybe younger. Shit, I'm not much of a witness, am I?"

"What about his voice?"

"Damn, Tanner, you've already asked me that. I've told you everything I know." Erik got up, skirted both his and Tanner's chairs and headed for the kitchen.

Jack raised his head hopefully as Erik approached, but rested it back on his paws when Erik didn't so much as look at him.

Tanner got up to follow. "I'm not being obtuse, Erik. I keep hoping as we speak that something will jog your memory more."

"Okay, formal. He was polite and formal. Not the way most young people talk, or old people, for that matter." Erik went to the fridge, opened the door and stood staring. Nothing had changed. Nothing had magically appeared since the last time he'd looked over an hour ago. Where was Rhyjl?

"Formal?" Tanner crossed the room and looked out

past the breakfast nook window to the sea beyond. His legs were slightly apart, his arms clasped behind his back. Ten´ Cheloveka had always spoken in a very formal manner. He and his companions had always joked that the Shadow Man thought he was a descendent of royalty. Perhaps a count. "Yeah, Count Dracula," Bass had said on more than one occasion.

Erik gave a slanted look at the detective. "Tanner, I get the feeling you've already got someone in mind."

Tanner pivoted. He suddenly felt very tired. He'd left all this behind, or thought he had. He'd wanted to live like a normal person with a normal life. Would he never be free? "I might, but I'd like more evidence before jumping to conclusions."

Erik reached in the fridge and pulled out a Samuel Adams. How was it that song by Alan Jackson went? *Pour me somethin' tall an' strong. Make it a "Hurricane" before I go insane. It's only half-past twelve, but I don't care. It's five o'clock somewhere.* Well, it wasn't even half-past twelve but right now he didn't care. He offered a second to Tanner, who shook his head.

"Enlighten me, Tanner, and forget the evidence part."

"That isn't how the law works, Arneson." He dropped into one of the dinette chairs and leaned forward with his elbows on his knees.

"Screw that! I didn't call the cops. I called you because this little quote, game, end quote we are playing has you smack in the center. Man to man now, Tanner, not cop to civilian."

"Fine!" Tanner threw up his hands in exasperation before letting them fall to his knees again. "I think your visitor last night and your hacker could be a man known as Shadow Man, aka Ten´ Cheloveka, aka Alexa´ Popov."

"Whoa! That's a whole lot of akas and at least two sound Russian. What the hell, Tanner!"

"Let's just say there was a time in my past where I had occasion to run into individuals like Shadow. They weren't always friendly meetings, either."

Erik pulled another chair away from the table and almost fell into it across from Tanner. "CIA? You and those dead guys?"

"Not quite so—shall I say—aboveboard as that?"

Erik couldn't stay seated, even though he felt like his legs might collapse from under him, and it wasn't because of the beer. He started to pace. His breath was coming fast, like he'd just run a mile. Shit, he knew Rhyjl shouldn't have gotten involved with this. His gut had been screaming at him, just as it had that summer his father forced him to remain behind rather than going with his mom. "Never mind, I don't want to know any more, except how the hell do we get out of this?"

Jack was now on full alert. He liked the man that had come to the house, but sensed the upset tone and pacing that Erik was doing wasn't right. The big dog rose and planted himself between his master and the visitor.

Tanner didn't move. Erik let his hand rest on Jack's back. "It's all right, Jack. Daddy is fine. Go lie back down."

"Daddy?" Tanner laughed, while continuing to make sure he remained non-threatening.

"Yeah, Daddy." Erik shrugged. "That's what Rhyjl started calling me around him. You know, 'Go find Daddy! Where's Daddy? Daddy will feed you.' It kind of stuck."

Jack responded well, but he refused to return to his favorite place near the food dish. Instead, he plopped where he stood.

"So," Erik said, returning to his chair. "This is beginning to sound like something out of one of those espionage thrillers. But this guy didn't sound Russian." Tanner lifted his brows in a question. "Okay, yeah, he had a bit of an accent, but he sounded pretty much like an American."

Tanner laughed again. "Which part of America, Arneson? New England? Boston, with your dropped R's that mysteriously end up on words ending in A's or W's? Or perhaps the South—deep Louisiana or perhaps Texas?"

Erik held up his beer in a salute. "Touché, Tanner. I got it and I should know better. But I spent a lot of time in some of those countries, as I told you, and most of the educated residents spoke English, but with a considerably British accent. This guy's speech was..."

"Which British accent? Cockney? There are about 56 main 'accent types' in the British Isles."

"F you, Tanner!" Erik's volume brought Jack up to a sitting position. "You are playing games with me now."

"Both you and your dog need to calm down, Arneson. Yes, I'm playing you a bit. To be honest, I wouldn't if it wasn't so damn easy to mess with that over-analytical brain of yours. And if I didn't need to take the edge off a little." Tanner shook his head, and laughed. "It's true, Erik. Like so many geeks, you want to think things out until they can be labeled and put neatly in a box. Life, real life, doesn't work that way." No one fits in boxes. Not Ten′ Cheloveka, not him, not Bass and the others. They had each been shaped, molded and broken like the rocks in a river by the water of life.

"Shadow's mother was a world-class violinist. She came to the States in the early eighties on a concert tour and ended up seeking political asylum. It took the fall of The Wall and a lot of work to later bring the toddler she'd been forced to leave behind to her home in Philadelphia. He was a teen by then. From what I gather, an angry teen."

"So he worked with you?"

"Hardly. He was educated here. He did become a citizen. Then, when he was in his mid-twenties, something happened to his father, who had chosen to remain in Russia. There's evidence he was part of the SVR. Shadow returned to Russia, presumably to pick up where his father had left off."

Chapter 17

Lost In Thought

Rhyjl took her time walking back to the house. The big clock standing sentinel in front of the Engineering building was a silent witness that half an hour had already passed since she'd left Marcus' office. She wasn't ready to face Erik yet. He'd be waiting, of course, to hear her news. He always believed in her. Cheered her on. But then, he knew what few others did. That she knew the truth of her findings by extraordinary means.

She knew without reservation that thousands of years ago, Caucasians from Sweden had settled in small bands on the northeastern shores of Canada and the United States. She'd seen them. Seen scraps of their lives replayed before her eyes, in a dimension that few—for she didn't know of anyone but herself and Erik's mother—had ever gone to. Were there others? Logic dictated that there must be, but it wasn't something you would want to parade around. Just as she kept it mostly to herself, it made sense that others did as well.

The monstrosity of a clock clanged the hour, breaking its silence and her from her thoughts the same way fingernails on a chalkboard might. She hated the clock, and never more so than now, when her annoyance level was screaming out of control. It was ugly! Well, to her it was. Completely out of sync with the rest of the campus. The chime wasn't the deep melodic tones of Big Ben or others she'd been around. It was a loud metallic clashing, just as the structure clashed with all the late nineteenth-century buildings surrounding it. The first time she'd come on the campus, she'd been struck with the incongruity of it. It looked for all the world like a giant digit torn from the hand of a mammoth robot and then stuck in the ground to tower above the campus. Just once, had any of the individuals creating it back in 1995 ever considered how out of place it might be?

Why did she care? Then it hit. She was sidetracking herself from what she didn't want to face. How was she going to tell Erik she was leaving for the Southwest in four weeks? That stopped her in her tracks. When had she made the decision? She stood looking off into the distance. Just off campus proper stood the gray Cape that she shared with Erik. It had become her home more than she ever thought it could. Most of that was because of Erik and Jack. What did they say? Home is where the heart is. And what of Jack? Could she take him with her, or would he need to remain behind? What would that do to Erik if they both were gone? What would it do to her if they both stayed?

It was as if the bench pulled her to it. She sat, seeing nothing except an image of herself leaving. She felt the pain lance through her very core. She hadn't known this kind of pain since she'd watched her mother slip away so many years ago. Just like back then, life would go on. It was different in that if she stayed, she could avoid the pain. But go, she would. She had no recourse. She'd worked too long and hard. It was only for the summer. Only three months and then...

Her fingers found the bone nub warmed by the heat of her body. She'd forgotten it in all that had happened. Forgotten she'd slipped it in her sweater just prior to leaving Alice's lab. Why had she done it? The bone answered her back.

The bastard stood before him. Hair was the color

of sand. Features, strong with a squared jawline and
cheeks that were wide and chiseled. A nose like a raptor's
sat between two eyes just as piercing, and colder than their
golden brown would have otherwise suggested. This was
what death looked like. He felt the sleep overtaking him no
matter how hard he fought it. He'd always wondered when
it would come. How it would come. It wasn't supposed to
be like this.

"Miss Martin, Miss Martin, are you okay? Jeff,
maybe we should call 911. I don't know what's wrong
with her."

The voices were so far away. So far.

"Already did, Tragen. They should be here in the
next ten minutes. Put your coat over her to keep her
warm," said the second man.

No, she couldn't let the medics arrive. They
couldn't help. Not here. She was drifting somewhere
between. She was still with him, but also within herself
again. No, not the medics.

"I think she's coming back around. Miss Martin?
Can you hear me?"

Rhyjl opened her eyes. There was the strong scent
of sweat and unfamiliar cologne coming from the collar of
the coat just under her nose. Two worried men hovered
above her. They were both dressed in the overalls the
campus gardeners wore. She knew the one. Tragen was
muscular, tall and ebony-skinned. She'd greeted him in
passing on her way to Marcus' earlier. The guy with the
dusty man bun, black rings that retained the huge holes in
his ear lobes, and a bushy beard, she'd only seen around
the last couple weeks.

On the periphery, several people were gathering.
She groaned. Just what she needed—looky-loos.

One woman said, "Seizure, maybe? She just kinda

got this weird look and toppled over."

Another man answered, saying, "Yeah, probably. Isn't she the one they found at the bottom of the cliff last fall?"

"I'm fine," she said, pushing the coat off. She obviously had slipped from the bench to the ground. She'd probably end up with another bruise to add to the ones from the night before. That, however, was the least of her problems. "Seriously, I'm fine. I just need to sit for a minute and then go home."

"I think you should try to remain quiet, Miss Martin," said Tragen, who was trying to wrap his jacket around her once again. She'd thought he was a basketball player the first time she'd seen him. Instead, he tended the flower baskets that hung from every lamp post and entryway on campus. This morning, when she'd greeted him, he'd been preparing the flowerbeds and raking. Beads of sweat were forming on his dark forehead. His chocolate eyes were full of concern. "I don't know what happened to you, but the EMTs will be here in minutes and it's best to let them have a look."

Oh, if only they'd all just go away. Especially those who hung around, not out of concern, but curiosity. She hated those kind of people. She made an effort to move. She sensed Tragen's hesitancy about what he should allow her to do. "Just help me get back to the bench," she said.

In answer, he laid a gentle hand on her shoulder to keep her still.

She needed to get home. To get to Erik. She needed to call Alice and Tanner. She'd seen the murderer. "Really, Tragen, I'm fine if..." Her words were cut short by the scream of sirens. It was too late.

She was surprised that Erik hadn't clued in to the sirens. Especially with her being gone. He always seemed

to be overly alert since he'd met her. But then, their lives
the last six months hadn't exactly been trauma free, had
they. She'd guess it wasn't too outlandish he might be a
little overly sensitive. She expected him to show any
minute. To hear the panic in his voice. But her knight
didn't come and she was surprised to find she was
dismayed by that. The sirens' call, however, had drawn
other spectators. The earlier few had turned to dozens. Or
at least, that was how it felt.

Two Emergency Medical Technicians spilled out
of the back of the red and white emergency van. A third
hung back, encouraging the crowd to do so as well. The
first one to reach her was a woman who had left her
younger days far in the past. She cradled a clipboard with
a pudgy, yet well-manicured hand. Her graying hair was
clipped short—almost masculine. Her questions were
clipped too—Home address? Phone? Birth date?

The second man didn't look like he should be out
of high school. His hair had that windblown look, a dark
curly mass. French descent, her thoughts said. He gave her
a cursory look from dark caramel eyes, the kind that could
make a girl hungry. If he had the manners to go with the
looks, he probably had a lineup of beauties. Pulling
Tragen's coat from her, he wrapped a blood pressure cuff
tightly around her left arm. She winced as he began
pumping it up while peppering her with more questions.
He called out that her bp was 130 over 80. "A little high."
What did they expect? She'd become the morning's event,
with people gathering about like vultures.

She heard, rather than saw, the second vehicle pull
up. The thwump of the door closing. A strong,
authoritative voice demanding that people back away. A
cop? What the... He was dressed in blue from head to toe.
A light knit cap topped his military cut. His windbreaker

had the caduceus, with its two snakes and wings embroidered on the pocket. The emblem on his shoulder and the silver-coated brass name plate identified him as Joe Walsh, Paramedic. The EMTs parted like the Red Sea as he moved to kneel beside her. With one look, they nodded and reiterated the information. He nodded, gently felt around her neck with his fingers while studying her pupils.

"You look familiar," he said.

She was waiting for the obvious follow-up, referring to her fall from the cliff. It surprised her when he said instead, "You were at the shooting last night."

That drew forth a collective mumbling reaction from the crowd.

"Yes, but I don't remember you." She didn't. She didn't remember much except the gut-wrenching fear that Alice or Tanner had been killed. "Seriously, do you take calls that are over forty minutes away?"

He laughed. "No, that call was my job. Three days on and three days off. I fill in here as a volunteer one day a week. My town. The least I can do." His hands had traveled up to feel around her scalp. Her hair kept trying to entangle itself in his blue gloves. She winced as one strand pulled.

"Is that tender?" he asked, narrowing those deep blue eyes framed by long eyelashes that most women would envy.

"Only when you pull my hair."

"Ah, sorry. So what do you think happened here? Were you feeling faint? Headache?"

Headache? Yeah, she had one, all right, but that wasn't the reason. "Stress, not enough sleep and missed breakfast," she offered.

"Yes, I can see where that might happen after the

events of last night." He reached out his hand. "I'd like it
if you could slowly sit up. Let me know if anything feels
off or hurts. Okay? On the count of three." His hand
gripped hers firmly. "One, two, three..." He pulled her into
a sitting position. "How's that?"

The gathering of spectators had begun thinning.
She imagined them thinking, *how boring*. She wasn't
going to die or put on some dramatic show after all.

"I'm fine, really. I'm really sorry for all the fuss."

"No problem. If you do have any more incidents
like this, you really should see a doctor." He almost lifted
her to her feet while still keeping a careful watch for any
telltale signs. "Do you live close by? Has anyone been
notified?"

"Yes, and no. I just live over there in that gray
Cape," she answered, pointing across the green expanse
that edged the entire campus and separated it from her
home. "I'll be fine."

"I'll see her home, sir," Tragen offered.

Joe Walsh scrutinized the groundskeeper. Was it
caution or racism? It was hard to tell. Then Walsh held out
his hand. "You're with Company C, 1st Battalion 126th
Aviation Regiment."

"Yes, sir." Tragen accepted the handshake.

"Mille here," Walsh said, referring to the older
woman with the clipboard, "will get her paperwork taken
care of. Then you, Corporal, can escort her home."

~~

Rhyjl was thankful she'd accepted Corporal
Tragen Dickson's escort. She still was feeling a bit off. He
remained like a solid rock beside her, but didn't pester her
with questions. The vision she'd seen was still fresh. The

eyes of the murderer, smoky and cold. He'd killed before. She knew it. How, she wasn't sure, but she knew, just as she knew the moment she walked in the door that Erik might never let her out unescorted again.

Damn! Why had she let this happen? She'd been so careful. She could pick a bone up. Move them from place to place. That had been necessary in her classes. The key was not to linger. To never let herself be open and vulnerable. Not since she'd had that little incident at the Henderson Farm site three years earlier. The jolt had been minor. A sting, really, like catching a splinter from a broken glass. Her vision had wavered. Easily explained away. The temperature had been over ninety. She'd been working out in the sun the whole day. Not enough water. Not that unusual. She was also learning to be more careful about the fresh bones, as she was coming to think of them. The first time she'd experienced a fresh bone had been that incident in the bone lab. She explained that away to her audience as a spider sting. It had been a sharp jolt, but again, she hadn't lingered. Today, however, she'd slipped. She was already open to the barrage of her own emotions. She'd felt the bone in her pocket. She'd fingered it absently. Played with it, almost, in the same way Erik did his rock. The bone! She frantically reached for the phalanx. It wasn't in her pocket. Of course it wasn't, she'd had it in her hand. She stopped as if she'd hit a wall. Turning, she looked back toward the bench. It must still...

"Looking for this?" Tragen reached in his pocket and pulled the fifth distal phalanx of a right hand out of his pocket. He held it out in his palm. "I won't ask why you are carrying the tip of someone's little finger around with you. None of my business. But I figure it must be important, the way you were strangle-holding it."

"Guilty," she said. "I work in the bone lab. We

aren't supposed to remove specimens. I discovered it in my pocket just before passing out." Her excuse sounded lame. It was. But he accepted it, if only out of courtesy. It wasn't his business, after all.

"Nice ride," Tragen said, pointing toward her driveway.

The motorcyclist pulled out of the driveway just as she and Tragen were approaching. He was dressed all in black leather. The helmet was jet black. The bike was black, except for the silver chrome glinting in the sunlight. He looked like an assassin out of some spy movie. Her heart skipped a beat. Her mouth suddenly felt like ashes. "I've got to go!" She snatched the small phalanx from Tragen's grasp. "Thanks."

~~

The house appeared deserted when she opened the door. Jack was nowhere in sight. Papers were scattered throughout the living room. It looked like a minor tornado had hit. The apprehension squeezing her throat was suffocating. Suddenly it collapsed like a punctured balloon with a sharp exhale of breath she wasn't even aware she'd been holding. Man and beast were out in the yard playing a doggy version of keep-away. It wasn't obvious who was winning, but Jack was clearly very pleased with himself. His tongue was lolling out the corner of his mouth. His front feet barely touching the ground. Erik jerked the stick to the right, then left. He hesitated with his throw when he saw Rhyjl at the door. Jack took full advantage of the distraction to leap in the air and snatch the prize.

She wasn't fool enough, living on a small campus, to believe the events of the last half hour or so wouldn't eventually reach Erik. She was relieved that she would have time to craft the story so he wouldn't fly off the handle. In the meantime, he had some explaining to do himself. Who was the person on the motorcycle? Why was the living room a disaster? But first things first, she needed to call Alice. Alice needed know what had happened.

The call went straight to voice mail two times in a row. Either Alice had turned her cell phone off, or she was on another call. She thought about calling Alice's home. She had the number somewhere. She'd rarely used it. Alice once told her it was more of a private number she kept just for her family. Scrolling through, she found it. She pushed "dial." It rang six times. Alice's voice cheerfully announced she couldn't come to the phone and would the caller leave a message.

The back door opened. Jack bounded in.

"You're home," Erik said, with a mixture of relief and tension. His worry stone danced in his fingers and his smile didn't quite counter the strain of his brow.

"You had company," she stated, her hand going to Jack's shoulders as he leaned against her legs.

"Tanner." Erik moved to pick up some of the strewn papers. He'd meant to do it prior to her returning. Jack had other ideas. The Saint made that very clear by going to the doors and circling. Jack's need took priority. The break from the tension had helped him as well. His teeth no longer ached from the clench and grind. "I think you should sit down." His eyes and head nodded to the space on the couch he'd cleared before taking Jack out.

Rhyjl had never seen Erik so edgy, so tense. She sat slowly, as if there might be some danger in the room she was unaware of. "That guy on the cycle was Tanner?"

"Yes." He walked over to the chair he'd earlier arranged for Tanner by his desk and pulled it over to where she was sitting. He sat across from her and pulled her hands into his lap. "We're in trouble."

"Erik?" She pulled away. "What are... You're scaring me."

He attempted to claim her hands again. She countered by leaning further away, crossing her arms and tucking her hands firmly out of sight. Resolute as a stone, she waited. Feeling awkward, he fumbled for his stone.

"This case..." he paused, took a deep breath. The stone danced between nimble fingers. "It's a lot more than we signed up for. I called Tanner. He had some explaining to do. About last night, the tattoo, and why I..." The stone stopped. He looked at it as if surprised to see it. "We are being stalked."

"Stalked? I thought we all agreed that the shooting last night was about him. Why do you think it's not today? The guy you ran into last night? Circumstantial. We are jumping at shadows." Just as she'd jumped to the worst case scenario when she'd seen the motorcycle.

"Look, Tanner, well, he's got a past. A dangerous past with dangerous people. People that don't follow laws. People that don't care if they kill. Powerful people, Rhyjl. Government people."

"Well, we guessed as much. At least that..." The anxiety on his face was growing. "Erik, what's happened? You..." She thought about Alice and the unanswered phone calls. "Alice! Is Alice okay? Is that why Tanner was here? Has something happened to her?"

"She's fine, or at least as fine as any of us can be. There's been some trouble at her lab. Tanner told me that before he left her this morning, she got a call. She wasn't happy. They've taken the bones. It was expected, but I guess it didn't quite go down the way she thought. Whatever, with the removal of the bones, that kind of ends your part."

She thought of the fingertip in her pocket and almost reached for it. Should she tell Erik?

"But I don't think it is over for us, collectively," he continued. "They broke into my computer. Correction. He broke into my computer. Took it over. He warned me off. He called it a serious game and said that I'd left a trail but he had covered it up."

"What do you mean *he* took control of your computer? Tanner?"

"No, not Tanner. Someone else." He stood, walked behind his chair, then for a moment gripped the back, his hands, his knuckles straining. "I've been hacked, Rhyjl. My entire system compromised."

"You're not making any sense, Erik. How is that even possible?"

"I don't know. I've spent the last several hours going over everything. It's beyond me. My firewall is fine. I can't find a trace of the IP of my attacker. He's like a ghost. He's right, though, I don't know enough about this. I don't know if he's a black hat or white."

"What?" Rhyjl sank deeper into the couch. What more could go wrong today?

"In the hacking world they are called either black hats or white hats."

You're not serious? White hats? Black hats? Like one of those old B westerns? Scrubbing her face at the vision his words brought to mind, she managed a brittle laugh. "Gods, you are serious? Black being bad and good being white, I suppose?"

"I'm not amused here, Rhyjl. I didn't pick the names. But damn it, someone was into my system. Someone violated me."

"Erik, I'm not making fun of the situation." She reached out. His hands met hers. This wasn't the way she had envisioned their afternoon. Actually, what had she envisioned? Oh, Erik, I'm going to leave in just a little over four weeks to go across country. Isn't that nice? Or, I had one of my attacks. I'm sure half the campus is talking about it now. Well, that was a bit conceited. No, she just needed to be close. Maybe talk about everyday things like taking a walk or what to do for dinner. "I know this is hard for you. I just can't ... Well, perhaps he's a white hat. He did try to warn you. He did say he had cleaned up any evidence you'd left behind. Also, what makes you think it's a guy and not some gal?"

He abandoned his choke hold on the chair to come sit next to her. His arm circled her shoulder, pulling her close. She felt good. "I'm not sure, except that I think it's the same person I saw last night."

She looked up, hoping he was teasing. He wasn't. "Now you are giving me the creeps. Do you think he hacked the computer from inside the house? Erik, that's just not possible. I'd only gone to bed a few minutes before you came home."

"Were you in the living room the whole time?"

"Well, most of it. Still, even if I'd been in another room, I'd have heard something. I mean, I was listening for you to come back. Wouldn't it be more likely that he did it before we came home?"

"You think he was able to get past our locks and security system? Does that make you feel any better?"

She shifted and laid her head on his shoulder. "Not really. But you have to admit if he can get into your computer, our security is probably child's play. So what do you propose we do?"

"I think we do as he says and stay out of this mess. Last night we were shot at and hacked. I'm no coward, Rhyjl, but I'm no fool either. Something is really wrong with this whole setup. We need to distance ourselves from it."

~~

Rhyjl's call to Alice went to voice mail for the second time. The knot in her throat was growing. Soon, she might not be able to get words past it. She'd seen the killer. That kind of evil shouldn't be packaged in that fair a face. But it was. And now it was seared into her memory indelibly. Not with fire. This burn was cold.

Rhyjl could understand fear. She could understand hate. And if she worked at it, she might be able to wrap her mind around the type of greed that might drive a person to kill. But this was evil. It held no connection with any of the above. It was bred out of sick and twisted enjoyment. It took pleasure out of seeing the fear and pain of other living things. It fed greedily on it. The man wanted her dead. No, not her, the man named Bass. Bass had known him. But he hadn't thought of this demon by anything other than "the bastard." Still, there couldn't be many men that could rain fear into a man like Bass and have those features, that presence. Yes, that had been another part of it. The presence of the man. His demeanor was one of authority. Even Bass accepted that. This man had power. He could make or break lives in ways she or Bass couldn't begin to fathom, yet they both recognized it.

Erik had returned to fussing with his computer, the modem and anything else within feet of his work station. The tension in the room was sticky and overpowering. Erik had been violated by the words and presence of the hacker. What had he called them—hats? White or black, did it matter? She still found it somewhat amusing that new high tech individuals would resort to old western stereotypes.

But watching Erik, the way his nerves were like sparking wires, had vanquished most of the humorous aspect. He'd repeated that typed conversation so many times. The words were probably just as stark and cold in his mind as her vision was in hers.

She wanted to talk with him about her vision. She needed his thoughts, his unique way of seeing things. But Erik couldn't see beyond his preoccupation with the morning's hacking. The hacker might as well still be in the room with them. Erik was convinced the intruder would strike again. He'd tear the place apart until he was able to figure out what the guy had done, or worse, what he might do next.

"Erik, stop!" Rhyjl said. He'd taken his cell phone off his belt and was looking at it as if it had grown horns. "This is ridiculous! He's gone. He warned you. Told you to stay away. He's not out to steal your life's work or your life."

"But he could!" Erik laid his phone down on his desk, then snatched it up and shoved it back in the leather holster above his hip.

She hadn't thought of it before, but the phone's holder was another modern object they'd tacked an old Western name to. "No, he's gone. You won't see him again unless you meddle where you shouldn't. Where I asked you to." Guilt pinched her heart. "I'm sorry, Erik. I got caught up in solving a mystery. I shouldn't..."

"No, you shouldn't have, and neither should I. But we did." He shook his head, scanned the room and collapsed into his desk chair. "So where do we go from here?" His hand shot up to stay her answer. "I don't mean, what do we do about this case, but what have we learned, what are we learning from this? I know you think I'm overreacting."

Her head tilted to the left, her eyebrows lifting. "You think?"

"Yeah, I think. But it's not what you are thinking. It's not that I think the guy is still here."

Rhyjl's eyebrows shifted again with another little head twist and a slight grimace. "Really?"

"Okay, so maybe I'm still..." Closing his eyes, he dropped his face into his hands, his fingers scrubbing his forehead and combing back his hair. "I'm vulnerable, Rhyjl. If he could do it, others can. Cyber theft is electronic cancer. I've worked so hard to protect myself. What I've learned from this is that I'm not safe at all. Sophisticated firewalls, passwords, encryptions. All for naught."

She unfolded her legs from under her and moved from the sofa. "It's over, Erik. You were vulnerable because we went from the real world into some ..." She shrugged. "What? Superheroes and villains? I don't even know how to describe it. But in the real world you are protected. YOU hacked into their world. YOU are that good. But just like he said," she sat in his lap and wrapped her arms around him, "you were out of your league. So you attracted the attention of the super guys, non-mortals or enhanced mortals. It doesn't matter. You're just a fly to them. Stay out of their line of thought and view, and they won't even remember you're there. In the mortal world you hold your own."

Removing his hands from his face, he gazed into her eyes. He felt the warmth spreading through his body. Her countenance was soft, sweet. In that moment, he was overwhelmed with the love he saw there. He wanted to dive into it, feel it envelop him. But to do so could have repercussions, until she was ready. *Keep it light,* he thought, caressing her face, his smile turning playful. "No more *Marvel* for you."

She laughed and stood. "Your fault. I'd never heard of Hydra, the Avengers, or Shield until I met you. My interests were of a more serious nature."

"Well, you know what they say—all work and no play makes for a very dull..."

"That's it!" She lunged at him, her fingers going to his most ticklish spot.

Jack, refusing to be left out, jumped into the middle of the fray with huge, wet dog kisses. They giggled like children, legs and arms flailing in all directions. Pushing each other and the big furry mass who was barking as if all his squirrel dreams had come true. It left no room for the earlier specters.

Chapter 18

Death and Destruction

The back parking lot of the morgue was empty. No mute testimony of what had taken place the night before, but there was also nothing to warn her of what was waiting for her inside. Throughout her commute, she had hoped—no, expected—to see a black SUV, government issue. She had primed herself with demands. Someone owed her explanations. They needed paperwork. Someone needed to show they had authority to invade her office, her space.

She unlocked the door. The back entry hall was empty. Nothing out of the usual there. The tattoo of her stiletto heels echoed before her like a drummer before an advancing army. She was ready for battle. There were procedures and protocol to be followed.

Even before she twisted the door handle to her lab, she could hear a muted metallic clink and clack. Then there was a muffled curse, and then the sound of running water. The door swung inward on well-oiled hinges. Gene Haverty stood at one of the stainless steel sinks. It looked like he was simply washing his hands, until he turned slightly after hearing her entrance. There was blood there. Then her eyes swept the room. She gasped. The room was suddenly spinning. Debris was scattered everywhere. Broken vials and specimen dishes littered the floor. Papers, like spent confetti, lay forgotten. She took a step forward, more to catch her balance than anything else. She felt the crunch under the thin sole of her shoe. A bright tinkle like small chimes as more glass shattered underfoot.

"I'm sorry," Gene Haverty said. "I've been trying

to clean up the mess." He held out his bleeding hand. "The glass is everywhere. They weren't very careful."

Alice inhaled deeply. Vertigo still clung to the edges of her mind. "'Weren't very careful.' That's a bit of an understatement, wouldn't you say?"

He looked around the room, then back at her. He wasn't his usual cocky self. In fact, cowering puppy was a more apt description. "There was nothing I could do. They were already here when I arrived. As soon as I walked in I was manhandled into another room. They pummeled me with so many questions. Most of which I couldn't begin to answer. I..."

"Did you ask for ID? Did you demand the right to call me or Jim Ackerman?"

"No." His eyes darted from side to side.

Deliberately concocting a lie about the morning's events was just too much for him to process? She lowered her voice. "Why?"

"Well, they didn't give me much of a chance. As I said, they manhandled me into the waiting room and started asking questions."

She took a few careful steps further into the room, attempting to avoid the litter on the floor. Still, she inwardly winced at every crunch and tinkle. "Gene, you are a grown man. Not a child. You have rights. I have rights. OUR department has rights." Her voice was gaining in volume even though she had made a mental note to keep her cool. Too late, she saw her mistake. It was a wonder he hadn't already wet his pants. Her disgust was like sawdust on her tongue: caked and acidic. "We will discuss this further. If you are capable, try calling for housekeeping. They are adept at cleaning up other people's messes."

By the time she passed him and opened the door to her office, she had reached the end of her rope. The lab was her workspace. This was her personal space. Hers! Every file cabinet had been rifled. Files she had kept over the last four years were strewn about, their contents mingled with other files and folders. It would take days, if not weeks, to put them back in order. Her computer was gone. Pictures hung crookedly from their mounts on the wall. Two had fallen, the glass shattered. Chaos reigned. Drawers from her desk and the built-ins had been dumped and left. Books torn from shelves, their spines broken. Even the glass jars she had kept teas and cocoa in had been dumped. It could all be rectified. Put back. It would take lots of effort. Lots of patience. A virtue she didn't possess at the moment.

Amid the mess, something niggled at the back of her mind. She ran to her desk. Started shuffling paper. Moved the overturned picture frame with her family's photo. It wasn't there! She looked on the floor under the desk, beside the desk. It made no sense. Why would they take that? Then she glimpsed a partial wing. It had been kicked to the wall. Her special gift from her father the day she had graduated med school. Her angel. Delicate crystal wings folded at rest. The supple hands posed in prayer. A full skirt that formed the bell. Or correction, it had been an angel with wings and a full skirt. Only the head was intact.

"You will save lives now," her father had said. "Just like the angels." She hadn't told him yet that she wanted to go into forensics. His hope had always been that she would join him in his practice. When she'd shared what her choice was, instead of being angry as she thought he had a right to be for dashing his hopes, he said instead, "Then you will be an angel who brings closure to the grieving and justice to the wronged."

She cradled the head of the angel in her hands against her breast. Tears streamed down her cheeks as if from a fountain. She remembered she had forgotten to call her father this morning. He would be worried. She'd call him now. She wanted to go home.

~

Dr. Paul Merks answered his phone on the fourth ring. She was hoping to catch him before he went on his morning rounds at Brigham and Women's Hospital. "Daddy?" Her voice sounded mouse-small even to her ears.

"Alice! What's wrong?"

The story spilled from her amid hiccups and sobs. She had thought to be stoic. She'd failed.

"I'll be up as soon as I can get Bruce to cover for me and cancel the appointments that aren't critical. Should I bring your mother?"

"No. I want to come home for a while. I can see her then if that's okay with you."

"You don't even need to ask." His voice was strong, not angry. He was in control. That's one of the many things she admired and loved. Whatever the event, he rose above, never to be buffeted by the fates and winds. His only weakness was his daughter, but even today, as she had sobbed, he had been strong for her. His voice and words were the anchor she had needed to keep her from plunging into the abyss.

The phone on her desk rang. It shrilled a second time. Then a third. She felt torn. Like a Dalmatian's response to a fire alarm, she couldn't ignore it. Or, scanning her office, could she? Did she even care? Her father's calm voice was on her cell line outlining how the afternoon would play out. He'd be at her place no later than three. She should be ready so they could get back in time for dinner. Her mother was expecting company for dinner and then bridge, but if that was too unsettling...

"I, ah, let me get back with you, Dad. My office phone is ringing. It might be important." She gnawed her upper lip. Released the tension from her shoulders, and caught the call on the fifth ring. "Dr. Merks."

She recognized the officer's voice before he identified himself. He rattled off an address, more of a description, since it was on a back road. "Suicide," he pronounced. "Male. Mid-thirties." His voice grim.

She entered the information into her cell phone as he spoke. The mapping app gave her a rough idea of how much time it would take for her to get there. She was familiar with the area. A few scattered homes, many of them trailers. Not prosperous by any stretch of the imagination. Booze helped ease the pain. Sometimes, drugs. Not often. DUIs were common. The area was more or less a poster child for Drinking and Driving Don't Mix. Rock walls and sturdy pines weren't very forgiving. Adjusting the drive time with her prep time, she gave an ETA of twenty-five minutes.

She called her father. Explained that she wouldn't be coming down. At least, not today, but would like to keep her options open. She gathered a few things from the rubble for her bag. She grabbed a tissue, wiped the smeared mascara from below her eyes, gave herself a quick once-over in the mirror and walked out, locking the door behind her.

The officer had said it was a suicide. His voice had been strained. Suicides did that to people, Alice thought, stepping into the hall. Did anyone really understand what could drive a person to take their own life? Is that why it rocked us? Why even the most hardened cop couldn't just walk away without feeling something in their core. Or, as she thought so many times, did we fear it because deep down we all knew and understood it too well?

In the lab, a subdued and pathetic Gene was still picking up the larger pieces of glass. He rose from his stooping position as she entered. "Did you call housekeeping as I asked?"

"They said their contract is for evening hours, and they don't have anyone available at the moment."

"Did they?" Alice raised her eyebrows. "Well, call them back and tell them they had better find someone. I have a case coming in and I want this lab cleaned and ready to work in by the time I get back. They have just over an hour."

"But they were very insistent there was nothing they could do."

There was that pathetic puppy look again. No, not puppy. He wasn't that cute or appealing. Rat. Sneaking, conniving rat that's all puffed up and pompous until cornered.

"Gene, you are going to be very insistent that they get someone here immediately. That they will be compensated. That their job depends on it. And so does yours. Do I make myself clear?"

For just the briefest moment she saw a spark of anger flare in his eyes. It was so short-lived she almost could have missed it.

"Yes, Dr. Merks. Abundantly." He turned his back to her and grabbed the broom handle he had leaned against the narrow edge of the stainless steel table. "Anything else?"

"Yes. How do you think you would do flipping burgers?" She shut the door on his dropped-jaw expression.

~~

Dark, heavy clouds were gathering on the horizon. Just the right atmosphere for how she was feeling, and the scene she had just pulled up to. It was a lonely place to die—a narrow black ribbon of road that seemed to lead to nowhere. There were no houses on this stretch. Just a mile or two of wind-stunted trees and a long open clearing where giant power lines ran. A few scant patches of snow still clung desperately to shaded spots near rock walls and tree roots. If it rained, as it would surely do, by the color and size of those clouds, these stubborn remnants of winter would be gone by the end of the day.

There were two police cruisers and one unmarked detective's vehicle that reminded her of Mike's. Unfortunately, it wasn't. The detective who stood with his hands resting akimbo on his hips was Al Devners. She should have expected this. Would have, if her mind hadn't been cluttered with the circumstances of the morning. Of course, with Mike on leave, Devners would be taking Mike's calls. Mike's territory.

The victim's car was a late model GMC Terrain SUV. She'd actually considered buying one a few months prior, after the rental people had given her one as an upgrade while she was attending the Forensic Science Symposium in San Antonio last fall. She'd fallen in love with it. They weren't cheap cars, so the guy either had money, or had been in big debt. The latter could contribute to depression: overwhelming debt, struggling economy, perhaps a job loss.

Bud Wilks was walking to meet her as she stepped from the Body Wagon, the nickname the crime guys had pinned on the ME's Savana van. Middle-aged, with a nice build, he filled out his uniform nicely. "Dr. Merks," he said. His spring-green eyes, clear and observant under rust-colored brows, were filled with concern. "I just want to say how sorry I am about recent events."

He was holding up the yellow crime scene tape so she could duck under. For just a moment she was taken aback. Had word spread that fast? Sighing, she realized he'd meant the shooting. "Thanks. I'm fine, Bud. What have you got?" She fell in step with him as they crossed the narrow road.

"Straightforward suicide, Devners says. I've got to agree. One shot. Close range to the left temple. Looks like a Glock 36, 45 caliber. It's down at the guy's left foot. CSI should be here soon. I called them right after I spoke with you."

As if on cue, the state-owned Ford one-ton drove up and parked behind her rig. Two guys got out and busied themselves getting equipment from the back and suiting up into their whites.

"Doctor." Devners gave a slight nod. His lips resumed a hard, solid line. The jaw muscles were working as if he were chewing grit. He was not happy to have her there. But it wasn't his choice. She'd pegged Devners long ago as the kind that didn't like his authority or his plans challenged. He hadn't failed to live up to that assessment yet.

"Morning, Detective. I hear we have a suicide?"

"Doesn't get any clearer unless we have a note. And we will. I make the death at about midnight."

"Why's that?" Alice said, looking through the open window of the Terrain. The victim's head was at a slight angle, leaning back against the head rest. A raw entry wound was just above and to the left of the man's left temple.

"The driver's window is open. His jacket is wet,

but that appears to only be on the side near the window. We had a storm pass through here a little after midnight. "

"Anything else, Detective?" Alice smiled.

"Well, as you can see," Detective Devners' large fleshy index finger pointed at the face of the man, "He's gone into rigor mortis. We are at..." Devners twisted his arm and pushed back the cuff of his coat to expose a nice gold-plated wristwatch. "Ten thirty-five. The body is cold. I'm putting it at least eight hours ago. That pushes it back to around two a.m." He shrugged and moved his hand dismissively. "Storm and rigor."

His attitude was so smug, Alice wanted to go on full attack. She took a deep breath, exhaling slowly. Her smile was thin and spread too tightly against her cheeks. "That's good, Detective. Looking for a career change?"

"Just doing my job, ma'am."

She ignored the slight, pulled purple latex-free gloves from her pocket and stretched them on her hands. "Anything else you want to impart to me, or can I do my job?"

"Pretty open and shut as Bud told you. Suicide. The Glock is right there on the floor at his feet. We haven't found the spent casing yet, but ..." He cocked his head to the side, shrugging again. "Not really that important. I'm sure the CSI guy will have it in no time."

As you told Bud to tell me. "Still, if you don't mind, I need to make these observations for myself. I'm sure you understand. I mean, you wouldn't want me filling out your reports for you."

Again with the shrug, he walked away to speak to CSI. Alice was certain he was telling them how to do their job as well. She knew it wasn't personal with him. Just the way he was.

The man was dead. Single gunshot to the head

likely cause of death. The gun lying at his feet, the most likely used. Rigor mortis had set in, but it wasn't as simple as Devners believed. Sex, age, build and ambient temperature were all key players. Time of the storm? The open window? Yes, that could all play in. Still, something bothered her. The apparent angle the bullet had entered. The way the hands and arms were positioned. She pulled her camera out of the pack she'd slung over her shoulder and took numerous shots.

"What do you think?" asked Jimmy Jansen, or JJ, as he was called. He was one of her favorite CSI guys. Sharp, thorough, he never jumped to conclusions.

"I think we have a fellow who is sitting in a car, dead from an apparent gunshot to the head," Alice answered.

"What I thought." JJ nodded. "Devners there," he glanced and crooked his neck in the direction of the detective, "is putting it down as suicide."

"Yes, I know." Alice placed the lens cap back on her camera. She let her mind and eyes wander over the scene again. "Was this guy a southpaw, do you suppose?"

"Why, Dr. Merks. I would have never figured you for a baseball fan."

"I'm not. My dad is. He dragged me to every Red Sox game they played at home when I was a kid."

"Ah," JJ said. "So why do you think he might have been left-handed?"

"I don't, not conclusively. But something's not right about the hand positions. The left is dropped in his lap between his legs. So yes, he shoots himself with his left hand. Hand falls and gun ends up down there at his feet. Seems obvious enough. But studies have shown that not all suicide shootings are done with the dominant hand. So, is it possible he might be right-handed? Now look at his right hand. It's laying across his lap almost as if he was reaching across his body or resting it there. If you were going to shoot yourself..." She moved slightly to give JJ a better view.

"Yeah." He nodded. "I think I see what you mean. It's a tough call. But yeah, I don't think that right hand would be like that."

"There's also the angle of entry." She pulled a penlight from her coat and pointed it at the wound from different angles. JJ was good and caught her meaning immediately.

"Yeah, yeah," he said. "Doesn't quite look right either. Sooooo, are you thinking maybe suicide isn't what we've got here?"

"What I'm saying, JJ, is that I want you and Mark to go over this scene with a fine-tooth comb."

~~

Arriving back at the morgue, Alice backed the Body Wagon up to the back door. JJ and Mark had helped her load the body. She'd need Gene to get the victim into the lab. She made her way down the hall to the lab door. A quick glance told her very little had been done since she'd delivered her parting speech. Her heels clicked ominously until she reached the carpeted waiting room. Only Judy, her part-time secretary, was there to greet her. Judy was a middle-aged dynamo. Her hair was dark brown, short, almost spiky. Her complexion was tanned, since she'd spent half the winter in Florida, and the wrinkles were skillfully hidden by well-done makeup. She could bring an office and stacks of papers and correspondence to heel in an extraordinarily short amount of time. Exactly what the office required in this age of budget cuts.

"There have been four calls for you since you went out. Four messages are waiting. Jim Ackerman has called three times. He left two of those messages and called again about," Judy looked at the basic black clock on the wall, "eight minutes ago. He seems on edge," she confided, with brows furrowed and a slight frown.

"Where's Gene? We have a client that needs to be brought in."

Judy puckered as if she'd just sucked a lemon. "Out. He stormed out of here just a few minutes after I arrived. He said I could give you a message."

"Is that one of those messages waiting for me?"

"No, and it's not one you're going to like hearing. I'm guessing you two had a parting of the ways, and if not, will have when I tell you what he said."

Alice felt an explosion about to take place in her chest. The little bastard wanted war. His disappearance, along with several messages from their boss, Jim, were probably connected. "Keep the message, Judy. File it under scumbags. Do you know if the cleaning crew will be coming in soon?"

Judy's face crinkled. "Cleaning crew?"

Chapter 19

Just Hold Me

There was something entirely sinful about lying peacefully in bed in the middle of the day when you were neither sick nor injured. Rhyjl stretched her arms languidly above her head. Erik gave a little grunt, his arm constricting possessively around her waist. She hadn't shared with him the details of her morning and was even more reluctant to do so now. There was time, she thought, to break the news of the upcoming trip to New Mexico or Arizona or wherever this job would take her. And break was the operative word. All hell was going to break loose. She knew it. They'd already tentatively discussed their plans for the summer. He was going to finish and publish his patent idea. Then they were going to take a long trip to Sweden. Gotland Island, specifically, where she would get together with the two individuals who had been helping her with her research for her thesis. Frieda's work with DNA was crucial, as was Petra's research into late Neolithic and early Bronze Age settlement and expansion.

The vision of the raptor-faced man insinuated itself into her mind. He was someone she couldn't put off. Her public collapse was the other. Erik hadn't gone out yet, but as soon as he passed through the door of their home, that event would find him.

"What's on your mind? I can hear the wheels turning from here." His voice was low and husky, still sated with sleep.

"I didn't get a chance to tell you earlier. I had an episode on the way back from my meeting with Marcus."

He propped himself up on one elbow. The arm encircling her waist tensed. "What kind of episode? Why? Did you stop at the bone lab?"

"Marcus and I had a very interesting and provoking meeting. I can tell you more about it later. But it made me want to think rather than just coming straight home. While I was wandering and thinking, my fingers discovered something in my pocket. It was a bone from one of the victims. The tip of his little finger, to be exact. Out of the blue the scene was before me. I'm afraid... afraid I may have fainted."

"What you mean is you had an all-out episode. Damn!" He jumped out of bed, tossing the covers almost in her face. "What happened? I can't imagine it went unnoticed." His fingers were now raking at his hair.

"Please calm down, Erik." She swung her legs over the edge of the bed and gathered from the floor the shirt they had madly discarded only an hour or so before. She pulled it on. Then rose to go to the master bath.

"It's a wonder I didn't get a call from the hospital." He was pacing, buck naked, silhouetted against the glass French doors of their room. In their heated desire and rush earlier, they hadn't considered closing the curtains. But then the room was darker. The bright light outside would give the glass a mirror effect. And the green between them and the sea was private property. Still...

"You almost did." She looked from Erik into the bathroom mirror. Her hair was wild and tousled. Her eyes still had that soft dreamy look. She sighed. If only this feeling could last just a little longer. "The emergency people were called. One fellow, the paramedic, was actually at our scene last night." She was doing her best to keep it light. "If this keeps up, we are going to get quite the reputation."

"But you're okay?" he said, rounding the bed and coming toward her. "That's the main thing. I'm sure you managed to give a plausible and benign excuse, or I would have gotten that call." He turned on the shower. It hissed and spat against the tiles.

"Stress and low blood sugar."

"Of course." He pulled her top from her a second time and tossed it. Then gathered her into the steam behind him.

Discussion abandoned them, the hot water washing the initial tension away while recapturing the earlier sensations. But it couldn't hold the world back indefinitely.

"So what happened?" Erik toweled himself while watching her do the same. She had her back to him, but he could see her reflection in the mirror.

"To put it bluntly," she said, staring into his reflection's eyes, "I saw the face of the killer. Bass knew he was looking at the face of death."

The haunted look crept into her features. Tears welled up and threaten to overflow. He wrapped his arms around her. Felt her back mold against his chest. Sensed the effort it took as she tried to check her emotions. "Ah, honey, I'm sorry. What did Alice say? I'm assuming you called her right away."

"I did. Several times, but her phone went straight to voicemail." She trembled, kneading her towel for comfort. "I even tried her house phone. But as expected, I got her answering machine. That kind of worried me. Then I saw Tanner's motorcycle, which I didn't know at the time was Tanner's. That had my heart skipping a beat out of concern for you, and I kinda forgot Alice in all that followed." New guilt slithered unwelcome into her thoughts. Turning to Erik, her voice and eyes pleaded with him to reassure her. "She's okay, isn't she?"

"I'm sure she is." He hoped he was correct. "Dry off. Try again. She may have been on the road in to her office. You know using a cell phone while driving is anathema as far as she's concerned. Then, there's that mess with the remains being picked up. I'm sure there's plenty of red tape to cut through there. She's probably swamped."

"You're right," Rhyjl said, shedding the towel to the floor and reaching for the blue silk robe he'd bought her for Christmas. "I'll try her again."

As an afterthought, as she left him standing alone with his mirrored reflection, he added, "And when you do break through the sound barrier, with everything going on, perhaps you shouldn't go into details over the phone. Tell her we will meet her somewhere. I bet she hasn't had lunch either."

Chapter 20

Ol' Buddy

The ride down from Erik's to Groton, Massachusetts had taken longer than Tanner planned. It wouldn't have had he taken the turnpike, but to his way of thinking, motorcycles were meant for winding roads that meandered through the countryside and small towns. Not the crazy rush and crush of six lanes and tolls.

Groton was a nice town. He'd stayed there a time or two. Even dated a pretty little gal who had lived in the center of town in a great big Greek Revival. It was a bedroom town. Most of the residents worked within the 495 beltway of Boston. It was probably most famous for the private school bearing its name that claimed a diverse alumni, ranging from famous actors to an impressive number of Roosevelts, including Franklin D.

Jamie's insurance business was run out of his home. It was a basic saltbox structure, most likely built somewhere around the late 1700's. Both the business and the house had belonged to Jamie's grandfather, then his father, and finally his mother before passing to him. The front door opened up on a wide entry hall that divided into a narrower hall and stairway. The room to the immediate right was the office area. It had probably been a large dining room at one time. The room on the left, just before the stairs began, was a living room with a brass placard that stated "private." It was from this door that Jamie appeared.

"Wow, what a surprise!" Jamie grabbed his old friend in a bear hug. "The north wind blow you in?"

Jamie and Tanner could have been twins. Except Jamie's hair was darker and his middle was getting a bit of a spread. Not quite what you could call a paunch, but no six-pack either. Tanner returned the hug with a final slap across his friend's back. "You might say that. An ill wind is more like it."

Jamie backed away. A look of wariness. "What kind of ill wind, Mike? Is this something solid, or your Spidey sense clicking in?"

"A bit of both, I'm afraid." Mike glanced over at the office door. "Are you free for the rest of the day? Is there somewhere we can speak privately?"

"Sure, this way." Jamie gestured with his hand toward the door he'd just stepped out of, then followed Mike in. "The office closes at six. Patty, she's my assistant, sometimes stays to clean up on a few things, phone calls, emails. She will close up there and won't be a bother."

The room was spacious. A man cave with big overstuffed recliners and a sofa that had one of those fold-down tables in the center for your snacks and drinks. There was a fifty-inch flat screen hung on the wall. PlayStation 4 paraphernalia was strewn around. Most of the games were the paramilitary type.

"Beer? Something harder? I was just about to have a coffee, but I'll be glad to join you if you'd like something stiffer." Jamie gestured to the sofa, then stepped around Tanner to cross the length of the room. He stopped and paused at a door leading to the kitchen.

"Coffee is fine. Thanks."

"One cup of joe coming up."

Mike looked around the room. Other than the big screen, there wasn't anything else on the walls. Then he saw it. High up in the corner, almost blending with the crown molding, was a camera. He'd noticed the security at the entry. Security camera, motion sensor that set off a low beep when someone crossed the threshold. He'd put it down to security for Jamie's insurance business. But why the living room? He could almost bet if there was one in here... His Spidey sense was tingling.

Getting up, Tanner walked toward the kitchen. Jamie was pouring water into a coffee maker. He looked up and gave a nod.

"Sorry, man, I've got to make some fresh. The stuff from earlier would curl your toes. It won't take but five minutes. Can I get you something in the meantime?"

"Latrine? It was a long ride."

Jamie cocked his head to the left. "Go through that door and make your first right. It's under the stairs."

Jamie's cell phone had been on the counter next to the coffee maker. The kitchen was pretty much like any other, except it didn't have any woman's touch—shades instead of curtains, nothing on the walls, not even a clock. Clean and simple except for another camera nestled at the top of an overhead cabinet. As Tanner entered the hall, he spotted two more. *Why all the security?* Tanner wondered. Insurance business couldn't be that tricky, or was Jamie just a little paranoid? Had Jamie suspected something was up? A few strange events in the last couple weeks, perhaps? The thing was, the equipment, while sophisticated, didn't look new. Was this just a higher-tech solution to his own precautionary slip of paper wedged in the door?

Before leaving the bathroom, he checked his phone messages. There were four. Three from Alice and one from Devners. He could care less about Devners. That confrontation could wait until tomorrow. Alice was a different matter. Her messages were short. In all three, she was distressed. Her office rifled far worse than she'd thought possible, wondering where he was, and one mentioned a new case. She wished he was there and Devners was a pain to work with. Her third said she was meeting Rhyjl because the former had some new insight.

New insight? He still wasn't sure what to think about Rhyjl's ability. It wasn't like anything he'd ever seen, but it sure explained a few things. He dashed off a quick text message—*At Jamie's in Groton, MA. Came down to warn him. Hope he might have some information I can use. Call you at 8 from my hotel.*

He was thinking of Rhyjl and her abilities as he walked back into the kitchen. Jamie was texting on his cell. The coffee maker was burbling and gurgling. The dark rich liquid was almost up to the halfway mark. Rather than return to the living room, Tanner took a seat in a high-back oak chair.

Jamie finished his text. "Dani," he said, sticking the cell phone back into his shirt pocket.

"Ah." Tanner smiled, picturing the curly-haired boy—correction, man. Aeisha's boy. Once they had been close. Tanner had taken him camping and taught him survival skills. Dani was the only person he could talk about Aeisha with. Those days had slipped away. Tanner hadn't seen him for almost three years. His high school graduation. "How's he doing?"

Jamie brought two mugs over to the table. "Sure you want to sit here? The living room is much more comfy."

Tanner shrugged his right shoulder. "Here's fine."

"Suit yourself," Jamie said, returning to pour the coffee. "He's at MIT now. Doing well. Gone into electronics. Always did like that stuff. Thinks he's going to make millions making games. He just might, too." He took a seat across the table from Tanner, filled both waiting mugs, and set the pot down between them. Cupping his hand around his mug, he appeared to be absorbing the warmth as if they'd just come in from the cold. "Different world than we were in at his age. It's all about computers and games."

"So, the games in the other room?" Tanner asked.

"His. Well, to be honest, they were mine, too. Kinda like reliving the old days. And Dani is good. He beats me repeatedly. I taught him all I know and pointed out inconsistencies. Of course the biggest one is that in the game, if you die, you get revived."

Tanner heaved a heavy sigh. "Yeah, a lot different. That's why I'm here, Jamie. I think that world may have circled around to bite us." He took his own cup, lifted it to his lips, then paused. It was ridiculous. It was born out of that world he'd come to talk about, but he wouldn't drink until Jamie did.

"Really?" Jamie's lips quirked. His eyes twinkled. "Old habits die hard. Still seeing spooks, Mike?"

"Yeah, one shot at me last night. And Keys and the rest of our unit, well, they are somewhere in a government morgue right now."

Jamie lifted his coffee. Drank deep. Lowering the cup, his hands a death grip on the mug, he cleared his throat. "That's the kind of news a man should take with a whiskey, not coffee. Are you sure?"

"I'm sure." Tanner drank. The words were right. Even the look of deep concern. But Jamie had always had a habit of clenching his jaw, the muscles twitching just under his ears when something shook him. It was missing. "I was there when they were exhumed."

"And you say someone shot at you?" Jamie's brow furrowed over narrowing eyes. "Last night? Any ideas?"

"Yeah, I only know two people who can shoot like

that."

Jamie chuckled. "What? You only know two people who can shoot and miss?" He took another sip of his coffee.

"Ha! Ha! No, I only know two people who can shoot that distance and hit exactly what they were aiming at. 'Shot at me' was a misnomer. The guy shot my tire. It was a warning. He even left a note inferring I was an easy target."

"So you think you have an idea of who it was, you said."

"Well, it was either you or Wolf. You up in my neck of the woods last night?"

Jamie shook his head, his brow furrowed further. This time those little twitches jumped to action. "It wasn't me. I was at dinner with an old friend down the road. You can ask him if you want, but I don't think it's me you really suspect, is it?"

"I don't know what to think, Jamie. But I don't think you have the time to be playing games up in Maine. So that leaves me Wolf."

Jamie got up and began pacing. "What games, Mike? Have you been shot at more than once?"

Tanner took another swallow from his mug. It was damn good. Jamie had always been the cook. He may not have been chef material, but it was a whole lot better than what the rest of them could come up with. "Things, happenings. Someone has been in my apartment. They haven't taken or left anything, but they want me to know."

Jamie topped off his coffee. "Okay, I can see where you might associate that with Wolf. He was always good at wearing his victims down. Make them lose sleep so when you do make your move, they aren't as sharp." He returned the glass coffee pot to its stand. "But it's not an uncommon ploy. So if it's Wolf, why now?"

"I don't have the answers." Tanner studied the glossy black coffee in his cup, swirled it around and looked back at his host. "I will add that I think Shadow is involved."

Jamie's features pulled a serious frown. "Shadow?"

"Yes. I was working with someone trying to get answers. They were hacked. Seriously hacked."

Jamie's eyes narrowed. A little quirk pulled at the corner of his mouth. "Who were you working with?"

"You should know better than to ask. I'm not going to give up my sources to you or anyone. First rule, remember."

"Yeah, but we aren't in the business anymore, Mike, unless there's something you aren't telling me." Jamie turned his back and opened a cupboard. He pulled out a bottle of Jack Daniels. "I think I need something a little stronger than this coffee. You?" he said, holding it out toward Tanner.

Tanner shook his head. His senses were still zinging off the scale. Something was wrong. He couldn't afford to let himself become clouded. "Nope, but some food might be nice. I saw Bruno's Pizza is still around when I drove in. Do they still deliver?"

Jamie phoned in an order. They talked small talk. Good talk. The kind old friends do. Tanner asked about the girl from the Big House, as they'd called it.

"What? You looking for another big dose of rejection, Mike?"

"Yeah, she did kind of let me know what a cold hard fish I was, didn't she?" Tanner chuckled.

"I think her term was frozen cod, but I could be wrong. Well, she found herself a live one. Moved away about the same time Dani went off to MIT. I will miss insuring that Jag of hers, though."

"Insurance business slow?"

"Nope. Booming. All's well there."

Something in the way Jamie said it, or what he didn't say, clued Tanner in that something wasn't good. He was just about to ask when the doorbell rang.

The pizza was just as good as Tanner remembered. He dug into it like a starving man. Jamie, however, hung back, picking at the one piece he'd taken from the box. "Something wrong?"

"Why did you come down here, Mike?"

Tanner felt the creases between his brows form. "I already told you. I wanted to see if you might know something about..." He put his half-eaten slice down. Gnawed at his lip. "About Keys and the others. And to see if you were okay."

Jamie was on his third glass of whiskey. He cradled his chin in his hand. His index finger absently massaged his lips, his eyes on the pizza between them. "I'm dying, Mike." He didn't look up. "Cancer. Stage four. I've been a walking dead man for over a year now. Just didn't know it until about eight months ago."

Tanner felt his gut twist. Was this what his senses had been picking up? "Ah, shit!" His pizza had turned sour. "I'm so sorry, man. Where's a glass? I think I'll join you with that drink now." He shoved his chair back.

Jamie beat him to it and went to the cupboard, withdrawing another glass. "Yeah, so I'm not too worried about meeting your killer. At this point, he would be doing me a favor."

"How long?" Tanner said, taking the glass and pouring from the half-full bottle. He took a long pull. Felt the burn down to his gut.

Jamie held up his glass in salute and took another one himself. He shrugged. "Year, maybe less. Irony is that it would have taken me by now if I weren't such a great physical specimen."

Tanner didn't know much about cancer. It wasn't one of those things that had ever crossed his radar. Death for him had always been fast tracked. First his parents in the auto accident. Then the parade of deaths in the battlefield, and finally his job. "You don't look sick. You still got your hair." He downed the amber liquid in his glass and poured another.

"I didn't have any of those treatments," Jamie answered, looking amused. "They said there wasn't much chance of me beating it. So hey, why poison myself? Besides, I've still got a few loose strings to tie up before I go. A few confessions to get off my chest. Reminds me of that song we used to play as a band. 'Sundown' by Gordon Lightfoot. Do you remember the words?"

"Yeah." Tanner put his glass down. Maybe it was the lack of sleep. Maybe it was the stress and shock over the last few days, but the booze seemed to be hitting him a lot harder than he thought it should. He scrubbed a hand over his face.

"Remember the chorus? *'Sometimes, I think it's a sin when I feel like I'm winning and I'm losing again.'* That's how I've felt for a long time, ol' buddy. You know, Mike, you were always the hero. Helping everyone. Making it happen when others thought it was impossible. I always kind of stood in your shadow."

Tanner's Spidey senses were no longer screaming at him. They were muffled and distant, as if coming from some long dark tunnel. He looked from Jamie to the digital clock on the stove. It was almost eight. He should be going.

"Why did you come down here, Mike? Was it to be

the hero again? To save ol' Jamie? Warn him that the big bad Wolf might pay him a visit? Did you ever wonder all those times how Wolf was often ahead of us? Just as if he knew our next move? Did you, Mike?"

Tanner squeezed his eyes shut hard. Then opened them wide, willing them to remain open and focused. "Yeah," he answered, his mouth feeling like dry tissue paper.

"I worked with Wolf, Mike. I've been working with him for years. I don't know who your stalker is, Mike, but it's not Wolf. And Shadow? Well, let's just say he crossed the wrong people at the wrong time. We all get careless at some time. Don't we, Mike."

"Jamie, what have you done? Why?"

"Why?" Jamie tilted back in his chair, his hands folded comfortably across his belly. "My dad. I know I told you all that he was missing in action. That's because that's what my mom and I were told. It almost killed her. She started drinking." He held up his glass, downed the remains and slammed it down hard. "It took years, but eventually the booze did kill her. We had the funeral. I kept noticing this guy hanging on the periphery. First at the church. Then the cemetery.

My training kicked in. I was in mourning, but still, when she was laid to her rest, I followed him to a cab. On the way back to the reception, I placed a few calls. The cab had dropped him at a motel at the edge of town. As soon as he opened the door, I realized I'd been looking at a younger version of him sitting on my mother's nightstand for years.

"It's a long story, but we still have time. He invited me in. Shared how his unit had been under mortar and gunfire. You know what it's like. He took a hit. When he woke, he said it looked like a meat factory—body parts everywhere. He'd sustained a head wound. Actually lost part of his ear. He was scared. So scared he shit his pants. There were no other survivors that he could see. He heard some far-off crashing through the jungle. Knew it was the enemy coming back. He ran and kept running."

Tanner's hand scrubbed over his face again. He was so tired. He was having trouble following and Jamie seemed to be headed down a rabbit hole. "I'm bushed, Jamie. Get to the point. What has this to do with Wolf?"

"This was a man I'd looked up to my entire life. He was the reason I'd joined the military over my mother's tearful protests. He was scared, Mike. That fear that freezes your brain and sends ice coursing through your veins."

"Jamie, we've all felt that fear. We didn't run."

"We didn't run—I didn't run—because we always had each other. We always had the hero to get us through. We always had you, Mike."

"Me? I'm no hero, Jamie. I was just as scared as any of you. I just did what needed doing. One foot in front of the other."

"Well, if not a hero, you were the glue. You set the standard. You inspired us to be the best by your example. But it was a high bar, Mike.

"After I found my dad, we kept in touch. We were careful. You know what happens to deserters. He was old, Mike, and he was ill. We weren't careful enough." Sometime during their talk, Jamie had switched over to water. He paused, took a sip and got a faraway look in his eye.

Tanner's mouth was tasting like steel wool. He wanted some water, but the energy to make the effort was lacking. He also wasn't sure how his stomach would handle it. The pizza, coffee and whiskey were battling it out.

"To this day, I don't know how he found out. I made a slip somewhere. That's when the threats began. 'Do it our way or we take your old man out.'"

"He? You mean Wolf?"

"No!" Jamie shook his head. "Granger."

Now Tanner's stomach twisted. He'd never trusted their handler. The man was too calculating. Too self-serving. "When was this?"

"Two years before Paris. Yes, Paris. The big turning point for us all."

"Where's your dad now?"

"Oh, he's long gone. Like me, cancer. Like father, like son, I guess. But if you are wondering, and I'm sure you are, it's simple. First, I did it to protect him. Cancer is tough, but add prison to that... Well, I couldn't let that happen. I couldn't. He'd suffered enough.

"Then by the time he was gone, I was in too deep. I'd become a traitor—to myself, my country, my friends. It wasn't Aeisha's brother or his associates that took her out that night, Mike, it was me."

"You loved her, Jamie. It's easy to take on the responsibility of blame. I know. I did it for years. I don't know what you let slip, said, or did. But someone else pulled that trigger."

Jamie shut his eyes, shaking his head. "Same old Mike." He laughed. "Always believing the best in those you care about. Some say it's your only flaw. No, I'm to blame. Not like you. Your guilt is because we used her. Put her in danger because of Granger's orders. You wanted her smuggled out, but he wouldn't allow it. She was still so useful. It ate at you. Using the only woman you had allowed yourself to love. But you're wrong.

"Earlier in the day, Aeisha was in the market

square. I didn't see her. My bad. But you know how those women dressed in hijabs all look the same. She saw me handing over an envelope to Wolf. She was far too smart, Mike. Too observant. But then, that's what made her valuable as an asset. It's also why you loved her. Later, at the café, she confronted me. She knew. Not everything, obviously, but enough to put two and two together. I didn't deny or confirm her suspicions. I knew. I knew she was going to tell you. She would describe Wolf. The game would be up."

Tanner's jaw was gnashing on words. He wanted to scream. He wanted to punch Jamie's face so hard they'd need plastic surgery to make it look human again. "So you turned her over to Wolf. You bastard!"

"Close. I did tell Wolf. But that's not how it went down. Later when she showed up at Rick's Americana looking as if she had the devil on her heels, you chased after her. We called a quick break. Bass went charging after you. I headed for the roof, grabbing my rifle on the way."

Tanner lunged from the chair. "Son-of-a..." The floor undulated beneath him. He grasped for Jamie, the table, anything that would break the fall. He hit the floor. There was a loud pop as his cheek met the worn linoleum. He wanted to reach up to touch it. His body wasn't his anymore. His thoughts turned vaporous. He couldn't hold on to them except one—*poison.*

Jamie rolled him over. He even winced as he saw where the impact had cause the skin over Tanner's cheek to split open in a nasty gash. "I'm sorry, ol' buddy. I really am."

Chapter 21

Circumstantial Evidence

Alice hung up the phone. *Well, that went well.* She'd intentionally delayed returning Jim Ackerman's call until she'd set a few things right in the office. She was hoping it would give her a chance to work off some of her steam and gain a semblance of composure. It had probably been a mistake. When she did call, Ackerman didn't give her much opportunity to explain the morning's events. That little rat, Gene, had bent Jim's ear with one accusation after another about her ineptitude in handling everything. He'd turned all his inept actions and her words back on her. It was her fault the lab was in disarray. If she had been at work on time. If she had called. If she had asked for ID so they would know who was responsible. And then to expect Gene to clean up the mess and harass the cleaning service. Finally in her frustration, she'd taken it out on him by threatening termination.

She was a wire stretched tight. Her blood pressure was climbing. Her temples throbbed. It was as if she'd gone through a calisthenics class with all the bending, squatting and lifting she'd done this morning. Her office was gaining back some semblance of order. It would take time. Staring at the empty space on her desk for the umpteenth time, she wondered if or when she would get her computer back. She'd never given it much thought before. Never thought of herself as dependent. It was just convenient, like expecting clean water to come out of a tap at the turn of a faucet. She'd gathered all the scattered papers, reorganized and filed them. Her tiny vacuum had taken care of the powdery hot chocolate mound and sucked the smaller shards of shattered glass off surfaces and carpet. At least it was ready for the cleaning crew when they finished with the lab. Thank God for Judy. Not only had she gotten them there quickly, but rather than just the usual two cleaners, the service had sent three.

The shooting victim had been placed in the cooler on hold until the lab was ready. Now, unless she could get Dr. Allen to come in and sub, she might be working until midnight. Ackerman had made it quite clear he wanted to see her in his office. That meant a long drive to Augusta. She'd made one ultimatum by the end of the call. Gene would not be coming back except to clear out his things. It was him or her. Jim said they would discuss it.

~~

Bruce Allen was a pencil of a man. His skin was pale, his hair more so. Too many years in autopsy labs and missed meals. She wondered if that would be her fate. She explained to him about the scene of the shooting and her suspicions that it wasn't suicide. It would have been better if she could have downloaded the photos she'd taken with her camera. Since the government had deemed it necessary to confiscate her computer, however...

"I'm really sorry to call you in at the last minute, Bruce, but I'm in a bit of a bind and need to get the autopsy done before Detective Devners declares open and shut suicide."

Bruce Allen laughed. It was a deep rumbling and shook his thin frame. "Old Wrap-em-up-quick Devners? He still out there? I thought with all that fatty fast food and that caffeine addiction he'd be retired by now, if not in the grave."

"Wrap-em-up-quick? You mean he's always been that way? I thought it might have something to do with him getting close to retirement. What do they call it? Old Timers..."

"Short Timers," Allen chimed in with a wink and crooked smile. "Devners always had a lazy and impatient streak. I can't imagine what it must be like now. I'll get right on it. I might not be as fast as you or even as good. Old Timers, don't you know!" He laughed again. "But I can have the preliminaries done by the time you get back this afternoon."

She wanted to hug him. Bruce Allen was a good man, a good doctor, and an exemplary medical examiner. It was never easy to step into another person's shoes, especially someone like Bruce. It warmed her that he was pleased with her.

She received the call from Rhyjl as she was going to her car. It was cryptic at best. Rhyjl believed she had a description of the man who might be the killer. When Alice pressed, Rhyjl refused to give her any more. What she did say only painted a deeper mystery: "In light of recent events, Erik thinks it's best we keep our cell and email communications limited. Could we meet for lunch?"

There would be no time for lunch today. Alice explained she had to run to Augusta on business and wouldn't be back until later in the afternoon. They discussed options to get together. They chose to eat in. She'd pick up BBQ on the way back from her meeting and join them at their house. Hopefully she'd get there by six.

Getting in her car, she made two more calls. The first was to her dad, telling him that things just kept getting uglier. He offered again to come up. She told him she'd be spending the evening with friends. As a last thought she said, "Would you still be interested in having me as a partner?" She knew the answer, but it was nice to have him affirm it.

The second call was to Tanner. It went, just like the other two, to voice mail. She told him Rhyjl's message. They would be meeting at Erik's for dinner. Said she missed him and wondered where he was. Then, as she shut her phone off and started the Savana, she hoped wherever he was, he was safe.

~~

Jim Ackerman's office was cool grays, whites and blues. There was a huge seascape of a watery sun partially hidden by ominous clouds, and a valiant three-mast schooner riding a wave-tossed sea. Vertical window shades were pulled, blocking the view of the building next door. The desk was sleek, clean, efficient. The bookcase behind the desk was filled with journals, a few sailing trophies, and small tokens of the sea. It matched the man well.

Jim Ackerman was relatively young for a man in his position. She knew he hadn't seen fifty, yet there were slivers of gray in his otherwise ebony hair. He stood as she entered, indicated she should take a seat on the pristine white sofa. She did, knowing it for what it was—a power move. He'd either walk, or stand so he was above her. Or if he remained at the desk, he'd still be at least a head above and also at a cool distance. Instead, he chose to take the chair she would have gravitated to near his desk, turned it to face her, and sat. His eyes were cool, troubled like the waters in the painting. His mouth was grim.

"I don't like trouble, Alice. I don't like employees of my medical examiners charging into my office before I've even finished my morning coffee. I take huge exception to a state-run lab being trashed and state-owned equipment appropriated."

She reminded herself she wasn't a schoolgirl. This man held power, but so did she. That knowledge wasn't doing much to quell the queasiness of her stomach. She crossed her legs casually. Forced her hands to remain easy in her lap. "I don't blame you. Neither do I," she said, utilizing her best Harvard accent.

He changed tactics. The grimness softened, as if he found something quite amusing. "Insufferable little man, your tech is. Indiscreet and no sense of loyalty. Reminded me of a snake tied in knots. I'm amazed you've kept him on as long as you have. Are things as bad as he claimed?"

He expected her to make excuses. To defend herself. She would not. "Worse, I imagine. The snake, as you say, hadn't seen my office. He was too busy being abused by government employees, I understand, to handle the situation or to call for help. However, I've taken steps to put things in order and get the lab up and running. Bruce Allen is working there as we speak, on a case that came in this morning. I did inform Mr. Haverty that his job would be terminated if he could not get the cleaning service to have the lab cleaned by the time I got back from this morning's call. Not only did he fail to follow through, but he was not available to help me unload the body once I got back."

"I see." Ackerman tilted back in the chair. It gave a mild moan of protest. "Alice, I've been getting a lot of disturbing messages lately. You are exceptional at your job. One of the reasons you've had death threats in the past. Sometimes people don't like what we find. Of late, however, I've received reports that you and Detective Tanner were shot at yesterday. Saturday, I was informed by certain individuals that four bodies you had in your lab were to be claimed by the feds. Then I hear whisperings of unethical practices on your part."

Alice's feigned composure snapped. "Unethical practices?" Shaking her head, she rose. Now she was looking down at him. "What unethical practices? What am I being accused of? Who is doing the accusing? Haverty? He wouldn't know what was ethical if it turned around and bit him."

"You are correct about Haverty. He did make a few suggestions as to improprieties. It's not his accusations that are concerning. It's the DOJ that is conducting the investigation."

She opened her mouth to speak. Or scream. Instead, she swallowed the bile building in her throat. "Why is the Department of Justice investigating me?"

"I'm sorry," Jim said, rising and placing a solid hand on her shoulder. "I can't tell you anything while you are under investigation. In truth, they haven't told me much. That's why I invited you to my office. I don't believe what I'm hearing. I do have to take it seriously. So do you. So let's start at the beginning. Tell me everything that has gone on over this last week."

Chapter 22

Dinner Revelations

Rhyjl sat munching on stale chips she'd found in the cupboard. She was curled on the couch, her legs tucked under, her leather journal in her hand. She'd been working for an hour trying to get the sketch of the man correct. She was no artist. Had never claimed to be, but she'd learned to follow lines as they flowed. She'd drawn enough sketches of bones as an undergrad. It was the best way to really learn them, especially when it came to faunal remains. A beaver's femur was very different from that of a dog. But a dog and a cat? They were so very close. Not just the size. You could have big cats and small dogs. The distinction could be made in the tiniest, most subtle of ways, such as the swirl pattern on the distal end of the femur.

Erik had gone to town to grab something for lunch over an hour ago. She'd waited a solid forty-five minutes, then had gone in search of something, anything, to ease the gnawing on her backbone. The chips helped some, but now she was thirsty. Her mind snagged on that thought and pulled her back into her earlier vision.

Keys had been thirsty. It had been the coarse sandpaper feel in his throat that had finally aroused him. Then, of course, his thirst hadn't mattered, had it. He knew the minute he looked into those pitiless eyes that he was dead. Knew a fear he'd never experienced.

They were deep eyes. She wiped the greasy salt from her fingers on a piece of paper towel and began drawing again. The brows where thick and curved like a raptor's wings. His cheeks were finely sculpted beneath. The nose was pinched and long. The nostrils went back and up at a sharp angle. His forehead was high and wide. The jawline was like the nose—long and narrow, yet squared. She held the drawing up. His face was the shape of a rectangle being squeezed into an oddly-shaped triangle. It was easy to see why she was reminded of a bird of prey.

She was so immersed in her thoughts, she started when Jack sprang to his feet, running to the door and barking. It was his welcome bark, tail wagging. Erik was back. Only Jack would have been alerted to the Tesla's whispered approach.

Erik entered and kicked the door shut with his boot. Jack fell in beside him, tail wagging and nose glued to the brown paper bag with a green, red and white-striped Italian flag. On his other arm he hefted a white plastic bag, and a black one she recognized was from Larson's Ace Hardware.

"I thought you got lost," she said, tossing the tablet on the couch while getting up to join the procession to the kitchen.

He set the brown bag from Vinney's down on the counter and carried the other two over to the little dinette. "I ran a few errands while I was waiting for our order." He pulled four thin rectangular boxes about as big as his palm from the white sack. "I thought we could start using these between ourselves."

Rhyjl dug into the Vinney's sack and pulled out two white takeout boxes. They were barely warm. "The food is cold, Erik." She was further dismayed when she saw that one held her favorite dish. Placing her arms akimbo, she glared as he unpacked one of the little boxes and held up a cell phone. "We have cell phones. Why do we need those?"

"They're burner phones," he said, with the same silly proud look that Jack got when he retrieved a treasure.

"Oooookayyy, and again I ask, we need these why?"

"Let's have lunch. I'm starving." He slid the phone boxes back into the bag. "I'll tell you while we eat."

~

"This is serious, Rhyjl. I think using a burner phone is the best way to communicate at the moment. They can't trace us, and they won't be able to tap into our calls." Erik took the last bite of cannelloni on his plate, then rested the fork he'd been waving around like a lecture stick.

Rhyjl closed her eyes and rested her head in her hand. She was fast developing a headache, the kind that screamed tension. "I'm just saying that I think you are taking this a bit too far, is all. You were hacked, not attacked. The bodies are gone. As far as we are concerned there's nothing more to do. I'll finish the sketch. I'll give it to Mike. He will take it from here. I'm pretty sure he will know who this guy is."

"I don't think any of our lives will ever be the same." Erik grabbed his dish and hers. He walked to the sink, rinsed them and put them in the dishwasher. "I see it this way," he said, turning to look at her. "Life gives us doors, or tipping points if you'd prefer. Sometimes they're pleasant. Take our meeting, for example." He'd crossed the room while saying the last. Reaching down, he pulled her from her sitting position into a warm embrace. "A very pleasant door. And, it changed our lives. You," he touched the tip of her nose playfully, "are the very best door of my life."

She smiled up at him. "I know where this could lead." She wiggled her eyebrows three times. "We could continue this discussion of philosophy somewhere more cozy."

"Ah, we could, but I don't think we would get much discussing done."

"Kinda what I had in mind." Wriggling out of his grasp, she walked from the kitchen. "I don't know if I'm up to the world according to Erik."

"Low blow. But seriously," he said, trailing after her. "Our lives have changed. Take Tanner as the prime example. With the death of these four guys, he's lost what was like family to him. He'll be different. He already is. You weren't here when he came. He was more talkative. He shared things I never would have expected. I mean he was black ops! He was doing espionage like the movies, complete with guys named Shadow and Wolf. He thinks it's this Shadow guy that got to me."

"So he's your new hero?" She stood with one hip cocked, her hands lifted waist high, palm up.

"No!" He shook his head. "Well, maybe a little. It's given me new insight into him. I thought before he was kind of a puffed-up cop playing the tough guy. But he is the tough guy. I'd think that being a cop in a backwater area like this is pretty boring."

"If you call getting shot at 'boring.' But yes, I get what you're saying. Perhaps he was tired of being Mr. Macho. Maybe he wanted quiet. I get the feeling that after that woman died..."

"Do you think he loved her?" He remembered his feelings when he thought he had lost Rhyjl. "That would mean another door. A catalyst. He went from one life to something different."

Rhyjl saw the scene unfold in her mind. The rainy

night. The dark, narrow street. The man she now knew was Tanner, kneeling on the cobbles. The pale hand of the dying woman reaching to caress his face.

"If he didn't, he still cared deeply for her." Rhyjl's playful mood took flight, leaving a dark brooding behind. She could clearly see where Erik was coming from. Her life might not be changed so much by this case. She felt no huge revelations, other than her abilities seemed to be morphing in subtle ways. Not like her life had changed last fall with the introduction of Erik, her first-time involvement in a murder case and her friendship with Alice. Now her life was at another threshold. Her acceptance or refusal of the job in the Southwest.

"What about Alice?" He walked over to the bank of windows. Jack padded over and sat beside him, wondering what his person saw, or if it meant game time.

"What about her?" Rhyjl joined them.

"Does he love her?"

～

At first Alice wondered if she'd gotten the time wrong. It was almost six, and yet she saw no lights on. Erik's blue Tesla was parked in front of the garage. She didn't see Rhyjl's Rubicon. Then she heard the barking coming from the back of the house. She left two big bags of Big Bob's BBQ in the front of her dark plum Nissan Juke and walked around the end of the house. Jack was bounding up the cliff trail. She watched as he raced ahead, lowered his head to his front feet in a good yoga imitation of a down dog, then bounced sideways with a loud 'wroof!' Behind him Rhyjl and Eric appeared, holding hands and laughing.

It did her heart good to see this warm scene. God

knew she needed it. Her meeting with Jim Ackerman had been less than satisfactory. Jim agreed to Gene's termination. He agreed, so far as he knew, that she'd done nothing illegal or immoral. She'd been called in on the case. She had transported and studied the remains. She'd gone through the usual procedures of identification. Rhyjl had been called in, but not until after the university had vouched for her expertise and he, himself, had given the go-ahead. It made no sense, but that's where it was. Jim had no choice but to place her on administrative leave, pending the results of the investigation. That was a knife blow. She understood, but felt as if it was almost like admitting she was guilty in some way.

After the meeting, she'd swung by the lab. Judy fussed like an old broody hen. Dr. Allen had been more stoic. He'd already received Jim's call asking if he could fill in. He'd also informed her that her hunch was correct. "Not suicide," he said. And that if the truth be told, he admitted, he might not have seen it if she hadn't clued him in. It made her feel smug. One point for her. After gathering two boxes of personal things from her office, she'd looked around, her eyes stinging. She didn't cry. She'd be back. If not, well, there was no shortage of opportunities.

Judy drove her home. The Body Wagon would remain with Bruce. The two women kept the banter light: weather, good reads, and the deplorable movies that seemed to be coming out these days. That last being one of Judy's favorite rants. Neither wanted to stir the emotional pot they were both stewing. Once home, Judy helped carry the boxes in the house. They hugged. Judy promised to keep things in order, then left.

All Alice had wanted was a hot soak and a good cry. It would have been better if Tanner were there, or at least if he would call back. It was not to be on all three. So she had backed her sporty Plum out of the garage and headed for Bob's BBQ.

"Hey there!" she shouted, waving her arm. Jack's head popped up. He shot toward her like a speeding freight train. She braced for impact. He stopped just short, tongue lolling in expectation. Ruffling his furry head, she spoke in baby talk. "Waza good boy him iz." Then she greeted his owners with hugs.

"No Tanner?" asked Rhyjl.

"Nope, and I have to admit, I'm a bit puzzled. I haven't been able to reach him all day. He's not returning his calls. Have you seen or heard from him?"

"He was here this morning," Erik offered. "I had a problem and he came over on his bike to help me out."

"His bike?" He'd talked her into going for a ride with him last summer. She had been terrified the whole time. 'Death traps,' her dad had always called them. She was in complete agreement.

"Yeah, a sweet all-black number with shiny chrome."

"Mike is Erik's new superhero," Rhyjl said, in response to Alice's puzzled expression.

"Because of the bike?"

"It's a long story. Let's go in." Rhyjl hooked her arm in Alice's and they began walking toward the back sliders of the living room.

Alice took about three steps, then stopped. "The BBQ! It's in my car."

Erik offered to get it and lock her car while he was at it. Alice tossed him the keys. The two women mounted the stairs. "Before we go in..." She paused, glancing back at Erik. "Erik got hacked this morning. He's been a little bizarre and paranoid all day. Just letting you know."

"He was hacked?" Alice grabbed Rhyjl's arm just below the elbow. "How?"

"That's what has him flipped out. He doesn't know. Whomever it was, was a professional. They warned him off of this case."

"They threatened him?"

"Well, that's a little strange, too. It's like they warned him, but as a friend might, and then said they had cleaned up his tracks, meaning the codes he used to get us that info."

Now Alice did feel like crying. It was just too much. "I don't know..." She screwed up her face and bit at her upper lip. "I just don't know how this day could get any worse."

After Erik wrestled the four sacks containing their dinner to the kitchen, they shared their battle stories of the day as they unpacked containers of beans, ribs, and potato salad. Alice had brought enough to feed a small army, but then she always did. All three agreed that Alice's day was by far the worst.

Around six-thirty, Alice's phone alerted her that she had a text message. It was like a part of her had been holding her breath all day. Tanner was at Jamie's in Massachusetts. He'd call at eight when he got back to his hotel.

"I wish he'd waited until I could show him this." Rhyjl retrieved her journal with the sketch from the sofa and showed it to Alice. "He would have had something more to go on."

"For someone who can't draw," Alice said, studying the drawing, "this is pretty good. If it's accurate, I could pick this guy out in a lineup."

Erik came and looked over Alice's shoulder. He hadn't had a chance to see what Rhyjl had been working on all afternoon. "That is good. The guy's a shoo-in for the next Dracula movie."

"Not quite my thoughts, but he looks like the type that would step on the Tooth Fairy and spit in Santa's face." Alice offered the journal back to Rhyjl. "I can see why you had your episode. I might have had one if I'd experienced this guy in person."

Rhyjl looked at the face staring out at her from the page. It was good. Good enough to send icy fingers playing along her back. She slammed the journal shut and put it aside on the end table near the sofa.

The ribs were juicy and tender. The potato salad was just right. Unlike their other meals where the three of them would have almost talked over each other, there was very little chatter. What little existed was between Rhyjl and Erik. Erik brought up the burner phones and his theory of why he felt the necessity for them. Rhyjl rolled her eyes and reminded him they weren't characters in some Baldacci novel. Alice hardly touched the ribs and spent most of the time pushing the beans and salad around the plate.

When Erik's first helping was gone, he shared his surprise at seeing Alice's car instead of the Savana. "Nice rig, but I never pictured you for a purple type of person," he said, not catching Rhyjl's warning shake of her head in time to avoid the mask of despair on Alice's face.

"Plum, not purple," Alice corrected, her voice barely over a whisper.

Sensing his faux pas like a sharp jab in the side, Erik wandered back into the kitchen. Rhyjl was pretty sure the potato salad was calling to him, and hoped he might return with a bottle of wine. It probably wouldn't be the quality Alice would have served, but at this moment, she didn't think Alice would care.

"Look, I don't know who you are! If you want to help, then step up and give me something more than that!" Erik demanded from the other room. "How do you know who is doing this? If you're so sure, then you call the police."

There was a stretch of silence. Both Rhyjl and Alice gravitated within feet of where Erik stood braced, looking as if he were taking on the Devil.

"So how am I supposed to know if what you are saying is the truth, and not some kind of scam?"

Rhyjl pantomimed that Erik should place the call on speaker. He did.

"... and death. But if you don't care, then fine. Take a chance. He'll be dead by tomorrow if he isn't already." The call went dead.

"My hacker," said Erik. The women's faces were chalky, especially Alice.

"Is he talking about Mike?" Alice's tone of voice pleaded for denial.

"What else did he say?" Rhyjl asked, placing her arm firmly around Alice's shoulder.

"He says Mike is in trouble. He wants us to call the police."

"If he knows that, why doesn't he do it himself? This is really odd, Erik."

"That's what I said, Rhyjl. He told me he didn't dare get involved any further than he already has. Says he's exposed himself too much already."

"Erik, I thought I heard you say something about knowing who it is. Does the guy know? Did he say anything else?" Rhyjl asked.

"Something about a guy named Granger."

"Granger! You sure it was Granger?" Alice's balance wavered.

"Why?" Rhyjl reached out a steadying hand. "Does that name mean something to you?"

"Mike was talking about a man named Granger last night. He didn't like him much and I kind of got the strong impression the feeling might have been mutual."

"So who is this guy?" Erik asked.

"Mike's old handler."

Alice pulled out her cell phone. "It's almost a quarter of eight. Mike texted he would call at eight. He's at his friend's place in Mass., but I don't know the number."

"Call," Rhyjl coaxed, squeezing her shoulder tighter.

Tanner's face appeared on the screen. Alice hit the green phone symbol next to it. The call jumped to voice mail. She tried again. The same. In her heart she hoped that meant he was trying to reach her. The choking grasp around her heart told her the opposite.

"Call his friend." Rhyjl tried to cut through the shock Alice was slipping into. Alice's hand was shaking. Her finger hovered over the glossy face of her phone, but appeared paralyzed. Rhyjl clamped down on her desire to steal it from her friend and do it herself.

"I don't know his number!"

"What do you know? The guy's name? His address?" Erik was already at his keyboard. "Alice! Stay with us. What's the guy's name?"

"Jamie. I don't know his last name." Alice was gnawing her upper lip, her brow furrowed, trying to remember anything Mike might have said. "He lives in Groton, Massachusetts and has an insurance agency."

"Okay." Erik's fingers flew across the black keyboard. "Come on, come on. Got it! There's only two in the town. One has a James Lyster as agent owner. James could be Jamie."

Erik read off the number listed. Alice dialed. It went to voice mail.

"I've found a cell phone listing. Try this."

This time the call went through. "Hello? My name is Dr. Merks. I'm looking for Mike Tanner?" Alice strained to pull her professional voice from the depths of her despair.

Rhyjl's finger slipped to the phone's screen and pushed speaker.

"I'm sorry, you've just missed him. Is there something wrong, Doctor?"

Rhyjl and Erik shook their heads in unison. Alice replied that there was no emergency. "He has some information I need..." She fumbled, seeing the warning look Erik was shooting her. "On a suicide we are working on."

"You MEs work late hours. Well, maybe that's why he insisted on heading home tonight. I'd say he left about forty minutes or so ago. I thought it was foolish, this time of night on a bike. He won't be back home until after midnight, I'm sure. Sorry I can't be more help."

Erik was frantically slashing his fingers across his throat. Alice thanked the man and hung up. "What's that all about?" she asked.

"How did he know you were a Medical Examiner? You said doctor."

"I don't know, Erik. Maybe because Mike told him? Or, I did say suicide. That could have clued him in."

"Or, he knows because..."

"Drop it, Arneson!" Rhyjl gave him the stink eye. "You're scaring us with this ridiculous and infectious paranoia of yours."

"Look, we got a phone call from a hacker who

claims that Tanner is in big trouble. Tanner's last known location was this guy's house. I'm not taking a chance on anything. It would be foolish to do so. I think we need to call the State Police in Augusta. Tell them we think Tanner is in trouble and what his last known whereabouts were. The guy has already been shot at. They'll take it seriously."

"It's almost eight. Can't we wait until then? He said he'd call," Alice pleaded. "He'll keep his word even if he did decide to drive back rather than stop at a motel. We will feel pretty foolish if we raise an alarm before then. What's five minutes more?" But she knew what difference five minutes could make. Still, she held out hope this was all some mistake. She had to. Mike was fine. She'd see him tonight. Then she'd give him an earful about the dangers of riding so late at night on a motorcycle. After, of course, she held him with all her might.

They argued back and forth until the big grandfather clock struck the hour with eight sonorous bongs. The next few minutes stretched on with no sound but an occasional whimper from Jack and the brush on the tile from his paws as he dreamed of chasing something.

"That's it." Erik's tone was firm. He dialed 911. "This is an emergency. State Police, please."

Chapter 23

Old Grudges

He was in a sea of red. His eyes burning. His head felt as if he had battled with a porcupine. It was all good. It meant he was alive. Where there was life, there was hope.

He needed to get his bearings. Focus away from the pain. Not trivial. The pain was huge. Popsicle-cold muscles were cramped and complaining from being in an unnatural position for too long. Zip ties bound his hands and ankles. Not close together like handcuffs, but each hand and ankle were securely anchored to separate legs and arms of the chair. At least it was wood, he thought. Metal would have been damn cold against bare skin. The absurdity of that thought under these conditions was almost enough to make him smile. He wasn't ready to let them know his condition, yet. Whomever had tied them—and he had no doubt Jamie had an accomplice—had made sure he wouldn't be getting loose. Just the slightest movement of his fingers, which were partly numb, caused sharp needle pricks where the plastic scored flesh. His waist and hips were also secured with rope. No chances taken here, he thought.

He kept his eyes closed. He knew as soon as he opened them the bright light would slash his visual senses to shreds. It was a trick that served to disorient and isolate. He needed to think. Act. Not react.

He called on his other senses. He was naked. Well, mostly. That was an old trick too. People were more vulnerable uncovered. A lot easier to torture, as well. His feet were resting on damp earth, but something else. Sawdust? There was a stale odor of urine. A stronger, more acrid smell of diesel. A more general all-pervasive musty scent. The miasma choking his brain was lifting. Jamie had a barn. One of those old New England-style barns that sat on a bit of a rise, allowing an under-cellar. Jamie had given him the tour long ago. The walls had been created by placing stone so well-fitted it didn't require mortar. The downside was that with all the freeze and melt over the years, many of the old barn foundations of this type had collapsed.

"I think he is coming around." Jamie's voice sounded so far away.

"Good, then the fun can begin."

Mike Tanner knew that voice. He hadn't heard it in a long, long time. But not long enough for his liking.

"Why can't we just do it and get it over with?" Jamie's tone would have been wheedling, if not for the nervous edge.

"I'm surprised, Jamie," Granger said. "You've waited so long for this, and now you want it over and done so quickly?"

"This wasn't how we had it planned. He was supposed to die in a failed attempt at saving that lady doctor friend of his. The hero was supposed to die a failure. That bitch knows he was here. She called. If he doesn't return, they will come here. I want him dead. Done. No escape! And a hell of a long way from here."

"James, calm yourself. We don't have a problem. It doesn't matter if she does get suspicious. He's only been missing for a few hours. No law enforcement agency takes a missing person report seriously for at least twenty-four hours. You know that. So we have plenty of time to have a little fun with him. I know it's not the revenge you wanted, but you should know well enough by now that there are times we need to improvise. Mike moved up the timetable."

"We HAD twenty-four hours. The clock is ticking. I say we kill him now and get his body as far away from my place as possible. I'm telling you, that woman has connections. Tanner is a cop now. That can be a game changer."

"Relax. My source tells me that by coming down here, Mike went a little bit rogue. Was always one of his faults, and I should know, having had to deal with it for too many years while he was under me, how damn irritating that can be."

"Your source? You're telling me someone else knew he was coming down here?" Jamie's whining had been knocked up a notch.

"No! You're more of a fool than I'd believed if you think I would pull anyone else in on this. I made contact with the officer who is investigating the shooting. I made the call shortly after you told me what Mike had told you. I said my agency was interested in Tanner and there was a rumor that he was operating with some foreign operatives. It was possible that one of them might have been involved. The man I spoke with said he had plenty of questions to ask Tanner. He thought it was all a bit fishy. Then he admitted that Tanner had not shown up for the interview this morning. They didn't know his whereabouts after the officer sent to escort him dropped him at his apartment. The officer said Tanner received a phone call from someone who sounded like they were upset. Tanner told the officer to drop him at his apartment instead of taking him to the office. So you see, unknowingly, Tanner played right into our hands. Another plus in our favor is that Tanner rode his motorcycle. Motorcycles are notorious when it comes to accidents, and I know just the place Tanner will meet his fate.

"So here it is in a nutshell. Epitaph to Mike Tanner. He talked with you. Told you some of his suspicions. Remember, the more truth in your story, the better. Tell them he thought this might go back to some old Russian operatives he had tangles with in the past. You couldn't help him. You know nothing. The two of you had drinks. He became more agitated—again all true. He'd already told you he was going to stay at a local hotel. You weren't worried, since it is only a few blocks away."

"Except you forget that I already told her that he had headed home and that I thought it foolish."

"Another plus in our favor. Stage has already been set. It's a long way back to Maine. So stick to that story."

"Stop treating me like an amateur at this, Granger!"

"If I am, it is because sometimes when things get personal, you don't take the time to think things through. Like Aeisha. You could have told her you were handing off information to another operative because you were concerned there might be a leak. I, of course, would have backed that. But you went off like a loose cannon and killed her. The woman you loved."

Tanner didn't need to see Jamie to know the reaction. It was pretty much the one he might have had. The fact that their old handler wasn't lying in the sawdust with his neck twisted and awkward, his eyes glazed, was a testament to...what? Fear? What could Granger possibly do to him? Even if there was something, Granger's death...

Tanner's temples were hurting. Soon he wouldn't be able to control his teeth chattering like a pair of Spanish dancer's castanets. Granger was wrong about Jamie, though. He'd hadn't been in the field all those times when Jamie's cool and collected head had saved their skins. It was jealousy that pulled the trigger that dropped Aeisha.

"Anyway," Granger continued, "Tanner, here, is going to leave on his cycle. He's been drinking, stressed, and appeared agitated. It's dark. He must have decided to head home to be on the road at that hour. He hits a pothole. We all know how bad they are this time of year. He goes ass over teakettle off the road. His body and bike ignite when they hit the rocks below. He won't die the failed hero but... Shouldn't the drugs be wearing off by now?"

"If I know Mike, he's probably been listening for a while and planning his strategy."

"Huh. You think so?"

Tanner felt as if Granger's scrutiny was like fire ants crawling over his skin. Pain shot through his shin and up his leg as Granger's shoe delivered a swift blow.

"Oh look, I think he is waking up. Good evening, Mike."

Mike groaned and shook his head as if just coming around. Jamie was right. He'd needed them to believe he was still out while he surreptitiously tested the binding on his wrists and ankles. Listened to their plans. His assessment? He wasn't going anywhere until they moved him to meet the arranged death Granger had just spelled out. Until then, he had something they needed, or he'd already be cinders along with his bike. He didn't plan on compliance. "Granger, you son-of-a-bitch. What hole did you crawl out of?"

"Now, now, Mike," his old handler said. "There's no need for vulgarity."

Granger caught Tanner's cheeks in a pinching vise grip, forcing his lips into a fish face. "I want to know how you found the team's remains. I want to know why you think Wolf and Shadow are hunting you. It wasn't your time yet. You know, everything in its season." Granger gave a hard shove, snapping Mike's head sharply back. "I'm supposed to be at an important event with a special lady tonight, that could move me up in the food chain in Washington. Not here with you." His hand connected with Tanner's left cheek.

Tanner felt blood mixing with the saliva in his mouth. He spat it as far as he could. It missed Granger, or he would have heard a curse. His defiance earned him a backhand on the other cheek, mixing with the fiery pain already there. "You are so damn smart, figure it out. I gave..." He coughed. Blood was dripping from the corners of his mouth. He guessed he probably looked like one of those horrid characters on the book cover of a zombie story. "I gave Jamie enough details." And he had, because he hadn't believed Jamie was mixed up in this in any way, except as another possible victim. Or had he? He'd known something was wrong. His Spidey senses had been screaming. He'd watched the food, the drink. He'd known. Damn! Damn! Damn!

A hard kick landed on his shin a second time. Bone snapped against the hard surface of the chair leg. A cry escaped his lips before he could stop it. *I'm getting soft,* he thought.

"Now let's try this again. You have a lot more bones and teeth. Someone has been snooping into my personal files, checking dates and times I was working with you, Jamie and the band. Someone knew where Jamie and I buried the bodies and fed you information. Someone has been warning you. Someone knows just too damn much! I need to know who."

His eyes were still swimming behind blood-red lids. Pain seared his brain, slowing his thoughts. If he was going to survive, he had to think. Alice had called. She'd get help. He just needed to stall.

"I can't tell you what I don't know. That's why I'm here. I thought Jamie... oooooph!"

The blow struck him in his midsection.

"Try again. How did you find your buddies?"

"A call. Burner. No ID." He'd already given that information to Jamie. It wasn't worth another blow.

"Why did you think Wolf was after you? Did you see him?"

The air was getting colder, yet sweat was forming on his brow and upper lip. It made the cold seem that much colder. "Someone shot at me."

"Wolf doesn't miss."

"He meant to. Left me a mocking note."

There was blessed silence for a moment. Or, was that ominous? He tried to steer clear of the pain. To slip through it as if it were fog. Except the fog was red and filled with icy splinters. Instinct screamed at him to open his eyes, to use that sense to get his bearings. His training knew different.

"So you have no idea who called or shot at you?"

"No." Blood mixed with the word, making it sound like he was speaking underwater. He spat again, more with the need to clear the blood before he choked than as an insult. Of course it wouldn't have hurt his feelings if Granger had been hit. But again, he knew he had missed. There was no expletive.

Silence. Then footfalls. First the lighter tread of Jamie in his soft-soled loafers. Moments later, the tread of a hard sole, which he surmised was Granger. Without his sight, he could only assume there were just the two men. But there could have been a third. He'd used that tactic before. Take the sense of sight, then have one person remain quietly like a fly on the wall to observe. Let the interrogatee think he was alone. Let him drop his guard.

So many things could be ascertained during those moments.

Chapter 24

A Little Help

Erik listened to what the captain had to say. This was the fourth person he'd been transferred to. It was getting old, and Erik's temper was reaching critical mass. "Okay, I hear what you've been saying, but let me repeat myself. Tanner was shot at last night. He was trying to follow up some possible leads today. Now he is missing. He hasn't returned any calls. His phone goes straight to voice mail. He didn't phone Dr. Merks at eight when he said he would. When we placed a call to the individual in Massachusetts where Tanner was last known to be, the man acted strange, like he wasn't quite sure what his story should be. What would it hurt to call someone down there to run a quick check?"

Erik's finger hit the screen with such force, Rhyjl was amazed it didn't shatter. "No luck?"

"No! You'd think it would take an act of Congress, and all that crap about 'you can't just invade a private citizen's home without due process' blah da blah da blah. I think we should jump in the car and head down..."

A snatch of "Clair de Lune" broke into Erik's tirade. Alice scooped up her phone as if her life depended on it. "Mike! Oh, Dad, yes, yes, things aren't going so good. Mike has disappeared and the ..." Sobs overtook her. Her speech was almost impossible to decipher. If Rhyjl couldn't understand half of what she was saying on this end, it was doubtful that a distressed father on the other end would get much at all.

Rhyjl grabbed the phone. "Dr. Merks? Yes, my

name is Rhyjl. Oh, Alice has mentioned me. Yes, I'm afraid she's overly distraught. We all are, actually. Mike Tanner has gone missing. He was shot at last night. Yes, we are pretty sure it was meant for him. Today, he went down to Groton, Mass to get some information from an old friend. Yes, that's the last we have seen or heard. Uh, huh. Uh, huh. Yes, we have the address. But we don't think the guy is on the up and up. There's another thing. Mike and his friend were both in black ops at one time. We think this has something to do with it. No, the police won't have anything to do with it at this stage. Oh, really? Well, I also think I've got a sketch of a man, possibly named Granger, who we think might be behind all this, but we don't know anything else about him. We were going to turn it over to Mike. Yes, we can send it to you."

Alice's sobbing had turned into sniffles and hiccups. She reached for her phone and Rhyjl handed it back. Erik was already gathering their coats from around the room, checking to make sure Jack had water before being kenneled. Rhyjl wondered if they wouldn't be better off just taking Jack along. They didn't know how long they would be. She'd tell Erik that as soon as she finished listening to Alice's side of the conversation.

"Yes, Dad, I'm sorry. It's just been such a stressful day. You did? When? ...hiccup... Why? If I wasn't so thankful, I might be a little upset with you for invading my ...hiccup... privacy. No, he wasn't driving a car. He was on his motorcycle. Yes, I'll give them your email and we will send the sketch out right away. I love you, too, Dad."

Erik's answer to everything. He returned from the kitchen with a large glass of water and exchanged it for Alice's phone. "Drink," he ordered. "The whole thing without taking a breath. It will help."

Alice did as instructed. When she finished, she

followed it with a gulp of air. "Thanks. So, my dad has hired a private investigator. An old friend of his. I guess the guy used to work intelligence for the army. He's had the fellow checking on Mike since this morning."

"Really?" Erik said, taking the glass back. "So he wants us to send him the sketch?"

"Yes, really! And he wants Rhyjl's drawing right away. He also wants Mike's last known location and Jamie's name and address."

Rhyjl won. Jack was loaded in the back of the Tesla. Erik had sent the information out to DrGoose, a name he'd raised a skeptical eyebrow at and which Alice told him she would explain later. Erik checked the doors a final time and they were soon on their way.

Chapter 25

Unexpected

Tanner heard the muffled voices outside. There was some banging and clattering, and then a curse from Jamie. "Just get the damn key and I'll ride it up into the back of the pickup."

"Shut up, you fool. Do you want to announce it to the entire neighborhood?"

Granger's words were barely audible and he was correct. Jamie was being a fool. If anyone ever did come sniffing around to ask questions, at least one of the neighbors would remember hearing the motorcycle start up, maybe even catch a snatch of Jamie's comment. They probably wouldn't remember the exact time. Most people didn't pay that close attention. They would associate it with something they were doing, however, like watching a certain show on TV or a shower or even that they'd just gotten home. If asked when, they would be able to give a roundabout guess. Not that it would do him a lick of good. He'd be crispy at the bottom of a hill. But hopefully Jamie and Granger wouldn't escape.

Minutes later, the rumble of his motorcycle growled into the quiet, along with a clunk of the board ramp biting into the truck's bed. Then nothing.

His head was becoming clearer with each passing moment, but his time was running out. Testing his bonds had failed again, with the exception of making his wrists slick with his own blood. His shoulders burned, and his right tibia was most likely broken, since the pain he'd felt earlier had become almost numb. Or maybe that was the shock or mild hypothermia. He was sweating, even though the temperature was reaching refrigerator settings. Alice would know which it was. A vision of her swam before the red curtain of his eyelids. Her smile, the way her nose sometimes crinkled when that smile was about to turn into a laugh. The way her body fit with his so well. He didn't want to lose that. Not when he had finally found that precious something only she could give him. Anger shot through him like a heavy punch. The bonds cut deeper into his flesh. He felt something give in his leg.

The door creaked on hinges. "Now, Mike, it's not going to do you any good. Just accept that..."

Granger's speech was interrupted by a loud "ummmmph" and the sound of the door slamming against stone. The blinding light crashed to the floor. The red curtains fell into blackness.

"Your friend's down, Granger, and don't count on the fact that the dark will stay my 45."

"I don't know who you are, but you know who I am. This is government business. You have no jurisdiction interfering in it."

"That might work on some johnny cop, but not me, Granger. This isn't government, it's personal."

Tanner felt the slight movement to his right. Granger, like the snake he was, was attempting to slither quietly away, either to escape or use him as a shield from the stranger. He opened his senses wide and waited. He felt the air shift, the heat change almost imperceptibly, but still change. He also knew his ally was doing the same. Would he really take a shot in the dark? Risky business, especially when there was a good chance of hitting the wrong person.

For a breath length, the chair only gave a pathetic wobble. Then seconds exploded into grappling sounds, a muzzle flash, and stars. The last thing he would remember as the chair crashed into Granger was his head hitting those perfect stones and the crack reverberating through his mind.

Chapter 26

Changes

The room could easily accommodate twenty people. The colors were a soft blue and mauve. Three huge windows looked down from the fourth floor onto the awakening Boston skyline. For a surgical waiting room, the furniture was unusually comfortable. Considering they had been waiting for almost six hours, that was a blessing.

Rhyjl looked around the small huddled group of her closest friends. Alice sat wringing a handkerchief that Rhyjl was sure wouldn't be much more than shreds at the end of their vigil. Her mother, a gentle woman who looked like she'd just stepped out of a salon rather than her bed at two a.m., sat next to her with one arm around her shoulder, the other wrapped around her arms. Both their heads were bent, making soft muffled sounds only meant for their ears. It made Rhyjl yearn for her mother as she hadn't for years. Not even when she'd been hurt. But it was seeing that bond, that closeness. She sighed and looked at Erik. He stood resolute. His hands were semi-clasped behind his back, the marble-sized Turritella agate he always carried slipping absently between his fingers. His gaze lost on the city. Only she knew it wasn't. Perhaps he, too, was thinking of his mother. This was his hometown, after all. Out there somewhere was the mansion his grandparents had built. The home he'd grown up in, and the home where his father still resided. A home that someday would be Erik's. Or maybe it wouldn't. Only time would tell.

The police had come and taken their statements hours ago. The man who stood in the corner was the only one who had been able to give them real facts. Rhyjl had studied him these last several hours. There wasn't much more to do. There was no one else in the room. Surgeries weren't that common at this hour of the night, even in a city like Boston, where a segment of the city's more seedy side never seemed to sleep. Erik had once shared with her that the mansion he'd grown up in not only had high-tech security, but armed guards. "Boston," he'd say, "was no worse nor better than any other large city, but it only took one crazy who decided that an Arneson would make a good target for ransom, to become a problem."

They all owed Jason Rashner a large debt of gratitude. And Alice's dad, for hiring the private investigator. His quick actions, both at the scene and afterwards, had saved Tanner's life. He'd done it all without taking a life. Jamie and Granger were both in custody. Jamie was being held at the police station back in Groton. Granger had been transported to the hospital along with Tanner. His gunshot wound was superficial, but he'd taken quite a blow to the head when, according to Rashner, Tanner had sent them both careening into a rock wall.

A tall man, six foot three if he were an inch, walked into the room. His hair was as snowy white as the long coat he wore. His face was narrow, the nose slender with almost a little button on the end. His smile was soft and immediately put everyone at ease. He was the kind of guy she was sure could even take the blow out of a tough diagnosis. The coat made him look stockier than he was. From his hands, wrists and pants, she knew he was slight of frame. It was easy to see why many of his child patients had started calling him Dr. Goose. Well, that and the fact that Alice said he was an awesome storyteller.

Alice jumped up, shedding her mother like a sweater in an overheated room. She met her father halfway

across the room. Rhyjl expected a hug. Instead, Dr.
Charles Merks cupped his daughter's face in between
those surgeon's hands and nodded. He then looked up to
address the rest of them.

"Mike Tanner has come out of surgery well. They
are just finishing up the last sutures and Dr. Abrams will
come out and speak with you more. What I will say is that
we are very fortunate to have had Dr. Abrams on hand at
such short notice."

Rhyjl knew what he was neglecting to say was that
without his influence and pull, they wouldn't have been so
fortunate to get Abrams on board.

"Most of Mike's wounds were not life-threatening.
He may have a few new scars as conversation points, but
as a whole, he made it out pretty unscathed. With the
exception of his broken tibia. We see this type of injury
more often in breaks of the femur, where the femoral artery
becomes severed. In a case like Mike's, where due to an
injury and break of the tibia, a popliteal artery trauma
occurs or in layman's terms, a break in the artery behind
the knee, are very rare. We see them more in cases of a
gunshot wound. Due to the remarkable advances we have
made in the last forty years in vascular surgery and the skill
of surgeons like Abrams, amputation is not as common as
it was back when I was a surgeon in Vietnam. At that time,
thirty-seven percent of these cases did require amputation.
His injury will take time to heal and physical therapy will
be necessary, but he should gain complete use of his leg
and might forgo the limp."

A collective sigh of relief filled the air, to be
replaced by happy chatter and mutual hugs. Alice looked
at her father as if he were radiance itself, wearing a halo.
Charles Merks hugged his daughter, then his wife, then
crossed the room to shake hands with Rashner. The two

men spoke in hushed tones. When they had finished, Rashner patted Merks on the shoulder, nodded to those who were watching and slipped out the double doors.

"Now that I've shared the good news that Mike will be fine, I have some other news as well. It seems that Mr. Richard Granger has been busy stirring up all kinds of troubles for the four of you. Rashner has it on good authority that Granger was behind the DOJ investigation of Alice, which included Rhyjl as a possible accomplice. The FBI investigation of Mike suggested that he had a conspirator when it appeared that some government data banks had been hacked. Granger didn't know who, but if I can make an educated guess, I'm sure federal agents were able to as well, Mr. Arneson. They thought they had Mike's accomplice on hacking charges, I guess, but whatever evidence there was seems to have vanished."

"Erik, sir. Or Professor Arneson. Mr. Arneson is my father."

"Yes, of course, Erik. So, now that the truth has come out, and I'm sure there will be a lot more to this than meets the eye, all of you should be fine. You, Rhyjl, were luckier than the rest. It seems any charges that might have been conjured against you couldn't stick any better than a fried egg on Teflon. But don't think Mr. Granger didn't try."

Rhyjl closed her eyes and took a deep, deep breath. These few days of trepidation were over. They could get their lives back. Then she remembered that wasn't quite so. She still needed to share her trip to work in the Southwest. But that could wait until they had all caught their breath, had a good long sleep and the dog...

Jack! Oh poor Jack. He'd been stuck in the car in the parking garage for hours!

~~

"It could have been worse, Erik. He could have chewed the upholstery," Rhyjl said, as they made a third trip around the two-block hospital campus.

"But I just got those new Bose bluetooth headphones. He's never done anything like that before."

"Well, we've never left him stuck in a car for six hours either."

"So, speaking of we, why didn't he chew something of yours? Like that bag of reading you brought along but didn't use. He could have munched on bones in a literary sense."

Rhyjl laughed and felt whatever tension there was left flow away. "Because it was your fault he was in the car, I guess."

"How do you figure that made it my fault? You were the one that insisted we bring him along and said we wouldn't need his crate."

"Because it was your car and you were the driver. That makes you the responsible party."

"Ah, huh, and I suppose he told you that?"

"Just a little doggy psychology."

~~

When they returned to the waiting room, Alice and her parents were waiting for them. Abrams had come out and spoken with them while Erik and Rhyjl and been out with Jack. Tanner was in recovery and would probably be able to have visitors later that afternoon.

Alice's parents, as Rhyjl suspected they would, offered their hospitality and a bed. Erik thanked them but said he had other plans. They, of course, assumed he meant that he would go stay with his family. Rhyjl didn't have a clue what he intended. The women all hugged. Charles Merks and Erik shook hands and it was agreed they would meet again later.

"So where are we going?" Rhyjl said, as they walked to the elevator to go back to the parking garage.

"A hotel. I booked a suite down at Long Wharf. It was where my mother liked to stay when she was home."

"When she was home?" Rhyjl asked as the elevator doors opened and Erik guided her in with gentle pressure on the small of her back. The doors closed. She turned to him and he knew without her uttering a word what her next question would be.

"The last few years of their marriage were, shall we say, strained. She didn't stay at the house. Neither did I, as a matter of fact. Mother preferred to be near the water. She had a small boat—easy to handle—that she kept there. She was comfortable entertaining her friends there. I was able to pull a few strings. I got the same suite and permission for Jack to stay with us."

"I guess the name Arneson does carry a lot of weight in this town."

"Not Arneson, but my mother's influence. She was very loved by those who knew her."

~~

The phone call came in around one, just as they were finishing lunch. The number was blocked. Erik hesitated, then thought it might be Dr. Charles, as he'd taken to calling Alice's father. As soon as he heard the voice, he put it on speaker and pulled Rhyjl close.

"Good work, Professor. Saved the day and your own skin as well. I hope you and your lovely lady will retire from affairs that don't concern you. Somehow I have a feeling that won't be the case."

"Wait! Why are you helping us? What's in it for you?"

"Just paying some old debts. Righting wrongs, you might say."

"You knew the victims, didn't you. You are somehow connected with them and Tanner. I get that. But why me?"

"The friend of my friend is my friend. The enemy of my friend is my enemy. I'll be around." The line went dead.

"What does he mean by he will be around? Are we going to be stalked?" Rhyjl asked.

"Got me. But he's friends with Tanner, I guess. Even that wasn't really clear. He did warn us. Maybe he even tried to warn Tanner."

"Do you think he was the one that made the mysterious call about the bodies? Or, could he have been the one that shot at Tanner? Alice said on the way down that Tanner suspected it was a warning, not a threat."

"Could be. He could have done a whole lot of damage to my system, but he didn't. He did let us know that Tanner was in trouble, and he knew Jamie and Granger were the offenders. But if he's working just on his own, he must be pretty amazing. Computer hacking and sharpshooting."

"Yes, that's all true, but he's just a little too cryptic for my liking."

The phone chimed again. The caller ID was the same—blocked.

"Now listen!" Erik started, and then heard a familiar voice.

"Erik? Is everything okay? This is Charles. Mike is

awake. We are on our way. Meet you there?"

"Ah, yes, Dr. Charles. Everything is fine. Thanks for letting us know. We'll head over in a few."

~~

The hospital room looked just like any other. A picture of some bucolic setting with copious flowers and a fountain hung on one wall. A TV was mounted near the ceiling on the wall directly opposite the bed, so the patient could watch while lying down. A window that overlooked the city was on the far wall. Alice stood beside the bed holding Mike's hand. Her parents stood at the end of the bed.

"I was just telling Mike he couldn't bring up your being too young to be involved with forensic crime investigation anymore after this. Especially if almost getting yourself killed is an indicator," Alice said, with a wink and smile.

"Well, I don't think he will have to worry. Rhyjl and I are swearing off that sort of thing," Erik replied, giving Rhyjl's shoulders a brief hug.

"I think we all might be," answered Alice. "I've notified Jim Ackerman that I won't be returning. I've decided to take a position with my dad's clinic."

Rhyjl looked from Alice to her parents. The shared look of joy on their faces said it all. They were getting their little girl back.

"Mike also won't be returning to work."

"Now wait a minute, Alice. I said I was considering it," Tanner said through bruised lips.

"You said it would be pretty hard for you to remain at work after what happened and how you felt they had 'abandoned' you. You also said it would be difficult to remain up in Maine with me down here."

   "You impressed Rashner, Mike," said Dr. Charles. "He said he could use a partner like you when you get back on your feet."
And so the banter went. Everything was changing, Rhyjl thought. There would be no more Thursday night dinners at Vinney's. No more girls' lunches. She realized that Alice and Tanner were a part of the fabric that held her in Maine. She had assumed that even with her leaving for the summer, they would be there when she returned home. Home. The home that she and Erik shared. Would that fall apart when she told him about the job, or would he understand? Only time would tell, but as evening approached and they cruised the Tesla along I-95 with a happy Jack snoring in the back, she decided that topic could wait for another day or two or even possibly a week.

About the Author

JM Meigs has always believed that human and animal remains each have their own stories to tell. Combining her love of archaeology with her second passion of storytelling, has led her to develop the Rhyjl Martin mysteries.

She lives in the Pacific Northwest with her family and a menagerie of pets.